AF224928

The More The Merrier
ISBN 978-1-909934-08-5
Copyright©2013 Barry Lowe
Cover art and design by Dawné Dominique

First published by loveyoudivine Alterotica

Published by
Lydian Press 2013
Find us on the World Wide Web at
www.lydianpress.com

THE MORE THE MERRIER

Gay Gangbang Erotica

Barry Lowe

Lydian Press

CONTENTS

Page

1:   Marine Biology †

19:   Flesh for Fantasy † *

39:   Buck's Night †

65:   Four On The Floor †

81:   Sluts & Satyrs †

101:   Framing the Picture of Dorian Gray †

143:   Fuck Buddy †

177:   Seven Card Studs †

205:   Dude, Where's The Bar? †

225:   New Year's Steve †

† All previously published as individual eBooks by loveyoudivine Alterotica.

* First published in a slightly different form in Cargo #11 (BlackWattle Press, 1991)

DEDICATION:

*To all the men past, present and future who
had/have/will have their way with me, and to Wally,
the one man, past, present and future who has
always been there for me
(even if he wasn't always at the groups)*

Some guys simply can't get enough!

Marine Biology

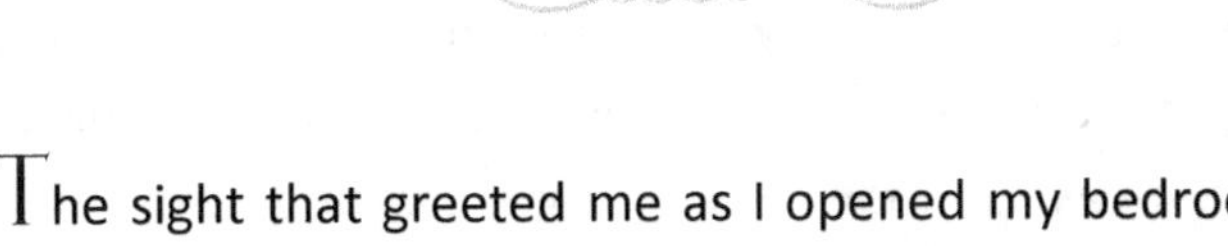

The sight that greeted me as I opened my bedroom door was the hairy butt crack and dangling scrotum of my beefy big bro, Karl. There wasn't time for it to register as erotic as I watched him slide the entire length of his substantial cock into his *girlfriend du jour* before he screamed, "Get the fuck outa here!" That he'd glanced over his shoulder to see who the intruder was meant that he didn't mind sharing. Just not with his kid pro bro.

If I hadn't forgotten my key, of course, none of it would have happened. But I was in such a hurry to surprise my parents for their thirtieth wedding anniversary, I pretty well floored the Toyota Camry for two hundred miles from my uni campus in the capitol to Redneck Central, as I not-so-fondly called my home town.

It didn't feel much like a home town any longer. I was particularly out of favor with the populace, as I'd become an outspoken opponent of the country's military policy. Perhaps not a good idea in a town that supplied a rather large contingent to the Marine Corps. They were heroes. I was a traitor. They'd seen action in a war zone. I'd been on the receiving end of a police baton charge at an anti-war demo. I had a cabinet full of swimming medals. Karl had a chestful of bravery awards. It was a no brainer.

My brother and his marine buddies are all big gorillas of men. Karl is 6'4" of almost solid muscle and, I'm pleased to say, an increasing amount of fat, and weighs in at 240 lbs. Cropped dark hair and an attitude so belligerent that it would feed the messianic zealotry of any medium level dictator. Naturally, he attracts chicks like horse manure attracts flies.

Me, I take after mom. She's petite, dwarfed by my dad, with blonde hair and the friendliest disposition you'd ever care to meet. I take after her—except for the disposition. Like my brother, I get that from my dad. And, of course, like my dad, I have a dick. Besides that, I have blond hair, a slim pro swimmer's body that weighs in at 120 lbs, and a face that's much too pretty for its own good. Got me beat up a few times. And it's a constant source of friction between me and my bro and his buddies who call me 'Pretty Boy' to my face, as well as behind my back. It's not meant as a compliment.

Our parents discourage mutual homecomings, and we're both happy to oblige. This, however, was one occasion where there was a scheduling error.

Lights blazed in the house; the music was thumping a bass line so loud it could be heard by the deaf in Middle Earth. The laughter was raucous and the language blue enough that our fundamentalist neighbors had locked their windows, drawn their blinds and turned up the volume on their Christian cable channels to drown out the profanities.

No one would call the police. These marines were heroes to the town of 'true believers.' It was just the boys home on leave and blowing off a little steam. Tomorrow they would settle down and become law-abiding rednecks. Tonight? Well, what we don't see and hear...

I cursed. Dad's SUV was missing from the driveway. Even my parents tended to leave the nest when Karl returned in Caesar-like triumph. They'd come back and sweep out the debris of sexual, alcoholic and narcotic excess and quietly pay the girls who knew the routine and waited patiently for their due. It was my parents' ritual, accepted as part and parcel of the sacrifice of having a decorated war hero for a son.

Now the 'wrong' son was crashing the party. I could have turned around and driven away to a hotel or back to the college, but I was simply too stinking tired. And too stinking poor. I banged loudly on the door and there was a whoop from inside. "The chicks are here at last!"

The door was yanked open. The smile of expectation became a snarl of recognition.

"Cool it! It's not the girls," Dean, one of my brother's marine buddies, spat out. "It's just Pretty Boy home from college."

There was a moan from the living room, plus a tsunami of cursing.

Dean still blocked the door and made no effort to move.

"I'd like to come in," I said as firmly as I could.

"I don't think you'd like it in here," Dean said. "It's full of misinformed military muscle." He was quoting from an editorial I'd written for the campus newspaper which had earned me a rebuke from my father, a look of pity from my mom, and the everlasting enmity of Karl and his buddies.

"Or maybe that's what Pretty Boy really wants. Military muscle," he said as he grabbed his crotch. He was borderline drunk.

"Leave him alone, Dean," a kinder voice said. "And get out of the doorway and let him in. It's his home."

Dean sulked away to be with his buddies, who were getting hot and sweaty watching porn in the living room.

"Welcome home." Sam smiled and shook my hand. He was one mean motherfucker. A tank of a man. And one of the nicest guys I knew. Every time I saw him, I just wanted him to sweep his huge, black arms around me and make me feel safe.

"Not the welcome I expected," I said, shouldering my bag to the vestibule floor. "Where are they?"

"Karl shouted them a week in Hawaii for their anniversary. They left this afternoon."

I shrugged. "I don't have that sort of money."

"You don't owe me any explanations." Sam read my mind.

That's when I'd gone upstairs to my room only to find my bro performing the testicle tango as only he knows how. Although the two of us did not share any common political or cultural ties, we did share a bedroom. I guessed I wouldn't be sleeping in my bed tonight.

There was nothing else for it. I would sleep in the car. Sam caught me sneaking out and put a sweaty arm around my shoulder. Ah, that brought back the memories, and I immediately got a boner in my jeans.

"Where ya going, buddy? The party's this way." He steered me into the living room, a garbage dump of cheesy pizza boxes and leaking beer cans littering the furniture and the floor. My mom would sigh at the damage to her new settee and forgive 'the boys.' There were four of them, all in various stages of undress—and arousal—as they waited impatiently for the girls. Gino, the most extroverted of the bunch, was smokin' and strokin', his vision glued to the porn DVD on the flat screen television, which had tell-tale smear marks where he'd been rubbing his greasy, uncut cock against video screen mouths or else had been licking spread video pussy. It was his famed party trick.

Sam nestled me in an arm so muscular it would have snapped my 5'9" frame like a twig if he flexed. It was comfortable cradled there. I'd always liked Sam, and to be in close proximity to his unapologetic maleness was heady. Especially now that he was stripped to the waist and smelled of beer and testosterone.

In my teens, I had jerked off over fantasies of Sam and me together. The big hulk fucking me hard and heavy; ever since my parents had insisted that big bro Karl and his buddies take me on one of their camping trips. I hated the open air, and Karl and his buddies hated having me along on their booze fest. Plus they intended to get to a town, any town, where there was ample pussy to go round and there was no way they could do that with me tagging along.

Karl had made the trek a misery, hoping I would turn back and go home. Round the fire the first night, he told stories about wild animals and monsters that patrolled the woods looking for kids just like me. I was a gullible fifteen-year-old, so what did I know? Except that the sounds that came from outside my tent sounded strangely close and incredibly dangerous. Naturally, I screamed and Sam came belting to my rescue. He chewed out Karl because I was shaking so much in fear I had pissed myself.

Sam had let me move my sleeping bag into his tent. I'd gone to sleep easily, knowing the big, muscular marine was there to protect me. In the morning, I'd seen him through the tent flaps as he pissed and wiggled his flaccid cock to get rid of the last drops. He'd given it a few tugs and it grew in size. I couldn't believe how big it got. He moved his hand up and down, slowly milking his huge weapon. I'd gone hard in my sleeping bag. Sam glanced over at the tent and saw me watching. He quickly put his cock away and pretended like nothing happened.

For years, I treasured a fading photograph of that camping trip: skinny me hanging off Sam's bicep. He'd flexed his arm, and I'd jumped up and swung from it. I had never been so happy. Sam was thirty then—the oldest in the group.

"Why don't you come over and help me out, Pretty Boy," Gino suggested without even looking in my direction and without missing a stroke. I knew from my brother's tales he could keep it hard for hours. "Just 'til the girls arrive, you understand." He laughed. If I'd thought there was even a modicum of real intent in his invitation I would have jumped at the chance.

The one thing college had taught me was that I loved cock. And Gino's large, uncut beauty was exactly the sort of cock I liked. Hell, if I was honest with myself, I subscribed to that old adage of Will Rogers: I've never met a cock I didn't like. But then, I haven't met them all yet.

"Hey, Gino, I think he likes. He can't take his eyes off it." Brad snickered.

Gino looked over and smiled. He milked his cock in my direction. "Come and get it, Pretty Boy. Come and take care of Gino. Be Gino's boy pussy." The air was electric with expectation.

"Cut it out, you guys," Sam bellowed. "This is Karl's little bro you're talking to, not some faggot slut."

The moment vanished like a summer storm.

While I appreciated Sam's brotherly interest in my welfare, I knew he was as big a homophobe as the others. I'd once overheard him discussing me with Karl. "You think Pretty Boy is a faggot like they say?"

"Why?" my brother asked. "You want to fuck him?"

Sam had flattened him for that. He was the only one of the group who could take on Karl and better him.

Gino shouted across the room, "Why don't you see if Chip's awake, then Pretty Boy could use his mom and dad's room instead of sleeping in his shit heap of a car."

Now the one sacrosanct commandment is that my parents' bedroom is strictly off limits. Even I didn't dare contemplate breaking that number-one-with-a-bullet house rule. Gino had let slip that Chip had.

Sam read my mind again. "He was just feeling a bit under the weather, buddy, and he needed somewhere quiet away from the boys. He's not with a chick or nothing."

"Come on guys," I said as they all awaited my reaction. "It's none of my business. You know the policy: Don't Ask, Don't Tell."

"You better go get him anyway," Gino suggested, and Sam lumbered out of the room.

"Now, Pretty Boy," Gino said. "How about it?"

He opened his legs wide to show off his stallion qualities. A quick glance around the room and I judged no one was going to beat me up if I did as I was invited. At least not before it was over. And I guessed they'd keep it secret from my big bro. I didn't care if they didn't.

Gino shucked the remainder of his clothes as if to show the encouragement was genuine. I hesitated a few seconds before kneeling in worship of a man I basically despised—but libido has no use of such niceties.

I gently tongued his balls, slicking them with spit, and then ran my tongue along the greasy shaft. It was already slimy with precum that he'd used as lube for his constant fist jack hammering. The other guys looked at each other, half in terror, half in expectation and turned to make sure Karl wasn't lurking in the background. Or Sam.

It wasn't until Gino moaned that anyone dared breathe again. As my lips engulfed Gino's weapon, my tongue tracing the ridge under the head of his cock, he sighed. "Oh, shit! Oh, fuck!" This was the connoisseur of sex giving me his seal of approval. I was a success. Hell, any hole would have been a success at this party, but I was now officially a bona fide Grade A cocksucker.

Gino put his hands on the top of my head and pushed me down onto his prick. I gagged momentarily, but soon got my rhythm in line with my breath control. We fell into an easy give and take partnership. The other guys came closer to watch, and Brad was even brave enough to sit next to Gino to watch from close quarters. He stripped to reveal a solid erection, which he was hoping might be next in line. I was sure the guys weren't this tentative with the girls they fucked, but unfamiliarity bred unease. As I bobbed up and down throat fucking Gino's cock, I reached over and wrapped my fist around Brad's weapon. It was fully loaded.

I heard Dean unzip. He must have been cautious in case a hasty retreat was sounded. I lifted my mouth off Gino who cursed and, without any foreplay, sank my hot mouth around the full length of Brad's eager cock. He had no technique other than ramming.

"Not so aggressive, dickhead," Gino said as he watched. "It's not a fucking race. You'll have more pleasure if you let the faggot do the work."

Brad snorted, "I just want to cum. And before Sam gets back."

"Sam will be okay with this once he sees the cocksucker's enjoying it," Gino said confidently. It had the desired effect. Brad slowed down and let me set the pace. Dean was so eager he was humping the side of my face seeking attention. I could have kept this up all night, tired as I was, but I could feel the urgency in the room—urgency to dump a load and to finish before Karl could enter the equation. They didn't know, nor did I, what his reaction would be to seeing his baby bro being used as a cum dump.

That's all I was. I knew that. Accepted it. I wasn't looking for roses and a commitment ceremony, especially not from these guys, hot as they were. Just as I was a convenient hole for them, they were convenient cocks for me.

I gave in to Dean's insistence and turned and sucked his cock. Thin and long, it felt at home in my throat. He just gasped. "Holy mother of God! Is this what a blow job should be like?"

Gino said proudly, "Pretty Boy here is a born cocksucker. One of the best, so don't bruise him 'cause, man, I ain't finished with him yet."

Dean didn't last long. The least experienced of the group, as well as the youngest, around 22, my age, he screamed "Holy fuckin' shit!" a couple of times then I felt his cock snot hit the back of my throat and trickle down into my gullet. I cleaned off his knob and slit with my lips and tongue, but he was obviously too sensitive and pulled away and zipped up.

"Go and keep watch," Gino commanded. Dean obeyed.

Gino watched impatiently as I swallowed Brad to his balls, stroking in time to my sucking. When it came to sex, Gino was a general; the other guys were just enlisted men.

"Don't take all fuckin' day, man" Gino grumbled.

"You told me to enjoy it, dickwad," Brad said and showed no inclination to cum to the party.

"You can take your time the second time around," he snapped.

There was going to be seconds?

I could see Gino was on the verge of shooting, but Brad was not going to give up his place at the head of the queue and resolutely held me in place.

"Selfish fuckin' asshole," Gino spat, but it gave him an idea. He quickly kneeled behind me and had my jeans and briefs off in one expert maneuver. He pulled my ass cheeks apart, spat at my hole and pushed his finger inside.

"Aw, Gino, that's real faggot stuff," Brad complained.

"You finished with his mouth? No? Then shut the fuck up and let me dump a load. I've seen you fuck ass before."

"Yea," Brad acknowledged, "but not a faggot's."

"An asshole is an asshole." Gino put paid to any criticism and spat in his hand a few more times until he had enough to slick his cock and lubricate my hole. It wasn't ideal, but I wasn't going to insist on stopping the action while we went in search of industrial-strength lube. I felt his cock head at the entrance to my guts and then...

I grunted my pain into Brad's balls and almost choked in the process.

Gino was only interested in his own pleasure now. It was okay to allow me to make the rhythm while I was blowing him but fucking, he was very much the aggressor. This wasn't about pleasure any more; this was about dumping a load.

"Fuck, Pretty Boy, your asshole is so hot and so tight. You like cock in your ass, don't you, Pretty Boy?"

I didn't bother answering because I knew the question was rhetorical, but I squeezed my sphincter around his cock anyway.

"Hot damn, you're good, Pretty Boy," he said and slapped my ass.

This was heading in a direction that was decidedly uncomfortable for Brad. He began slamming his prick in and out of my mouth to get it over with as fast as possible. Gino had invaded a 'no go' area and Brad wanted no part of it.

"Who's the pretty blonde chick?" I heard Chip ask in a drunken slur behind me. He must have thought the girls had arrived.

I heard the chuckle in Gino's voice. "Pretty Boy."

"You mean, Pretty Boy, like Karl's little bro?"

"Uh huh?"

Chip whistled. "Boy, you're in deep shit."

"Nah, he's clean as a whistle. I checked." Gino smirked.

"How long you been into fuckin' boy pussy, man?" Chip asked.

"When the fuckin' chicks don't turn up a man's gotta do what a man's gotta do."

Gino had an excuse to cover every variation of behavior.

Brad shot his load silently, not wanting to draw attention to himself and got up from the lounge so quickly I couldn't drain the last drops from his knob. He was still leaking as he pulled up his shorts.

I looked over at Chip, who was smiling weirdly.

"Hot damn, you got good action, boy." Chip was unsteady on his feet as he attempted to strip while Sam steadied him. I saw a flash of pain as Sam looked me in the eyes. He could tell this was consensual activity. Just a group of horny guys taking care of a faggot who wanted it. But that didn't make him like it any the better.

"What's his ass like, man?" Chip asked as he stroked his half-mast cock.

"Mmmm, tight. Sweet. Hot."

It's always an ego booster to get a good review.

"Move aside sonny and let a man at that boy pussy."

Sam grabbed him. "You're not gonna stick that thing of yours in his ass. It'd kill him."

"That boy gonna taste my cock or get it in his ass. Which you want, boy?"

He was waving his cock in front of my face.

"He's Karl's little bro, Chip. You can't treat him like those sluts we fuck off the base. You don't want to hurt him."

"He's just a cute little blond faggot slut as far as my cock is concerned. Fuck the consequences. Here, boy, slick me up."

He straddled my face as Gino watched. He liked watching Chip stretch small, accommodating holes whose muscles expanded like elastic bands to fit the monster cock.

I wrapped my lips around it. It wasn't the girth that was a problem. I've seen thicker—only in movies—but I knew the length was going to hit places that had never felt cock before.

Chip relaxed. "Hot damn that mouth feels good."

"You think that's hot, wait 'til you try his ass."

Before I chowed down on Chip's weapon, I glanced sideways to watch Sam. He seemed conflicted. The growing bulge in his shorts revealed the sight of my impalement on hot marine cock was exciting him, but his loyalty to Karl, and the fact I was like a young, albeit recalcitrant, brother to him made him guilty.

Gino had a mouth on him like a porn actor and was narrating in vivid detail the effects of Chip sliding his XXL cock into my size S mouth. My eyes were watering and drool slobbered from my lips, but I wasn't going to let the side down. It had gone past the point of enjoyment. Sure, my asshole being pummeled by Gino's gorgeous prick was still pure pleasure, but Chip's baseball bat cock was way out of the ballpark on the Richter scale of grunt and pain.

It wasn't exactly a chore; it was more something to be achieved. I wanted to plant a notch flag close to the root of his cock, I wanted to be the first to hit his nose against those wiry pubes and stake my claim to minor immortality.

"No chicks ever got that far," Chip admired. "Another inch and you've nailed it, boy."

It was a stupid competition, if I stopped to think about it, but I didn't intend on doing that. This was like being the first man in space, the first man on the moon, the first man to climb Everest. And if there wouldn't be blanket television news coverage, at least my achievement would be talked about in hushed whispers among aficionados at the barracks.

I filled my lungs with as much air as they could take and impaled my face on the cock. It scraped the back of my throat and kept going. Chip put his hand around my neck and squeezed.

"Hot fuckin' damn I can feel it way down his throat. No chick's ever taken it all the way. You're a real star, boy."

I choked and spluttered, but I held on until my breath exploded out of me. My face was a mess of snot, cum and puke. Chip cupped my face and wiped my lips with his big thumbs. With an automatic burst of "shits, fucks and cunts", Gino made a claim on my attention. I gripped his cock with my ass muscles and milked him dry.

"All greased up ready for you, man," Gino said as he showed Chip my oozing hole. Chip kneeled behind me, his cock slick with my throat juices. There were no niceties, just the barge of an impatient pole right into the innermost crevices of my ass canal. It winded me and Chip remained fully embedded until the pain subsided and I got my breath back.

"Come on, Sam. Give him something to bite on while Chip fucks the ass off him," Gino pleaded.

"Nah, I don't think so."

"Karl will never know," I said, finding my voice at last.

Dean and Brad pushed him toward me, but Sam crashed on to the settee fully dressed. I unzipped him expertly and felt for his cock. It was hard and leaking. He couldn't help himself. As I pulled it free from his trousers, it was the most perfect cock I had ever seen. The right length and thickness. I leaned forward to kiss it in appreciation. As my lips touched it, I thought Sam was having a seizure he bucked so violently. As Chip thrust into my asshole, he pushed my head down on to Sam's prick. I was the meat in a kebab impaled at both ends. Sam took Chip's hand off my head and allowed me to suck in time to the thrusts up my ass. Almost negligently, he began to stroke my hair and my face.

I could hear Chip's ragged breath, and then I actually felt the pulse of cum scudding along the length of his cock as it shot deep inside my asshole. I was sure Sam would follow shortly by shooting a load into my willing mouth, but our sexual gratification was interrupted by loud knocking at the door. Sam froze; Chip kept right on pumping his last drops into me while Gino went to the window.

"Shit, it's the chicks. They musta got lost."

Chip pulled out, gushing cum over the backs of my legs. There was a general scramble for clothing, and I was forgotten in the melee. Sam was inscrutable. I decided to take a chance. In the confusion and the impatient knocking at the front door, I grabbed Sam by the hand and led him out into the backyard. Out of view of the other men who had already forgotten their brief flirtation with faggotry, although I was sure I would hear from Gino again, if not Chip, I leaned into Sam's muscular chest and pulled his face down to meet mine. There was no reluctance when I pushed my tongue into his mouth. He reciprocated with all the passion I would have expected only of a starving man.

"Why do you let them treat you like that?" he asked, sad rather than moral.

"I guess I love cock," I said flippantly, but I could see he was pained. "And I haven't found the right man yet to settle down with."

"So, you're looking?" he asked.

"Uh huh," I nodded and sighed theatrically. "If only a good-looking guy like you was available then I'd settle down tomorrow."

He gave a little embarrassed laugh. I ran my fingers across his chest and down his arm to his marble-hard bicep.

"I remember when I was so young that ..."

Sam reached into his back pocket and pulled out his wallet. He extracted the photo of me swinging from his arm.

"Sam?"

"Was it me turned you gay?" he said with a catch in his voice.

"How?"

"You saw my dick that morning when I started to jerk off and I thought …"

"You thought it turned me gay?"

He shrugged. "I wondered."

"You and me have to sit down and have a serious talk some time about what being gay is all about."

"I'd like that," he said. He put his arm around me.

"Uh, you think I could be gay?" he almost whispered.

"Anyone can be gay," I said.

"Even a United States Marine?"

"Of course. I've even met a few."

His look of surprise said it all. I didn't think his education was ready for the news of a Gay Marine Support group and their civilian admirers, let alone Marine gay porn.

"You've been hanging around with Karl too long," I said.

"You think another guy could go for me?"

"Sam, you are such a gorgeous man you'd have them lining up around the block."

"Nah, I only want one."

Up until then I thought his interest was just general. Suddenly, it had become very specific. I wondered why he carried around a photo of me in his wallet. My heart thumped. I looked up at him. Really looked into his eyes. The moment lasted so long I thought I'd explode then, a slight nod of the head...

I jumped him, pushing him backwards. I was sitting on his chest trying to hug the big man. "You stupid bastard," I screamed with delight. "I've been jerking off over you ever since that camping trip. You know why I've never settled down? It's because no one ever lived up to you. I was always comparing my lovers to you."

He was genuinely surprised. "Really?"

I moved my lips to his chest and gnawed gently on his nipple. He wriggled at the unusual feeling, but it got hard, and I could feel something else get hard again in his shorts.

"It's okay," I said. "I won't tell the others."

"It made me sick to see the way them other guys treated you tonight."

"They didn't force me, Sam."

"I know, but I wanted you to myself. And I wanted you different."

"Like we are now?"

"Yeah, like that."

I held his face as I put my mouth over his lips and pressed my tongue inside. I felt all the tension go out of his body.

I may never get a medal for serving my country, but at least I can show my patriotism by serving the Marine Corps. Or servicing one member of it. Mom and dad would be so proud.

Flesh For Fantasy

"Great place for a mass murder," Robbo said as they pushed their way through the throng to take up vantage points for the annual Sydney Gay & Lesbian Mardi Gras Parade. They'd intended being early, but Robbo had decided they had better eat if they were going to party, party, party the night away, and what with his prodigious appetite, they'd ended up being on the ass-end of the stragglers for good spots.

They shoved their way into a mob of beer-swilling heterosexuals and stood on tiptoes surveying the crowds for signs of intelligent life.

They weren't in much luck on Liverpool Street and were contemplating moving to a more sympathetic atmosphere when the mandatory loose change buckets for gay charities were thrust at them. Robbo and Steven delved for loose notes and tried not to think of the drugs and alcohol they could be buying and ingesting with the proceeds. But then Steven remembered Peter, and Remo, and David and...well, this was a night for thanksgiving and solidarity. He shook the painful memories from his mind.

"The parade's started," Robbo shouted. Steven looked at his watch. It was early. First time in living memory.

Steven was a sucker for a good parade. He'd watched one as a toddler when the queen had made her first visit in the 1950s. He'd got a nosebleed and some nice people in a house elevated above the general rabble had invited his mum and the rest of the family up to watch the parade while little Steven recuperated. But his major memories of that event had been waving a Union Jack at the young woman about whom everyone was saying, "Ooooh, isn't she lovely?" in a tone usually reserved for new-born babies and soft puppies. That and the giant double-page, color painting of the Royal Yacht Britannia in Sydney Harbor that his grandmother, in her fervent devotion to royalty, had framed from the *Women's Weekly*.

By the time the queen had been back a decade or so later, he and friends on one of their cruising escapades had stumbled across a ratbag collection of royalists at Circular Quay and had given the quickly retreating back of the monarch the finger. They'd laughed about it for days.

His second parade had been marching through the deserted local shopping centre on Anzac Day as a member of the primary school contingent making up the numbers. Too young to know what all the fuss was about he was more interested in walking along the double yellow lines in the centre of the street than the significance of the event. It was not every day you walked along the middle of the highway without being run over.

By high school, he had learned rebellion and pacifism and refused to march or even to bow his head at the school Anzac Day ceremonies although watching the big-city march on television with his father did bring a lump to his throat. Yes, he was a sucker for parades.

Later came the Waratah Festival parade named after the state's floral emblem and in homage to...after all these years he couldn't remember except that it had been an excuse for colorful floats and costumes, and hordes of parents lining the roadway cooing to their children, "Ooooh, isn't it lovely?"

Lovely was not the word most of those solidly suburban parents would be using to describe what he was watching now. Still it brought genuine emotion to his throat, something he'd never told anyone before, especially not Robbo, who was prone to laugh at any overt display of feelings.

He was soaking it all in, trying to ignore Robbo's criticism, "Not as good as last year," which, from recollection, he'd been saying now for the past six years, though Steven had to agree the floats and the participants seemed to be rushing past with unnecessary haste. He was getting old. The liver spots on the backs of his hands were testimony to that. Perhaps his memory was not what it had been. Maybe his reflexes were slower, making everything appear to be going faster, birthdays tumbling over one another in the race for sixty. And he noticed he used a lot more moisturiser on his face to keep the skin supple, the wrinkles having become crevasses rather than mere indents.

He banished these ideas because it was the one night of the year when he felt young, well, youngish again, and he could unabashedly ogle those gorgeous near-naked male bodies with a lust that would have got him abused or punched out on any other occasion had the recipient of his admiration noticed it.

Steven was mellowing, mellowing to the extent he refrained from thumping the drunken yobbo next to him who kept saying, "Here come more poofters"; and to a lesbian mother, "How did you manage that without one of these?" before grabbing a handful of his own genitals and thrusting them forward. Finally, the sheer numbers overwhelmed the heckler and, thoroughly defeated, all he could mutter in wonder was, "Where do all these poofters come from?"

"Robbo!"

Steven clutched Robbo's arm. He'd seen a vision. He'd already fallen in and out of love half a dozen times with the unattainables on the floats, although Robbo was of the opinion, unsubstantiated, that everyone is haveable, particularly if they're drunk enough.

He'd seen what Steven meant. "Wow!"

The glittering gold shorts clung to the slim, smooth body with the beginnings of definition, hair bleached to within an inch of its life, a pout that screamed come and get it if you think you're man enough, a crotch packed appetizingly, and an ass that had to have been designed in heaven.

"I'm in love," Steven wailed as the tightly compact ass wiggled toward the appreciative masses. Instant hard-on time.

"He's nothing but a little tramp. Look at everyone slobbering over him."

"He's an angel. Perfection itself! The personification of beauty."

Robbo pouted, miffed that Steven had seen the vision first. "I thought you didn't like blonds?"

"Oh, it's not for me personally, but wouldn't he be ideal casting as Tadzio in my musical version of *Death in Venice*."

"Your what?" Robbo laughed. "You're not serious?"

"I've been slaving over it for months, and all we need for the workshop is a little blond spunk who looks young enough to pass for Tadzio, and who's such a turn on, the entire audience will want to fuck him."

"Mmm, does he meet all those criteria, or is it just that the author wants a bit of ass? Anyway, you don't know if he can act."

Who cared? Steven had already cast him as the all-silent, all-dancing fantasy Tadzio followed by an obsessed von Aschenbach around the decaying and diseased back alleys of pre-World War I Venice.

As soon as the last float had pelted past, Steven grabbed Robbo and ran toward Oxford Street.

"What float was he on anyway?" Steven was trying unsuccessfully to appear nonchalant now.

"Is that why we're hurrying? To catch up to the little tramp? Listen, he was wiggling his cute little ass for all and sundry. What makes you think you're gonna get a piece of it?"

"You're the one who's always saying that they're haveable,"

"Yeah, but in his case I think you'll have to join the queue."

"I think it was the RAMS float they were on. That's the gay bowling team. Come on."

They pushed their way through the heavy peripheral crowd negotiating cans, bottles, abuse and vomit with a deftness that comes from years of experience, stopping at The Exchange so Robbo could bop to "I'm Too Sexy." Then a little further on so Steven could be tongue kissed by a guy who'd fucked him at a party in full view of all the guests; finally by a group of his friends who were eager to tell him about the cute, young blond who, they were sure, was going to cop it good and hard in the toilet at the party.

Everyone was talking about him. Everyone wanted him. Well, not everyone, but he certainly was a focal point and that pout...Steven was hoping he could satisfy that pout.

Having caught up with the object of his desire at Taylor Square, Steven kept pace with the truck, watching intently for any signs of imperfection. But there were none, although his shorts by this stage were creeping up his ass, *deliberately*, Steven thought, as a tease.

"Well, if it isn't Steven."

It was Matt. Yup, yup yuppie, Matt. Steven hadn't seen him in years, not since their tragically mismatched date in the bushes of the urban forest in Moore Park where they'd both wanted to fuck each other and neither had been willing to offer his ass for penetration. It had been a match made on the spur of a drunken moment when both were boozily horny and a quick fuck was all that was on the agenda. They both wanted to get their rocks off and get home. As a result of the impasse, pride had been lost on both sides. Steven didn't care if it was centuries before he saw Matt again. "Had your eye on the little blond did you?" Before Steven could offer any excuse.

"Yes, we all have. What a shame."

"What's a shame?" Steven said.

"That float."

"The gay bowling team?"

Matt guffawed theatrically. "Gay bowling team? Oh, love. It's not the gay bowling team. It's just initials. Don't you know what it stands for? Rights for All Male Sexworkers. He's a pro, lovey. They're all pros on that float. Don't tell me you didn't know? Oh, wait'll I tell the boys this." Cackling like the Wicked Witch of the West, Matt pushed his way into the crowd calling, "You couldn't afford him anyway, lovey. Takes more than your meager salary."

"I only want him for a musical I'm writing," Steven shouted to the snickers of those around him who'd heard the exchange.

To rub salt into the embarrassment, Matt tossed Steven a ten cent coin with the parting shot "To help you with your savings. You're going to need it."

They'd lost the blond during the contretemps with Matt, and it was at the Showground they found the already deserted truck still blaring its disco music guarded momentarily by the float's marshal getting changed from the official T-shirt into something more glitzy, more in keeping with approaching party mode.

"Norrie?" Steven shouted over the din. "Is that you?"

Steven had dumped Robbo somewhere in the park area trying to cadge a giant pair of fluorescent lips. He gave Norrie the third degree on the whys and wherefores of the young blond.

"Cute, isn't he?" Norrie teased.

"Yea, I suppose, but I'm interested because I'm doing a musical version of *Death in Venice*, and I need a Tadzio. Do you think he can act?"

"What about that performance on the back of the truck?"

"Yes, but real performing?"

"Why don't you ask him?"

"Because I'm shy."

Norrie laughed. "Not when you asked me to go to bed with you."

"And he's gorgeous. Perfect in every way."

"If you say so."

Robbo came over as Steven thrust a card into Norrie's hand. "If you run across him give him my card and tell him to ring me if he wants to be an actor."

"Oh, brother, have you got it bad. That's the tired old line you used on me," Norrie said.

"Let's see if we can find him," Robbo said as they made their way to the party.

But they didn't. Steven became more and more convinced, courtesy of an overactive imagination and a quantity of recreational chemicals, of his undying love for the blond, and that his concern for him was purely artistic. Steven likened the fair-haired God to a beautiful piece of sculpture. You admired it, certainly, and perhaps you ran your hand over it, but you certainly didn't fuck great works of art—no matter how much you were aching to.

It was all so immensely pleasurable and non-threatening in his eccied state he was sorry when Robbo, whom he'd lost earlier in the melee, rediscovered him and grabbed him by the arm. "I've found him," he shouted in Steven's ear. "Come with me if you want a piece."

Steven didn't like the way Robbo was speaking about the man he loved and told him so.

"What have you been on since I last saw you?" He looked somewhat disapprovingly at Steven's lack of self-control, for Steven hadn't kept count of the drinks or the...what were they...he'd taken.

"Where is he? Do you think he'll be interested in me?"

"I'm sure that when you're chock a block up him and you whisper in his ear that you'd love him to play Tadzio in your new musical he'll be overwhelmed. That's if he even knows what a Tadzio is because I suspect the little bugger can't even read yet."

"Where are you taking me?"

"Round here," Robbo said and shoved Steven into the fray. He stumbled and fell into the guy at the end of the queue.

"I don't need to go just yet, Robbo."

"Just get in line and shut up. And here."

Robbo pressed something into Steven's hand. Instinctively, and without hesitation, he put it in his mouth, spitting it out almost immediately afterwards.

"Are you trying to poison me or something?"

"God, you're so orally retentive; everything goes straight into your mouth," he said retrieving it.

Steven looked at the wrapper in his hand: it was a condom.

"I'm not into eating these any more. Anyway, it's empty."

"See that shock of blond hair down there and those ghastly shorts in the dirt?"

"Oh, he's over there," Steven cried with joy and made his way toward the blurred outline of the blond. He was immediately manhandled back to his place with grunts of, "Wait your turn," or "Quit pushing in."

"We're in a queue," Robbo said with remarkable patience. "We're the ass end. That line over there is for his mouth."

It finally penetrated Steven's dizzy brain as he looked at the men in front of him, all in various stages of erection, playing with themselves in preparation for the main event, that the young blond was spread over an upturned garbage bin just a few minutes ahead of him. Now he could hear the groaning. He could make out the men in the other line thrusting into a willing mouth and throat, and he found himself getting aroused.

"Now put it on," Robbo commanded.

Gingerly, Steven unzipped and took out his erection even though the ambience reminded him more of a supermarket check-out than anything even remotely erotic. He felt his shirt pocket for his business card, which he would give the blond as he talked to him about the great role and opportunity he was offering him in his new musical.

"Don't just play with it—put it on!"

Steven was so full of eccy love he wanted to embrace the whole world. He supposed it was only fair that Robbo was making sure he did it safely.

"Here, give it to me." Robbo grabbed the condom from his fumbling fingers, and in a few deft strokes had it on him.

"That one's taking his time," Steven said counting off the number of men in front of him. "Like those people who don't have their money ready when they get on the bus." That thought stayed with him right up until it was his turn.

He bent over the blond, who was otherwise engaged slurping on a cock as if it were a giant ice cream and said into the one available ear, "My name's Steven, and I want—"

Robbo grabbed Steven around the waist and with a deft maneuver guided his erect cock up the blond's ass. "Talk to him about it later. Right now, you've got more important things to do."

It was warm and squishy, but Steven managed to take the card out of his pocket and wave it in the general direction of the blond's face all the while keeping up a running commentary on how famous the young man would become if he were to put himself—

"For Christ's sake just shut up and get on with it, mate," said someone in the queue.

"We haven't got all night," another yelled.

"Shit, the speed's starting to wear off," cried a third.

Steven felt his cock being squeezed by a more than willing asshole, which was begging him to get about his business. But it wasn't right. This wasn't the way to cast a play, buried to the hilt up the person you wanted to be your leading man.

Meaningful conversation, as opposed to one-sided blathering, seemed a remote possibility, but the gods were kind. As Steven continued to mechanically pump away, his mind concentrated on making verbal contact when, fortuitously, the chap on whose cock the blond had been sucking grunted briefly, dumped a load and withdrew. Steven's opportunity had arrived.

"Look, I'm casting a play and..."

Before the ever-willing mouth could be accommodated again, the blond turned to reprimand Steven for his crassness during what was meant to be the erotic experience of a lifetime. Steven immediately lost all interest. It was the wrong blond!

Then his stomach told him what his brain had been reluctant to acknowledge: that a belly full of recreational substances and the very rich Singapore curry that Robbo had insisted he shout before the parade...well there was only one way for it to go. So while the ass in which Steven was embedded wiggled its insatiable demands, and the young blond's face was well and truly skewered on a new cock insisting on attention, Steven just had a chance to admire the youth's tanned and slender back before vomiting copiously all over it, thus bringing to a standstill one of the year's most talked about party orgies.

Still reeking of half-digested eccy, alcohol and curry, Steven fled with the curses of thwarted lust ringing in his ears, although he noticed fleetingly that one or two of those in the line, including Robbo, were holding their ground and had no intention of allowing this little incident to dampen their ardor or relief.

After he'd washed up, he ran into Norrie who, an encyclopedia of gossip and already privy to details of his disgrace, told him he thought the blond's name was Wayne and that he hadn't come to the party at all but had gone to the Exchange with friends.

Steven burped his thanks, bile rising in his throat, waved sickeningly, walked out into the fresh air, and immediately left a new deposit, which narrowly missed the shiny black boots of one of the security guards.

With no idea how he'd negotiated his way back toward Oxford Street, Steven saw his blond dream talking to a group of youths his own age near The Flinders. Steven waited, attempting to look inconspicuous while examining the display window of a furniture showroom, in particular an antique settee he could not ever hope to own even if he worked for the next five hundred years. In fact, he examined it so closely while waiting for the blond bombshell's friends to move off that he grew to positively hate the piece. Eventually the friends dispersed and the blond, wiggling his cute little ass, disappeared up one of the side streets. Steven followed into the dark laneway.

It wasn't until he came upon the blond leaning against a back paling fence smoking that he realized he'd made the second major mistake of the evening.

The savage blow from behind felled him. He'd been followed by the blond's mates. They rifled through his pockets for his tabs of eccy, his money, and his credit cards. The pain in the back of his head throbbed numbly because he was so out of it, but his attackers were far from gentle. When they'd finished ransacking him for booty, Steven looked up as the blond slowly walked over to him smiling.

The blond stood over him, smoking. "Sorry, mate. Nothing personal. We're all out of cash and promises and what's the one night of the year without either? No fun at all," he said. "No recreational substances, no party fun."

The young blond squatted across his chest close to his face and blew smoke at him. "You older guys are just so predictable. You have the money, the power, the experience, so you think all is fair in love and seduction. You think that's enough."

Steve blinked his eyes to get rid of the grit and dirt blurring his vision. He was lying in the gutter being lectured philosophically on a sexual variation of Adam Smith's capitalism on Mardi Gras night?

"Shit, he's laughing," one of the attackers said. "He's fuckin' mad."

"You hurt badly?" the blond said, offering his hand.

"Mainly my vanity. A few bruises. And my lip's bleeding." Steve touched it gingerly and felt the swollen plumpness as he sat up.

"Come on, Todd, let's get going," one of the gang said impatiently.

Todd, looked up at his mate calmly. "You stupid fucker! Now, he knows my name."

"Sorry, Todd," the chastened mate said, compounding the crime.

Todd shook his head in exasperation. "Good help is so hard to find these days."

Steve hated himself for it, but he smiled broadly. If you're going to die, perhaps it's less painful with a smile on your face.

An air of panic agitated the gang. "What are we gonna do? He can identify us," one of them moaned.

"Not if we do a little body modification on him." Todd moved the butt of his glowing cigarette closer to Steve's eyes and his butt closer to Steve's crotch. He had to admit the close proximity of Todd's inviting package close to his mouth and the muscular butt on his chest, had hardened not only his resolve but his conscienceless prick. As he blinked a little in fear, he caught a brief wink from the blond. What was he playing at?

Todd stood suddenly. "Wait for me at the Oxford." He opened Steve's wallet and took out the bundle of cash, handing it to them, giving them instructions on what drug pusher to seek out for their party substances. "I'll take," he looked at one of the credit cards, "Steve here, down to one of the automatic tellers and see what else we can fund tonight."

"Then what?" an aggressive voice asked.

He waved the cigarette in Steve's direction again. "We'll come to some agreement that's mutually attractive to both of us." He ground his foot into Steve's crotch unobserved by his mates.

"I don't think you should hurt him," one of the more timid members of the group said.

Todd's smile was like a shark's. "I won't." He took a long drag of his cigarette, then added. "Unless I have to."

He sat on Steve's groin, obviously feeling his victim's hard cock pushing against his butt crack, although he gave no indication of it. Leaning forward, he stubbed his cigarette near Steve's head, so close that he felt a little flair of heat against his ear.

Todd pulled his shirt over his head revealing a taut, hard body with abs so perfect Steve almost drooled. Flexing his butt muscles, he squeezed Steve's cock before leaning forward again, mouth open, to lock their lips together. Steve winced at the sudden pain, relaxing a little when Todd ran his tongue across his bleeding mouth, sucking away the anger and humiliation, the metallic taste transferred from his lips to his tongue.

Todd wiped the residue from his chin across the back of his hand, before admiring it, and lapping it off with his tongue. "You taste good," he said. He ran his fingers across the hard cock in Steve's jeans. "You feel good, too."

Steve opened his mouth, but Todd placed a finger gently against his swollen lips. "No questions."

Steve nodded his agreement.

The threat of physical violence still hung over Steve. Todd could be a psycho, but, if so, he would relax and enjoy his last moments. In fact, the uncertainty of the situation made it more exciting, more real than many of the purely mechanical sexual couplings in which Steve had indulged recently. The proximity to hundreds of thousands of revelers just an alley-length away, the danger of a young man intent on who knew what, and the fear of his gang returning, added spice to an already dangerous mix.

He stood, towering over Steve, his tanned muscles outlined against the night sky, showing that he clearly dominated in all respects: youth, beauty, strength, physical prowess, and, when he pulled down his shorts, priapic proportions. Steve was no slouch in the dick department, but

Todd was magnificent. Turning his attention to Todd's butt, now in its naked splendor, here was an ass of the gods, sculpted from honey and hardened through rigorous use.

"Promise me you won't make a bolt for it," he said softly.

Steve hesitated.

"Say it," he demanded, as if anything said under duress had any validity.

"I promise."

He pulled Steve into a sitting position and removed his T-shirt to give him better access to the nipples he took between his teeth, biting down harder than his victim was used to. Steve sucked in a breath, but made no objection. He ran his hands across Steve's chest, squeezing his pecs hard until he gritted his teeth and pushed him back down to the pavement. He unfastened Steve's belt, unzipped and dragged his jeans down to his ankles, before pulling them right off. Steve worried about them until he remembered he had nothing left to steal.

Reaching for his own shorts Todd scrounged a condom and a small sachet of lube. Steve took the opportunity to get more comfortable, the gravel was causing severe discomfort pressing roughly against his back and ass cheeks. Todd tensed as he saw Steve move, but as he made no effort to spring up or topple him, his concentration went back to tearing the foil condom wrapper with his teeth.

As he squatted, Steve felt Todd's breath moments before his tongue snaked out to lick the head of his cock. He must have liked what he tasted for his lips wrapped around his hard dick and slid down to the base in one fluid motion. A "mmm" of approval escaped from his throat. Todd's lips vacuumed back up Steve's shaft until he was harder than he ever recollected being.

Satisfied with his skill in bringing him to full erection, Todd unfurled the condom on Steve's cock, impatiently ripping the lube open to slather the gel on the rubber before dousing his own asshole, inserting a finger to smear the interior.

He squatted his butthole above Steve's eager prick, slamming his full body weight down so that he was penetrated brutally. He gasped at the suddenness of the invasion before Steve felt him relax his tight sphincter muscle. Steve marveled at the strength with which Todd was cramming his asshole with cock, milking it. The guy was a power bottom hell bent on draining Steve's balls. Steve decided to go along for the ride, pinching Todd's nipples savagely until his face contorted with pain.

Steve wrapped his hand around Todd's powerful prick and began to jerk it in time to his cock plunging to the depths of Todd's anal chute. This was one of the most intense fucks of his life, and Steve knew he wouldn't be able to hold off much longer, especially when Todd began to swirl his butt around to piston down from a slightly different angle.

He wiped his fingers against Todd's greasy ass and transferred some of the gel to the cock he was jerking. It made the action slicker, easier to control, so that it was a matter of moments before Todd yelled "Holy fuck!" and shot his load across Steve's chest and chin. His anal muscles contracted so tightly around Steve's pounding cock that he began to squirt violently inside him. Steve held Todd down on his weapon until it was milked dry then the young man collapsed against his chest.

A whistle came from the mouth of the laneway. Todd quickly released himself, disposing of the creamy condom, and dressing in record time while Steve attempted to retrieve his clothes. Todd kneeled quickly, giving Steve a brief but passionate tonguing. "Thanks, mate," he whispered. "I needed that." As he stood up, he apologized. "Sorry about before, but you know, drugs, booze and Mardi Gras. It can be a lethal combo."

He handed Steve back his wallet. "Hope you're not too pissed off. We need cash to have a good time. Life can be cruel when you're sober."

Steve nodded as if he knew what the kid was talking about, grateful to have his wallet back, but more pleased that all he'd lost were a few party drugs, some cash, and his dignity. After Todd disappeared without so much as a backward glance, Steve stood up, a little unsteady on his feet, and felt for bumps and cuts on the back of his head wondering if he'd been suffering from concussion and had imagined the entire experience. What he did know was that he was going to be very sore in the morning.

The next day Steven nursed numerous abrasions and counted his blessings, as well as the number of bruises. He wasn't dead—he just felt like it—as Robbo tutted at his indiscretions and plied him with bandages and platitudes, making him laugh with tales of his own torrid exploits.

"You know your trouble? You're jealous of the young and you avenge yourself by falling in love with them."

"The odor of youth can never be disagreeable," Steven finished Ned Rorem's homily for him.

But as he parroted the words he knew they weren't strictly true. There was a malodorous stench that youth gave off as well, the rampant testosterone of unfettered selfishness, the odor of self-importance. The gangrenous stench of envy.

He and Robbo watched the parade on the TV news, catching brief glimpses of their idol who had disappeared into the night as thoroughly as any masked superhero after his task was accomplished. But Steven knew that soon the popular Mardi Gras blond would be all his. His pout, his ass, his body...

Later, alone together, Steven displayed his rampant cock to the adoring adorable blond, who wiggled his arse in appreciation and screwed up his face just as Steven blew a gooey white load all over him.

Then, in silent worship, Steven kneeled and licked his sticky love off that beautiful face and body captured for eternity on freeze frame on the flickering screen of his television.

BUCK'S NIGHT

"Suck it, slut," Walsh demanded none too pleasantly.

I didn't want to, and I sure wasn't going to without permission. It was six months to my final exams, and I had no intention of spending them on the street. I glanced over at my boyfriend Rhys. He shrugged, but smiled encouragement. I noticed, too, that he was hard as stone in his jeans. I didn't like this change in the schedule, but I had to admit my socks were bulging with cash, so a quick mouth job on the wedding boy, and then out of there. I'd kept my identity secret, coincidentally making enough in tips to see me through next semester. I'd actually be able to contribute to the household budget for a change.

It had all begun when Rhys had that fucking whine in his voice again. "What else can I do? I'll have to resign from the faculty. My career is over."

"Don't be such a drama queen," I admonished. I'd been putting up with this all morning since the stripper had canceled. "Just ring and get another one."

He exploded. "You don't think I've already tried that? It's Saturday, for fuck's sake. They're all busy. And most of them don't do gay. This same-sex wedding shit is all uncharted territory. Who knew there would be a demand for gay bachelor parties?"

"Some enterprising gay stud with more sense than money," I said. Sadly, I hadn't seen the trap coming.

"Someone like you, Cal?"

In a way it was my fault. I was doing a major in Small Business at a medium-sized liberal arts university and I'd facetiously suggested as a subject for my end-of-year paper, emergent small business in the gay wedding industry. Not the catering, reception, photography, or all that pomp and paraphernalia that goes with any gender's wedding, but small businesses that were intrinsically gay. Gay men catering to bachelor parties, for example.

I wasn't surprised to discover a few of the local gay male sex workers had taken to advertising their services to this burgeoning field of endeavor, those of the get-rich-quick mind set, showing how little they knew about the inherently stingy nature of gay men when it came to sex. With the rush to gay marriage before the law could be overturned by a fundamentalist backlash, there was a scarcity of the raw commodity—strippers. Considering the reputation that hetero buck's nights had attained, I was surprised any monogamous gay man would allow his partner the opportunity to indulge.

Rhys and I had been together almost eighteen months, all of them filled with constant whingeing when he didn't get his way. I was trying to make our liaison work as best I could, but I was green. This was my first relationship of any duration, a weekend being my previous longest. At twenty-one, I suppose I was too young to put down roots. Plus, and I say this in all modesty, I'm quite a catch. In fact, Rhys couldn't believe his luck when I said 'yes' to his offer of a place to live.

Truth be known, my agreement was to a place to live and that alone. It's not much fun for a poor boy trying to get by on two part-time jobs and a scholarship so measly I had to borrow lube just to party. When Rhys offered his spare room at a nominal rent, and, I assumed, services rendered, I jumped at the opportunity. Rhys was pleasing on the eye, and we had already been there, done that, and enjoyed the experience. Now I could get it on a regular basis, ensuring I didn't have to trawl the bars and waste my time and money, and I had regular meals and a nice, warm apartment with my own room.

I may have seen us as fuck buddies, unfortunately, Rhys saw us as a lot more. He saw me as a boyfriend. I argued against it as best I could, but the comfort I was experiencing as opposed to my hand-to-mouth existence prior to my move lulled me into a complacency that eventually saw Rhys move my belongings into his main bedroom. There I stayed, putting up with the odd shag and the incessant whingeing ever since.

He was a youngish lecturer at the university, fifteen years my senior, madly seeking tenure so he was sucking up to every benefactor and faculty member who could advance his career. I suspect that on the odd occasion Rhys had literally sucked, possibly even bending over and touching his toes for a few of the older gay gentlemen on the board. Rhys would not have considered this as being unfaithful to me: all was fair in the pursuit of his career. Not that I cared particularly, except for the hypocrisy, although I was expected to remain as monogamous as a monk despite the snotty-nosed faculty members groping me and suggesting clandestine assignations behind Rhys's back.

At first I told him about them, but his distress was obvious, and he blamed me for encouraging them with the way I dressed or my supposed slutty behavior. He was in major denial. His future mapped, he would do everything to make sure he fulfilled that dream, his every action motivated by that need. My needs, my wants, were secondary, subordinated to his career advancement as well. This was a cause of friction in our relationship. That, and the fact I would not legally marry him. When he'd asked to legalize us, I realized Rhys was not the person I wanted to spend the remainder of my life with. It had hit me hard, and I'd begun experimenting behind his back.

Not with any of the faculty who would take great delight in reporting my sexual misdemeanors, nor with any of the students he favored in his lectures. I wasn't what I would call promiscuous, although I was in heat most of the time because Rhys's sexual exploits with me were perfunctory and infrequent once he'd moved me into his bedroom. I was a trophy, just like his academic qualifications and his athletic prizes.

Problem was, I kept getting hit on everywhere I went. Not my fault I'm cute as fuck, and I keep my body in good shape. I'm young, so what do you expect? I'm a trim, taut and terrific 5'10" with light brown hair, cool green eyes and skin smooth as a billiard ball. My body looks like I work out, but it's natural: the biceps from years of manual labor as a teenager in the foster home where I grew up and from which I was forcibly expelled when it was discovered I was gay. The six-pack comes from crunches I do every night before bed, and the dimple in my chin that gives me a cheeky look and draws attention to my cocksucking lips is courtesy of my mum and dad—whoever they are.

Oh, did I mention I have the bubbliest butt this side of the Pecos and a cock that simply won't rest? It's always hard and easily triggered. It's a nice mouthful at seven inches.

You can see I'm quite a package, but modest to go with it. And still too young not to be easily manipulated. I hate confrontation. But I hate whining even more.

"Do this for me, Cal. There's a lot riding on it."

"And there will be a lot of strange men riding me if I do what you ask," I said with distaste.

Rhys laughed. "You're kidding me? Is that what you think? Hell, if I'd known that I could have put your mind at rest straight away. Professor Walsh is the height of respectability. There won't be any shit like that at his buck's night. His career couldn't stand the scandal. More importantly, his boyfriend would kill him."

I didn't doubt that for a minute. Walsh's partner, José, was noted for his possessiveness, his sharp tongue and the razor sharp stiletto he supposedly carried in his waistband, should anyone get too close to his beloved.

"So why have the party?" I thought it was a reasonable question.

"Look. It's my attempt to get in good with the old professor. He holds the strings for my tenure and I thought—"

"You suck up to the old geezer, but you want me to suck him off." Professor Walsh, my Business Studies professor, was one of the bastards who felt me up surreptitiously, suggesting extracurricular activity if I wanted better pass marks. My marks were good enough, thanks very much, without his kind of help, but I always turned him down politely in case he felt inclined to take his rejection out on my essays. It was one of the times it came in handy saying that I had a boyfriend. He seemed to accept it in good grace.

Not so for Professor Brooke, my English Lit professor, who simply would not take no for an answer and began to mark down my assignment work in proportion to my reluctance to accept his invitations. Eventually, I had to go to arbitration, which meant my artificially low marks were elevated, much to his chagrin. He hated me now.

"Look, if it will make you feel better I'll ring Kevin. You know Kevin, who's organizing the bash, and ask him what's expected of the...um...entertainment. You can listen in."

That seemed reasonable enough. It also seemed my resolve was wavering.

Rhys made the call while I listened on the extension. "Hi, Kevin. Rhys Llewelyn here. I'm just making last minute arrangements for tonight with the stripper. Can you just confirm what's expected of him? He wants to come prepared."

Kevin laughed at the double entendre. "Nothing like that Rhys. This is a reputable crowd. It may get a little raunchy, but all he's called on to do is a few bumps and grinds, flash a bit of dick and ass, and treat the Professor Walsh to a special show."

"What does that entail exactly?"

"Let the old guy touch him up a bit, I suppose. Maybe slap his dick across the old man's face."

"But no sex?

"God, no. The old boy would probably keel over. Or José would put a blade through his heart."

Kevin and Rhys laughed.

"What was the fee you negotiated?" Kevin asked.

"A thousand dollars," Rhys replied. Fortunately, they didn't hear my sharp intake of breath. If I'd been vacillating before the phone conversation, the price tipped me over. "Plus tips, if anyone wants to put cash in his jock strap or his socks."

Kevin was beginning to pant. "If he's that good, they might."

"Oh, he's that good all right." Rhys winked at me. "He'll be wearing a mask; hope that's all right."

"As long as his body is smooth and muscular and his cock on the biggish side, it's perfect. He's not one of the students is he? Because it could be dangerous if he is."

"No, not a student," Rhys lied. "But well known in the town and –"

"I understand."

That clinched it.

"Oh," Kevin hastened to add, "if he's going to come masked you might try to persuade him to come as a superhero. The old prof is a mad keen comic book collector."

"I'll see what I can do," Rhys said before hanging up the phone.

The best Rhys could do was not much. The town's major costume hire store was just about all out of superheroes. There was a moth-eaten Spider-Man outfit, which would scarcely have allowed me to breathe let alone reveal my salient points, and a Batman mask made of a plastic so brittle I cut my hand on the pointed ears. Hmm, on reflection they both had their attractions.

"We do have another costume out back, but it's not very popular with the guys around here," the shop assistant said.

"May we have a look?" Rhys asked.

When he brought it out, it smelled of mothballs and reeked of 'gay.' It was the costume worn by one of the most popular cult superheroes of the past twenty years: Buck Naked. Popular with teenage geeks and horny gay men. His superpower was his genitalia. He could fuck anything male, female or alien into submission. And if that didn't work, his asshole would milk them to the point of exhaustion. Yep, Buck Naked's superpower was Superslutdom.

"Um...I think that will give totally the wrong impression," I said, backing away from a costume that was as dangerous as if it were riddled with kryptonite.

Rhys sighed, a sure sign another whinge was coming up. "We don't have a choice. The other two costumes are totally unsuitable. This is the only one even approaching what we need. So, it's either this or—"

"Call the whole thing off."

"And go and live the rest of miserable lives in Outer Siberia."

I sighed loudly. "Wrap it up, we'll take it," I told the salesman. Rhys beamed his satisfaction.

I was secreted in the exotically tiled Balinese-style kitchen of Professor Walsh's luxury apartment, attempting to swat away Kevin's unwanted fondling of my ass as we waited for the signal to start the bachelor party entertainment. I blamed the costume, which consisted of little more than a tight hood that covered my hair and the top of my head to my eyes down to the tip of my nose in a deep shade of maroon; a matching pair of flared suede thigh boots that looked like the fins on luxury cars from the 1950s, a pair of the tightest burgundy shorts known to man from which the seat had been removed so that my ass was open to the breeze and the aforementioned Kevin's digital maneuverings, and finally, a tight waistcoat that showed off my chest and biceps and was emblazoned with a coat of arms, two crossed penises with the letters BN.

"Here, you'll need some of this," Kevin said, bending me forward. Before I could argue, he'd lathered my asshole with some sort of gel, inserting his fingers between my sphincter muscles. It felt cool as his digits probed deep inside me. It was hard not to react to his attention, and I guess I groaned a little as my cock began to harden.

"Why do I need that?" I enquired.

"Lubrication," he said as he smeared more around my asshole as well as internally. "It's a relaxant as well as a stimulant. And it will help numb the pain. And with an ass as hot as yours, you're going to need it."

There was a loud roar from the living room. Over the pumping up of the party music I'd chosen for my act, I shouted, "That wasn't part of the deal."

As Kevin shoved me through the door into the living room for my performance, I heard his reply: "We lied."

I was like a frightened animal caught in headlights, wondering whether Rhys was part of the lie. Then I realized he couldn't be, not with his rigid demand for fidelity. On the other hand, he'd do anything for promotion. But did that include pimping out his boyfriend?

My brain commanded my body to get moving, but there was no response. Just like the first time I had ever done anything like this. I'd been desperately poor and hadn't known where my next meal was coming from, so the promise of five hundred dollars was a promise of salvation. I'd answered an advert for amateur strippers at one of the gay discos in town. They were hoping to lure patrons with the promise of a free show and lots of hunky bodies in a naked if not an aroused state.

My poverty made me do it. That was my excuse. I'd been something of a joke growing up in the town, my chubby body the butt of many cruel jokes so that my self-image was at bottom of recession levels. But enough sex partners had murmured appreciation of the new, slick slimline me to know I wouldn't make a total fool of myself, although I still couldn't reconcile the muscular hot number that stared back at me from the mirror. Perhaps this competition would help me overcome my issues of self-worth.

I waited, third in line, before I was shoved out on to the dance floor beneath the shards of light reflected from the revolving mirror ball to the pulsing beat of loud rock music. I stood rooted to the spot, terrified, glad now that my street clothes had been augmented with a cheap plastic Batman mask so that no one would recognize me if I humiliated myself. But I hadn't. The crowd had waited—like they were now—until some exhibitionist gene kicked in and the music's rhythm took possession of my body. It had been one of the most liberating moments of my life.

The whistling and slow handclapping from the partygoers brought me back to the moment. I was standing as near to naked as legally permissible among a group that included my uni professors, my boyfriend, various faculty members, and students who were eager for me to go beyond the 'legal' requirement. At least one of them was expecting a little intimate contact. I'd admitted to Rhys that I would allow Walsh to feel me up, creepy as that might be, but secretly I was prepared to blow the ugly, old bastard for the hefty fee I was receiving, but I wasn't prepared to let his prick into my ass. And anyone else who had ideas of taking such a liberty had likewise better forget it.

My body's natural rhythm took over. I bumped and grinded my way among the guests who hooted and hollered their appreciation, expressing it with their fingers and hands, copping a feel or squeezing their fingers into my bubble butt. Their faces lit up like a Christmas tree as they made contact with the lube, sliding in easily, their expectations rising as rapidly as their cocks. It also lubricated their appreciation of my performance, which they began to show in a mercenary manner by slipping cash into the bands of my shorts or in the tops of my boots.

Reluctantly, I had to admit I was getting turned on by all the attention. All those hands caressing my body, rubbing my six-pack and squeezing my ass, fumbling attempts to prize my ever hardening cock from my shorts. I slithered over to Rhys, who sat a little apart from the others, and perched on his knees giving him his very personal lap dance. I leaned in to his ear. "Hope you're enjoying watching your boyfriend make a slut of himself." I knew he was as his cock twitched beneath my butt. I ground down extra hard. "Just wait until I get you home alone tonight." He groaned in expectation.

Truth be told, I was super turned on. Exhibitionism came easy to me now that I was no longer the tubby little butterball of my teen years. Those dreaded years in which I desperately hated to share the showers after sport because I was ridiculed and reviled, every glance in the mirror a constant reminder of my lack of desirability; those years were indelibly etched in my memory. As was my sudden sprouting at 16 and my appreciation of physical contact and my pursuit of the body trim, taut and terrific—mine as well as others. It now looked as if it had paid off and I was reaping the benefits... financially.

In the two sweeps around the guests in the room I had avoided Professor Walsh in order to peak his interest and also, hopefully, to get him so turned on a quick hand job or the briefest of blow jobs would have him squirting followed by my quick exit. I slithered toward him meeting his eyes. I didn't like what I saw. Here was a man used to power, used to dominating, and all I saw reflected back was myself as prey. *Let's get this over with,* I told myself, lowering my ass against his bulging Armani trousers. I ran my hands over his chest and was surprised by the hardness of his musculature. Where I expected soft and flabby, he was taut and toned. I undid the buttons to his shirt to reveal pecs that would have done a man half his age proud. A small smattering of hair, turning slightly silver, meant the old prof must have been quite a stud, and quite a catch in his day. This wasn't going to be as bad as I had expected.

Leaning in I washed his nipple with my tongue and felt the sexual electricity zap straight to his cock, which twitched angrily beneath my butt. I used my teeth to annoy the nipple I had left alone. Walsh sucked air through his teeth. Bingo! I bit down slightly harder, a barely audible groan escaping his lips. The balance of power was ever so subtly changing. Given time, I could control him, therefore controlling the situation.

My face was so close I could taste his breath. He looked me in the eye, flinty and questioning, whispering, "Where have you been hiding yourself all this time, my lovely?" before grabbing the hood and pulling my face to his mouth. His tongue stabbed between my lips as he overwhelmed me. I went with it, mostly in fear that a clump of hair would be yanked out by the roots if I didn't. If the skirmish was brutal, the execution was finesse itself. This man knew how to seduce with a kiss. I melted into him, lowering my defenses. His tongue gently, but firmly explored my mouth as my tongue parried. He sucked me in with just enough force to trap me there without pain.

Cupping my sheathed cock and balls, moaning his approval, he ran his hands lightly across my stomach and chest, hesitating briefly to pinch each nipple, before rubbing down my back to my ass. He pushed a finger between my cheeks. Feeling no resistance, he explored further, slipping two more inside me. I saw an eyebrow rise in surprise, but not wanting him to get the wrong idea, I slapped his hand away gently and whispered, "Naughty."

The catcalls and obscenities from those watching increased volubly as I rose from his lap. I pulled down the zip of his trousers, extracting his impressive, steely hard cock, and kneeled in front of the head of the department, in both senses of the expression. There was a whoop of delight. Walsh made himself more comfortable by pulling his balls out of his trousers, which made his cock even more impressive. I wrapped my hand around the loaded weapon, stroking it gently, tickling the head with my thumb. Walsh relaxed into the chair, his breath ragged. At this rate, my performance would all be over in a matter of minutes. I increased my pace. That was when he uttered the words that would change everything.

"Suck it, slut."

Rhys didn't call 'time out', so I got down on my hands and knees, doggy style. A sting and a rush of blood went to my butt as a couple of guys swatted my naked, tanned ass, indicating some of the party guests had moved closer to watch the action.

Okay, I'd give them something to talk about. I ran my tongue slowly along Walsh's cock from his balls to the glistening head, then licked the pearl of pre-cum and swallowed.

"Nasty," he said. "I like it."

I teased the knob with a slight biting action before placing my lips over the large head. He grunted as I slid my warm, wet mouth down the shaft. It tasted spicy. As I neared his balls, I gave him tongue action that made him buck in his chair, slurping up and down his pole for about five minutes as the rest of the party just watched in awe.

"Fuck, son. You have great technique. You're a real professional. That mouth, whoa boy, it was born to suck cock."

I hesitated for a moment, remembering I'd been assured everyone would keep their cocks in their pants. I'd never expected to enjoy sucking Walsh's cock. I had been hoping I wouldn't have to, but it was harmless enough I guessed, and I was earning big bucks. More importantly, Rhys had given his consent. Or I'd interpreted his behavior as such.

What worried me was that I was getting off on what I was doing. I was enjoying the attention. Hell, I was even enjoying chowing down on the professor's dick. He grabbed the back of my head and pushed my mouth right down to the base then thrust brutally into my throat.

He moaned. "That's some throat you've got there, son. Only a slut could take me like that without gagging."

He allowed me up for air, giving me an opportunity to glance quickly at Rhys. He had his cock out, stroking it, his eyes glazed over with expectation.

"Are you a total slut, son?" Walsh asked.

"Yes, sir. I'm a total slut." I was giving him the answer he expected.

Big mistake. Uttering those words was like giving everyone at the party the green light.

Kneeling left my ass vulnerable. That was fine while the party was strictly hands off, but after foolishly admitting I was a total slut, some of the more adventurous revelers decided I was easy meat. I wasn't. I was play-acting. Maybe a bit more convincingly than I'd intended, if the sound of descending zippers was anything to go by.

I felt hands on my ass cheeks, then a finger exploring my hole. I tried to swat them away, but Walsh grabbed my hands and held them. I looked over to Rhys for help. Surely, he didn't want to watch his boyfriend abused in front of him. His smile revealed his satisfaction with the way things were progressing. As did the action of his wrist.

Someone began seriously tonguing my hole. His technique was superb. A+ or higher. I relaxed and the prof let go of my arms. A little anal tonguing couldn't hurt. I'd have to draw the line shortly, but I consoled myself with the belief that at least the guys were getting their money's worth.

I put it down as research for my paper.

The tongue vanished, and I felt probing back at my asshole. I tensed and flexed my sphincter closed, but I was so slicked with spit and lube the finger slid straight in. Then a second. Whoever was behind me was opening me up. That couldn't be good.

I turned, appealing silently to Rhys for help. He just shrugged as if I was on my own, getting my just desserts. "Look, this wasn't part of the deal," I mumbled as I tried to squirm out of the vise-like grip of the guy behind me.

"Just add it to the bill," Walsh said. Before I could complain any further, I felt a cock pressed against my ass chute. A pair of strong hands gripped my waist, a grunt, and an almighty thrust. I felt a cock sink into my guts. I let out a roar as the pain seared my butthole and the sting of illegal entry burst in my brain.

It was one motherfucker of a cock I had wedged in my asshole. This guy was hung. He not only plunged his weapon deep into my bowels, but he rotated his cock so it entered from a slightly different angle each plunge. He pulled out then slammed it the full length in again, pushing my head down on Walsh's cock so it sank deep into my throat. I attempted to suck in air as my head was held fast and the prof spewed his cum into my gullet. "Good slut. Swallow it all," he said before extracting his still oozing prick to wipe his stringing cum along my cheek. He leaned down to kiss my cum-soaked mouth and sucked his slimy residue off my tongue, exploring the inside of my mouth searching for more. His cock stayed hard and before I knew it, he'd leaned over me to claim his bachelor party right. "My turn at the slut's ass."

I shivered in anticipation of his strong, hard cock slamming into my hole. Plus, I was hoping to find out who the stud was with the great fucking technique. Sure enough, he took the prof's place. I glanced up at him just before he pulled my face toward his cock. I was suddenly sick to my stomach. I wanted out of there big time. That slimebag Brooke was now offering me his sleazy cock that had, until a few moments before, been slamming my guts. I hated the man. No way was I going to suck his greasy prick. I looked over toward Rhys, who was grinning so totally I could almost hear him preparing a speech to accept tenure.

I struggled to put an end to the party games, but Walsh slammed his cock up my asshole while Brooke pulled my mouth to his cock. I tasted my ass funk on his slippery prick. I choked and gag spewed out of my mouth around his balls. He wasn't going to let me go. I struggled as I was pinioned between the two insatiable cocks attempting to bury themselves as far inside my body as possible.

"You're choking him," someone called from the guys watching my impalement, but still they continued.

Walsh grunted. "It's the hood. It's not letting him breathe." Before I could stop him, he'd grabbed the edge of my disguise and ripped it away. There was a gasp from the room.

Someone shouted. "Oh, my god. It's Freeman."

Walsh and Brooke didn't vary their rhythm until it slowly registered who they had skewered between them. "Holy fuck," Brooke exclaimed before his cock spat hot spunk into my mouth.

"Damn, Freeman," Walsh hissed. "You're even better in the flesh than the fantasy. Hot ass, Freeman. If only I'd known earlier what a slut you are."

I wanted to scream that I wasn't a slut, that it was all a terrible misunderstanding. I wanted Rhys to get me out of there. When Brooke finally let go of my head, I spat his cum at him and it puddled on his stomach. "Don't waste it, boy," he said, with a touch of steel to his voice. Walsh pushed my face in it while he viciously plugged my ass. He hit all the right spots and pre-cum oozed from my shaft, which had hardened under his relentless anal onslaught. Fuck, my body was enjoying it even if I wasn't.

I heard the door open and a sudden hush fell over the room.

"I see you started without me," José said without an ounce of jealousy in his voice.

Walsh was incredulous. "You knew about this?"

José began removing his clothes to get in on the action. "Whose idea do you think it was?"

Walsh was still puzzled. "Let me get this straight. You deliberately hired young Freeman here for my bachelor party knowing I'd fuck him?"

"What? You don't like him all of a sudden?" José stroked his thick, tan cock near my mouth. "Of course I hired him. You've been obsessed ever since he joined your class. I have to admit, he gets my balls churning, too. So..." he said with a shrug, "...what better wedding present than we both share him."

"And Rhys agreed?" Walsh asked the very question I was afraid of.

During the confab, Brooke had reluctantly made way for the youthful José to shove his cock between my lips. "Of course, he did. I didn't even have to twist his arm. He practically begged me to take Freeman. The only proviso was that he wear a mask in front of the other guests. We could remove it later after the other guests had left. Looks as if that part of the deal is off. Oh shit, his mouth is so hot."

My face dripped manslime, being battered by José's incredibly hard cock while I felt Walsh hesitating with his cock embedded in my ass. "And young Freeman here knew nothing about all this bartering? He didn't know Rhys had set it up?" he asked.

"Uh uh," José grunted.

Walsh chuckled. "How delicious."

I think that made his cock all the harder. He showed me no mercy as he slammed his prick into my sloppy ass. "And we get to keep him for the night?"

José grunted his reply because I was tonguing him with even more fervor in an attempt to smother my anger at Rhys's betrayal. While I could appreciate his single-mindedness in his pursuit of a career, I drew the line at lying to me on such a grand scale, and offering up my body for abuse. The law had words for such activity. Okay, I was prepared to enjoy my humiliation for the moment—the money made that worthwhile. I was being paid for a service I was supplying. *Being serviced.* I grinned at the thought, almost choking as José sank into my throat.

Brooke kept up a running commentary on what he wanted his friends to do to my body, and it provided intense aural stimulation. I've always loved dirty talk. Rhys's silent lovemaking inhibited me into holding back on moans of pleasure and gasps during my orgasms. My situation now was infinitely freer, and I took advantage of it with guttural sounds from deep in my throat. I was also grinding my ass against the body that was expertly fucking me, my cock drooling its approval.

I heard Kevin's voice nearby whispering to José and Walsh, "Um, some of the guys are wondering if it's okay to...you know..."

Walsh panted. "That's up to young Freeman here."

My head was unpinioned, and I nodded enthusiastically without thinking. My mind and my common sense were prisoners to my body and its desires.

"What about Rhys?" Kevin whispered.

It was doubtful even Rhys expected it to go this far, but what the hell? He was responsible for it. I would probably find myself out on the street, my ass sore for days, and some of these guys I wouldn't have looked at twice as sexual partners in the normal course of events, but I had a shitload of cash that would see me through to final exams. I was more turned on than I ever had been in my life, and I absolutely loved being the center of attention.

"Fuck Rhys," I spat.

Kevin passed on my agreement to the whoops from the party guests, although a few, whose relationships were not predicated on sharing extra-marital sex partners, quietly left whispering their farewells to a blithely unconcerned wedding couple, while others were content to watch the activity while remaining steadfastly clothed or else jerked off to the entertainment. The remainder opted for eager participation.

In no time flat, Kevin had shucked his clothes. If I was honest with myself, I'd always fancied the stocky footballer. He wasn't your usual jock boofhead; the man had brains, but he also had a body that was thick and bulky without being fat. He slid beneath me and wrapped his lips around my prick, slurping away the obvious signs of my excitement. In my peripheral vision, I saw a number of men stripping off their clothes or just their trousers, awaiting their turn at me by playing with their cocks.

It has always surprised me how many good ideas occur at the most inopportune moments. Well, not inopportune exactly. Here I was kneeling on the floor being cocked fore and aft with my prick being expertly tongued when I decided on a short-term career change.

I suddenly called a halt to the proceedings. José was pissed that he hadn't had a chance to blow his load. I stood and removed what little there was remaining of my costume, a costume I was determined to keep and which Rhys could bloody well pay for, and said to the horny fuckers, "Okay, tonight's not been what any of us expected. I may have been conned, but you paid for a bachelor party, and a real bachelor party you shall have. So, take a seat guys, and let's get the real show on the road." There was a scramble to grab the best vantage points in the living room by the dozen or so guys remaining as I grabbed Kevin by the hand and led him away to a barrage of the catcalls and whistles.

Once in the kitchen, I thrust my mouth against his, sucking his tongue like it was his cock. Releasing him, I explained what I needed him to do; a simple task of subdued lighting, cueing the music, making sure the guests of honor were seated appropriately and that I had a small area to strut my stuff. I asked him if he had any more of the gel he'd used when I first arrived. He smeared a good patina over my butthole before sliding three fingers inside me. He pushed gently to spread the lubrication, almost bringing me off in the process. This man had magic fingers. His mouth wasn't bad, either. I was eager to try his cock.

"Let's see if I'm ready," I said with a smirk. I bent forward, and he got the hint. He slid in with a minimum of effort, but not without a small amount of pain—just the right amount to make it pleasurable.

He was breathless. "Holy fuck! You're still so tight." I squeezed his cock with my ass muscles to show my appreciation then pulled away, much to his disappointment. I wanted this whole show to be public, to be talked about for years to, ah, cum. Kevin returned to the living room to the salacious comments of his friends. The lights were lowered, and I heard hard driving rock music pounding from the sound system.

I put my costume back on, gyrating my body in time to the music's beat and pushed open the door to thunderous approval. I grinded my way to the small area that Kevin had opened up for me. I teased, I bumped, I ground my ass against imaginary groins, I humped the floor like a horny groom on his wedding night, and then I stripped off each item of my costume until I was buck naked.

I got down on all fours, crawling my way to the wedding boys. I impaled myself on José's hard upright cock, slithering until his eyes opened in amazement as he shot in my guts. I hopped off, sucking his slimy cock clean before turning my attentions to Walsh. With my asshole dripping spunk down the back of my legs, I lowered my face into his groin and forcefully suctioned my lips along the length of his rock hard prick. I brought him off in a matter of minutes as he pig-grunted and shot his bolt.

Turning to the others in the room, I opened my mouth to show my gob was full of slime. I rolled it around on my tongue to the chant of 'Swallow it! Swallow it!' from the audience. Moving slowly toward Rhys, the cum dribbling down my chin. I faced him as I sat on his cock, mashing my open mouth over his. He bucked in an attempt to move his head away; he has always hated cum in his mouth, but I wouldn't release him until I'd made him taste the slimy juice of his boss.

Triumphantly, I turned to the crowd. With a mischievous grin, followed by an enormous theatrical gulp, I swallowed the warm cum stew sticking in my throat. The cheers were deafening. My face still sticky with jizz, I licked the silvery traces from Rhys's slick lips before leaning in to whisper in his ear,

"Make the most of this sweetheart, because it's the last time you'll ever fuck me. From now on my ass belongs to anyone who wants it." I was exaggerating, of course, but it did me good to see the flash of panic in his eyes. It was payback time, although even as I said it, I knew part of it to be true. I would never go back to the relationship with Rhys.

I rode him like I'd wanted to for the past few lackluster months of lovemaking; I rode him like I had when we first met, before he began taking me for granted. I wanted him to regret what he'd lost. But true to form, the only sign that he'd deposited a load in my ass was an inhalation of breath until his cock stopped twitching inside my ass, then a satisfied exhalation that was just as quiet.

I stood up, wiping my lips with the back of my hand before hauling Kevin to the front of the room. He'd set up the coffee table for me, with cushions for my knees, and had ascertained that it would comfortably hold my weight. In front of the guests, I kneeled and arched my back so my inviting asshole, dripping warm sperm, was vulnerable to any onlooker. Kevin took his place behind me like he belonged there. I moaned like a slut and beckoned Brooke, who had kept away from me since my unmasking, to my mouth. I opened up as he approached. The look of surprise said it all, but he eagerly poked his prodigious cock between my lips.

The remaining guests, no longer reticent, were eager to join the sexual fray. They moved closer to fondle my body and join the queues for my willing cum-dump holes. The frenzy ran for an hour or more until I was so sore I could not take another cock, and my throat was so coated with cock phlegm I thought

I would choke. I had cum twice myself. Once while Kevin's thick cock massaged my prostate and later when one of the guests decided I'd suffered enough and blew me while I had cock buried inside me.

Rhys had long since left the party.

It was the early hours of the morning by the time coffee and cognac were served. Don't you just love the behavior of the seriously cultured? José and Walsh continued to finger me even after I'd begged off spending the night because of soreness and willingly took a rain check. I did go back, a little over a week later, and learned they were sexual athletes who kept me on my back for almost six hours. Well, not always on my back, but usually on the end of one of their pricks. To my surprise, I also got to butt fuck José's tight little asshole until I had him begging.

They turned out to be considerate lovers, and very much in love with each other. I was lucky to share their joy and ended up being invited to their wedding. I'd moved in with Kevin, who continued to plow my hole whenever the mood struck him, which was often. He didn't mind that I would occasionally feel the need for something special, like Brooke's nasty pole jammed between my cheeks. For that, I expected no classroom favors, and received none.

My reputation spread, as I had intended. I didn't care for the 'slut' tag which Rhys, in his jealousy, spread about, but the reputation as a bachelor party stripper, now that was something else. I enjoyed the attention. I enjoyed the cocks. I enjoyed the fucking. Most of all, however, I enjoyed the cash benefits. I only did a buck's night every now and then because

I made so much money at it, I lived comfortably. So comfortably, I considered it as a full-time profession.

I'd already discovered that the global economic downturn had killed any prospect of a well-paid career, especially in my degree subjects. But I also knew that my options for continuing to work at engagement parties was limited in a town the size of mine. I needed a larger population in which to strut my stuff.

Upon graduation, summa cum laude, I packed my new fuel-efficient car, gave my ass up to my old fuck buddies, and even gave Rhys a thank you blow job, plus a weekend of the best sex Kevin was ever likely to have in appreciation for his friendship. Under different circumstances I could have settled down with him, but for the moment, I was young and in demand. My reputation preceded me, and my asshole twitched at the prospect of that great big world of cock out there waiting for me.

I checked myself in the rear vision mirror. I was ready. I pulled away from the curb, honking my thanks to Kevin, who waved until I turned the corner. I switched on the radio, singing along loudly as I headed for the highway out of town, hoping for a life of adventure. I was young, I was cute, I was fuckable. All I needed was men. And the world was full of them. No wonder I was smiling.

Four on the Floor

The First Chapter of Busting Billy's Butt

"Holy shit, man, get a load of that ass." Jerry focused the binoculars on the fourth floor apartment across the street. With the magnification of those suckers, he could see straight into the living room through the wide-open balcony doors. As wide open as the guy's butthole, if I had my guess.

"Here, let me see." Mike snatched the glasses from him.

"I told you he was something out of the box," I said from the corner bar where I was topping up our drinks. I threw the empty Bourbon bottle in the trash to join the earlier one we'd already polished off.

Jerry, my sleazy boss at Klassic Kars where I worked as a detailer, came back to get his glass. He's chunky, in his early forties, shaven head and a splash of body hair across his chest; definitely a daddy type, but not exactly "attractive" to go with it. "You weren't kidding, Steve. That guy has it all. I could fuck that."

I knew for a fact that Jerry wasn't fucking anything at the moment. He was always at me to set him up with one of my single friends. It wasn't gonna happen.

Billy sneered. "I don't think there's anything special about him." He hated it when he wasn't the center of attention.

"You're kidding, right?" Mike relinquished the glasses to Jerry, who definitely wanted another look. We'd met Mike at the showroom a few weeks earlier, when he'd come in to give a newly arrived 1956 Buick Century Riviera Four-Door Hardtop the once over. He'd bought it on the spot, counting out the price from a huge wad of high value banknotes he said he always carried in case of emergencies. This guy was seriously wealthy—or a braggart. Maybe both. And dumb as shit to carry around that much cash. Both Jerry and I had pegged him as gay, and Jerry had pegged him as available, something I wasn't, and flirted accordingly. Mike wore baggy blue jeans, navy sneakers and a black cotton T-shirt that hugged his chest so tight his hard nipples could have poked your eye out if you got too close. He looked to be around thirty with shaggy, black hair that he flicked with his fingers to keep it out of his hazel bedroom eyes. I would have been flirting as well, if I hadn't already been in a relationship, although said relationship was as rocky as a row boat in the North Atlantic at the moment. However, we liked to give the outward impression we were the perfect couple.

We had been when we first started out five years before. Billy was the five-feet-eight, tanned skinned, blond haired, blue-eyed beauty with the snug little body that had only gotten better and more defined when he'd 'discovered' the gym. I would have said 'obsessed' with the gym since his retrenchment as a sous-chef in a restaurant that didn't survive the economic downturn. That was just one of the problems. I was the other. I'm slightly taller, thinner and two years older at twenty-eight, with dirty blond hair matched with dirty blond eyes. That's what Billy called them when we first met at a bar that was so humid inside we didn't know whether the air conditioning had failed or whether we were so hot for each other we were producing our own power surge.

By the time we'd both emerged from our sex-addled euphoria, we found ourselves saddled with a substantial mortgage on a fifth-floor apartment in a high-rise development full of gay couples and solos, with minimalist but classy furniture, expensive cultural and social tastes, and maxed out credit cards. There is no way we could afford a separation, even if we'd wanted one.

We didn't. We were still comparatively happy together. We fitted, in the parlance of our friends and neighbors. We were popular. A little too popular. The apartment complex was a breeding ground of temptation and infidelity: attractive, buff boys of every color, class, creed and combination. I was like a kid in a rainbow hued candy store, and I wanted a taste of everything. Billy, however, was all eyes front, prim as a Sunday-go-to-meeting front pew fundamentalist.

Trouble is I was finding it hard to, well, get hard for the same old/same old boyfriend after all these years. No one wants to eat meat and potatoes year in year out, so why would they want to fuck the same ass regardless of how cute? The solution, we'd decided, was Paris, and not because of any overt familiarity with the city, but just a general romantic longing to spice up our lovemaking, which had become as stodgy as porridge. But financially, Paris was as far away as Mars.

That's why we'd been sniping at each other all afternoon, the atmosphere taut as tensile wire across a paddock, when an uninvited and unwelcome Jerry, with two new buddies in tow, arrived for an up-close-and-personal look at our exhibitionist neighbor.

"What's he doing here?" Billy hissed when I told him who had just buzzed our apartment. "You know I can't stand the ugly toad."

"I didn't invite him," I snarled back.

Just then he barreled through the open front door, and we both beamed our best imitation smiles at him. He was too crass to notice, but his buddies did.

"Knew you wouldn't mind," he said. "You know Mike already, and this is his young mate, Raoul. Where're the binoculars?" Jerry was all couth.

Raoul, about the same vintage as Mike, tattooed and twice as good looking, had an attitude to match. "If he's as hot as Jerry here says, why don't we go jump him and tattoo his ass with our spunk!" One look through the binoculars was enough to convince him.

"You sure you don't know his number, man? Or even his apartment, so I can go buzz him." Unluckily for Raoul, our neighbor lived in a security building, but that didn't prevent him from shouting obscene invitations across the street to zero success, and to my utter embarrassment.

"You should have bought extra binoculars and installed cinema chairs for the show." Billy was at his sarcastic stage.

"Hey, chill out," Raoul said. "This is some show."

"Tell me about it," Billy said. "I got up the other night for a drink and came out here to find Steve fully naked and jerking off while he watched pretty boy over there in action. He didn't even realize I was watching him until he blew his load in the Zamioculcas zamiifolia. And it's not the first time."

Raoul was getting irritable and horny. "In the fuckin' what?"

"Those plants over there," Billy said, pointing at our Zanzibar ferns.

"Sick, dude," said Mike.

"It's not like I do it every night," I said, trying to placate Billy and keep the evening peaceful. I didn't want an argument in front of the guests. "Anyway his show that night was something else. There was a group thing going on, and I was hard as steel."

"Glad something can still make you hard because it sure isn't me," he said.

"Oh, shiiiiit," Jerry said. "He's got company."

Even Billy moved to the balcony to have a look. Our neighbor never did it in the bedroom, always in the living room, either for our benefit, because he appreciated an audience, or maybe because he never washed his bed sheets. His brazen behavior encouraged mine and I no longer tried to hide the fact I jerked off to him.

Not any more than our little group was attempting to hide the fact we were watching him as closely as teen sci-fi geeks at a Star Trek convention.

Raoul moaned. "That's a great ass, dude."

"Not what I'd call a great ass," Billy said.

"Fuck, I'd slip him a bit any time," came Jerry.

I tried lightening the mood. "You'd slip anyone a bit any time."

"Just exactly what would you class as a great ass then?" Mike asked with an arch of an eyebrow.

Billy shrugged. "Mine, for example." He patted his butt.

If I'd been honest I would have agreed with him, but in a stale relationship the ass across the street was more appetizing than that readily available in my bed.

Mike laughed. "Yeah, right."

"We'll have to take your word for it," Jerry said.

Billy smiled. "Don't believe me?"

Mike looked from Billy to the exhibitionist across the way. He turned the binoculars on Billy. "I guess Steve will have to be the judge because he's the only one who's seen both."

I was angry our private life was being aired in front of my boss and virtual strangers. "Leave me out of it."

"You'd be biased anyway," Mike chipped in.

"There's only one way to settle this," Raoul said eagerly. "He'll have to show us."

I didn't like where this was heading.

"His visitor is porking his ass. Fuck, that is so hot." Jerry had turned back to the free show across the street.

There was a scramble. We grabbed the binoculars from one another for a close up of our neighbor bent over the back of his divan, a hung top pounding him from behind. Even without the aid of glasses, we could see it was quite a performance.

"I could give you a much better show," Billy said.

Mike chuckled. "Man, there's no way. That guy is hot. Just look at him."

Lightning fast, Billy had his tank top off to reveal his marbled six pack with the small fluff of blond hair that snaked down under his army fatigues, which just as quickly dropped round his ankles. All that separated him from total nakedness was his navy striped briefs that clung to his bulging package and hugged his ass like toffee to an apple.

"Fuck, I thought I was ripped," Raoul said and flexed his arm. His bicep was good enough to lick.

I gulped my bourbon. I was losing control of the situation.

Billy dimmed the lights and programmed the CD player. Suddenly, *"Sin"* by *Nine Inch Nails* thundered through the apartment. I watched horrified as he slowly gyrated his body and wagged his ass like some cheap pole dancer, miming the lyrics about being 'defaced' and 'disgraced' as he swayed around the room like an Indian cobra under the influence of a Hindu snake charmer. Mike and Raoul were in party mood, whooping and hollering. As my lover swept his hips tantalizingly within reach, Mike opened his wallet and tucked a note into the band of Billy's briefs. Raoul was keen to join the testosterone melee that was engulfing the room and grabbed a handful of cash to shove down the front of

Billy's increasingly revealing underwear while taking the opportunity to cop a feel. Jerry, as usual, was content to sit on his wallet.

I was acutely embarrassed. On the other hand, Billy's eyes shone. Before I could scramble to retrieve his clothing and drag him into the bedroom, even before telling everyone the party was over, he panted and patted his butt cheeks.

He smirked. "Well?"

Jerry adjusted his cock in his pants. I turned away, disgusted.

"Not bad. Not bad at all," Mike said. "But we still haven't seen the real thing."

Jerry sneered. "I can get ass and a blow job anywhere else for what you guys just paid."

Billy extricated the cash from his briefs and flourished it in the air. "You think I'm some two-bit whore?"

But even from where I was seated I could see it was a substantial wad.

Mike dared him by counting out two one hundred dollar bills. "How about this?"

"That's a lot of money just to look at someone's ass," Jerry said. He'd always been a mean bastard.

"What about me, man?" Raoul pleaded. Mike counted out another two hundred.

"You want to see it?" Billy asked Jerry.

The idea of my plug ugly boss ogling my boyfriend's ass turned my stomach. When Jerry hesitated, Mike snapped, "It's only fuckin' money. For that, you get a moment in ass heaven. Or else, you get your money back. Right?"

Billy nodded.

"What about him?" Jerry said, nodding toward me.

"Forget about him," Billy said. "He doesn't matter."

My presence was dismissed so completely, I was momentarily castrated of my balls and my ability to speak.

Jerry thought about it for a split second before reluctantly counting out his cash. "I'm in."

I finally found my voice. "Come on, guys." I tried to push the cash back into their hands, but there were no takers.

Mike smiled. "Hell no, the night just got real interesting."

"Now we can judge for ourselves whether this ass you're always bragging about is as hot as you think," Jerry crowed.

Billy took control. "Get them another drink, Steve. None of that cheap shit either. That good Scotch you save for special occasions."

I poured way too much liquor, hoping they'd pass out. Me, I poured an even stiffer one. I gulped it down at once, and it burned my gut like humiliation.

Billy lowered the lights further, small consolation, cleared a spot and had the visitors seat themselves on the floor around the edge of the rug that he was about to use as his stage. To catcalls and whistles, he ramped up the music and *Nine Inch Nails*, his favorite band, spewed out *"Closer"* as he circled the area, ferociously bumping and grinding to the anthem about wanting to violate, to desecrate, to penetrate, before hooking his fingers in the band of his briefs. Sidelined, I held my breath. Teasing like a professional stripper, Billy slid his hands down until he was stark naked, waving his hard cock close to the visitors' faces. But that's not what they'd paid to see. He swirled around and bent over, parting his perfect muscled asscheeks, daring them to touch him while, with perfect timing, he mouthed the lyrics "I want to fuck you like an animal." Raoul had already succumbed to a pheromone rush and was openly stroking his cock in appreciation, while Jerry kept looking in my direction, frightened of any repercussions.

Billy lay back on the coffee table. He raised his legs over his head, spread his butt cheeks with his hands, singing *"my whole resistance is gone"*. All attention focused on his smooth, hairless thighs leading to that inviting pink, puffy hole. He licked his fingers and started to prod them into his sphincter. He looked so fuckin' hot burying three up to the second knuckle. "I guess I win," he said as he finger fucked the ass I had neglected of late.

I suddenly got my balls back and went to the CD player to end the charade, but in my confusion, all I did was bump the disc up louder. Billy raised his voice over the music, "Are you sure all you want to do is look?"

I could not believe what I was hearing.

"Add another five, and I'll let you fuck me right here."

Mike didn't hesitate. He peeled off five hundred and placed it on the coffee table, then smugly peeled off another five hundred for Raoul. Turning to Jerry he asked, "You in?"

Jerry's lust to pork my lover overcame his natural stinginess. His voice cracked as he told Billy, "Come by my office tomorrow and I'll pay you what you're worth."

The hypnotic song had been edited so that *"I want to fuck you like an animal"* was on a loop, a constant sexual command, cock hardening and orgiastic. Billy writhed to the pulse of the music as Mike leaned forward, pushing his strong, thin cock against his well-lubed sphincter. He slid right in.

Mike gasped. "Oh fuck."

Raoul moved quickly to hold Billy's legs to give Mike better access. He sank right down to his balls.

"Oh, man, you gotta try this fuckin' hole. Hot as hell, dude. Fuckin' ace."

Billy groaned as Mike slid in, a sound I remembered from the first time I pressed my cum-drooling prick inside his eager guts. I shook my head in agony. Mike pulled out, hesitating a split second before lunging back into that slick ass chute. Raoul, not to be denied, slipped his cock into Billy's hungry mouth.

"That wasn't part of the deal," I mumbled.

Jerry was contemptuous. "Who gives a fuck? Always going on about how perfect your fucking relationship is and all the time your boyfriend's a cum dump. Panting for cock from every sick bastard in the neighborhood. Well take a good look when I shove the cock that was never good enough for you up your sweet little boy's fuckhole." Jerry waved his ugly, drooling, stubby cock in my direction.

"This—mouth—was—born—to—suck—cock," Raoul panted. "His—throat—is—slick—as—pure—fuckin'—velvet."

"So is his asshole, man." Mike was battering my lover's ass like a tornado in Kansas. "Sweet asscunt."

"I bet the fuckin' slut could take two in his sweet boy pussy at the same time," Raoul said. "That way we can all do him together."

"I want the fucker's asshole," Jerry said. "No way will I settle for a blow job. This was about his ass."

Mike assumed control. "Okay, but you'll have to take sloppy seconds."

Jerry nodded. "No complaints from me. I'll just get his mouth to slick me up while I'm waiting."

Mike pulled out and lay on the carpet, holding his hard, slimy prick upright so Billy could skewer himself on it. Once successfully kebabed, he leaned forward to make his ass vulnerable to Raoul's liberally greased, uncircumcised weapon that he squeezed against Mike's, already buried up the battered asshole. Raoul, straining against his elastic ass muscles, made Billy cry out in pain before he relaxed, murmuring with pleasure. Jerry moved round to the only hole still available. I watched, repulsed, as he forced his thick cock between Billy's lips.

Incredibly, I was harder than I had ever been in my life. Harder than when I jerked off watching our neighbor take cock with considerably less skill than Billy. Harder than when the two of us first met and went at it like proverbial rabbits. Fuck, the realization was like a cartoon light bulb in my brain: I got hard on watching. Sure, I was pissed big time about my lover slutting his body to two strangers, as well as my disgusting boss, but I was more excited than I ever had been when I fucked him. I liked, no, I fuckin' loved watching him take cock in his ass and his mouth. Cocks of strangers. Cock of an ugly brute of a man.

Billy was taking on three, severely stretching his limits. Stretching mine. My cock was feeding directly to my brain, admitting this new experience was the ultimate pleasure. There was no thought about the repercussions of what we were doing to our relationship—was it over? But all anger and frustration left me.

Raoul took over the rhythm of the assfuck, penetrating deeper and deeper, opening Billy wider.

"Fuckin' sensational," he praised as he slid his tan cock along the length of Mike's shaft, Billy's ass muscle stretching to take the two greasy pricks.

Jerry sounded like a bad porn movie as he viciously fucked Billy's mouth. "Fuck the little slut. Bury your cock in his guts. Ram his asshole."

Mike massaged Billy's slobbering cock as he and Raoul raised the momentum. I moved in closer to watch the two amazing slimy, hard pricks shafting their way into the needy hole. It was hot enough to be a porn movie; but knowing it was my boyfriend's ass that was copping a battering sent the sexual mercury through the roof. I was painfully hard. I stripped off my jeans and briefs and began to spit slick the knob. Mike smiled knowingly.

Jerry saw me as well, and encouraged by Billy slurping on his ugly prick like it was prize caviar, kept up his verbal humiliation. "Your sweet slut likes real man cock in his cunt mouth. Watch me slide it down his throat."

Billy didn't seem to care the real ugly fucker he was sucking was my boss, a man with biggest mouth for gossip in the county. It would be all over the showroom tomorrow that he'd fucked my boyfriend. Slamming into Billy's mouth, he held the back of his head, pinning him like a trophy butterfly. "Nasty. Just the way you like, eh boy?" Billy was turning purple from the fat fucker holding his face firm against his belly suffocating him with cock.

Billy gasped for air as gag puke drooled off his lips when Jerry finally let him free. He just wiped his mouth and plunged right back around Jerry's prick. He was oblivious to everything but cock.

The onslaught of Jerry's verbal abuse, plus the friction against his sphincter and his prostate knob buried inside his fuck canal finally pushed Billy to explode all over Mike's belly. That in turn contracted his ass muscles, squeezing his two synchronized fuckers until they screamed out their pending orgasm and shot almost simultaneously into his guts. They slumped, exhausted, until their shrinking cocks slipped out of Billy's well-fucked hole. Knowing how impatient Jerry was for his turn, they helped Billy back on to the coffee table and went to clean up, all the while keeping a watchful eye on the action.

Billy held his legs apart, his slimy ass canal dripping sex juice and begging to be filled again. Jerry grabbed me by the hair and pushed my face toward his prize. "You always thought this asshole was too good for me. Now look at it." Jerry shoved in his fingers, scooping out cum and forcing it into my mouth. I sucked his fingers clean.

"Too good for anyone but you. Now it's dripping with other fuckers' spooge. Not too good now, is it?" He pushed my face into Billy's crack, smearing my face in the ass spunk. I tasted Mike and Raoul. He yanked my hair again; my face was level with his prick.

"Now get me slicked up Mr. High-and-Mighty. Too fuckin' smug to suck the boss's prick, but now look at you." He shoved it between my lips.

I tried to make him blow so he wouldn't plow Billy.

He must have guessed my intentions because he pushed me away. "That's enough! Beg for it, baby."

Billy whimpered. "Fuck me, fuck me now. I need you inside me,"

"You want my cock, baby? You want my hard man cock?"

"Rape my fuckin' ass! I need cock bad!"

Jerry gave what sounded like a strangled rebel yell and plugged Billy like he was plugging a dam, knocking the wind out of him.

I watched, fascinated, as this ugly fucker rammed into my lover. No finesse, just raw animal fucking.

Jerry cursed the slut, keeping up a string of filthy talk until it became so rancid I knew he was shooting his cumsnot in Billy's asshole. He shuddered the last of his juice into Billy, then pulling out, he wiped his slime over my face.

Now that it was over Jerry could not look me in the eye. He dressed quickly, mumbled his farewell and headed for the door.

Billy lay exhausted, his asshole gaping and dripping spunk. Raoul and Mike, now cleaned up and fully dressed, stood surveying the scene as if it were a disaster zone. I was so shell-shocked by the whole experience I feebly offered them coffee like a good host. They politely turned it down and headed for the door.

"Worth every penny." Raoul adjusted his crotch, and was gone.

Mike hesitated at the door. "He's right you know. One of the best asses I've ever had. You're a very lucky man, Steve. I envy you. And Billy's a lucky man to have you."

When Mike closed the door, the silence was deafening.

Billy lay naked and still, his arm across his eyes, waiting for the storm he knew was coming. I picked up the cash and counted it.

"With that bastard Jerry's money tomorrow that gives us just about enough to take that trip to Paris we were planning for our anniversary." I said, scarcely daring to breathe.

Billy took his arm away from his eyes and looked at me, stunned. I smiled.

He returned my smile. Relieved. He looked at my aching cock. "Why don't you fuck me now."

Damn. We were back to the same old routine. I regretted we'd lost the moment for a new beginning as I slid into his sloppy asscunt.

Then Billy said, "I hear those French boys are really something."
I fucked him with a vigor I hadn't felt for a long time.

BUSTING BILLY'S BUTT

Is available in both eBook and print from
Lydian Press
and
Amazon

Sluts & Satyrs

Nat wriggled in an attempt to pull the hem of his cocktail frock down to a respectable length as a truckie kept pace with our car, blaring his horn in admiration. The big burly boofhead wasn't to know the gorgeous woman seated next to me was actually my boyfriend who was doing his best to hide his generously proportioned cock.

I laughed. "I told you that little black number you're wearing would scarcely cover your unmentionables."

Nat was lapping it up, telling me that dressing up actually had the strange effect on him of making him feel more feminine, more like a woman. He easily passed. He was pretty: very pretty. A young pretty woman. That's why he had been receiving his share of stares and cheers from passing motorists, the truckie just the most recent in a long line of admirers.

"I think maybe we should have been more careful about the sort of woman we chose for you to imitate," I said.

"Nah," Nat replied. "I'm having fun."

As usual, Nat thought he knew better.

We were headed to the annual gay charity fundraiser at one of the larger gay bars in the city. The theme for this year's event was Sluts & Satyrs. No prizes for guessing that Nat had chosen to go as a slut, something so foreign to his nature that his friends gaped in amusement when he told them. I was outfitted much more mundanely as a satyr, stripped to the waist to show off my gym-toned body and wearing furry underpants with a tail, plus a pair of lace sandals as footwear. My outfit was also Nat's choice. He loved to get me half naked in public, to show his mates how successful he'd been in ensnaring the most desirable gay bachelor in town. That would be me. He believed the easiest way to incite jealousy and piss people off was to parade me about on his arm in the least amount of clothing that was legal.

I'm in a rather staid profession – accountancy – so I have to keep my looks and, especially, my body in peak condition to overcome people's rather clichéd preconceptions. It helps that I own a company that handles the largest corporations in the country. The clincher is that I'm endowed where it counts thanks to the family genes and I have the stamina of ten men. That's what keeps Nat happy.

Or I should say I used to have the stamina of ten men. I used to keep Nat happy. Not that he was complaining, but chemotherapy does have a tendency to kill not only the cancer cells but the libido. Plus the ability to get hard, especially when you most need to. And Nat does like his sex.

We'd tried Viagra and its generics, porn, recreational drugs, you name it, but my sex drive was still as sluggish as a Soviet-era Lada Niva on a sharp incline. The more I worried about it, the more difficult it was to perform. We'd tried toys, but it just wasn't the same. Nat topping me was even more of a disaster as it went against both our natural inclinations. "We'll work it out," he reassured me, but I couldn't help worrying that he might leave me for someone more… um…potent.

Nat was my whole life. He was young and horny like most men his age. I say 'most,' because I'm his age, twenty-eight to his one year younger, but I never seem to get horny any more. Nat is horny and popular. He's such an extrovert, loves meeting people and partying, dancing the night away, whereas I have two left feet and thrive on small groups of close friends. It's a wonder we ever got together in the first place, let alone survived four years together. I had to worry because the survival rate of a marriage without sex was slim indeed.

He must have read my mind, for he took my hand, and I made a silent prayer that he would never let it go.

This was his first foray into a public arena in drag. In fact, his first foray anywhere dressed as a woman. 'Dressed' is probably too strong a word. All he had on was a very elastic brief black sheath of material sold as a cocktail frock. It barely stretched from just above his pumped-up pecs, which he'd not bothered to augment although he'd tweaked his nipples so they thrust their way visibly against the fabric, down to just below the curve of his ass. He wasn't going for verisimilitude, he was going for trashy. The one concession he made, and then only because otherwise it looked so obscene, was to flatten his rather large prick, concealing it beneath a penis corset. On his feet he wore a pair of vertigo-inducing crimson high heels that he could barely totter about in let alone walk from the house to the car, but they made his ass, one of his greatest assets, wiggle like jelly.

He'd gone to the trouble of shaving his armpits although I thought leaving them bushy would have added to the authenticity. He also removed the few hairs on his arms, legs and chest, sculpted his little rash of blond pubes into what he called a landing strip pointing straight to his concealed cock, and had me wax his ass. He endured the pain of that treatment because he knew how much I like a smooth, hairless crack and that was his gift to me for allowing him to make such a spectacle of himself.

He didn't allow me to see the finished article until he'd been made-up and gowned. Two women friends who did the make-up for his television appearances, volunteered to come over and help out with Nat's transformation. I expected him to look like some old boiler who sold blow jobs down a back alley for a buck a throw. Boy was I wrong. When I caught my first glimpse of him as he sashayed down the stairs, my intake of breath almost caused me to pass out; he was beautiful. A little too realistically female if we hadn't been heading to a gay bar.

Sue and Lainie had lengthened his straight blond locks with extensions, shaded his eyes subtly, and given his pouty, loud mouth the cutest shade of red that would have got Satan himself hard. The only dead giveaways were his Adam's apple which they'd attempted to hide with cosmetic shading and his flat chest although his muscular pecs gave him an intriguing cleavage.

One of the reasons for such a total disguise was that Nat's career was taking off big time as a television newsreader and his agent had let it be known it was not in his interests to be seen at gay bars, to become the subject of vulgar gossip. A stable gay relationship was one thing, to be seen socializing at bars too frequently gave the appearance of indiscriminate sexual partnering.

We both took the advice on board even though it would mean more at-home entertaining and less public appearances with our friends. We hated going back into the closet, even with the door half open, but it would only be until Nat became so established he could get away with just about anything, except perhaps Nazi sympathies. But there was no way he was going to miss this party. Normally we both would have avoided anything with even a hint of sluttiness or satyriasis, but it had been an intense few months for Nat, taking over onscreen news desk duties after the sudden death of a colleague. It had been a steep learning curve, industry jealousy and nervous cock-ups responsible for the floods of tears Nat shed in the privacy of our bedroom. But he had eventually settled into the job and critics were finally coming around his side, especially after the faltering station's ratings were increasing at the same rate as his confidence.

Right now, he needed to blow off steam and relax. Unfortunately for me, it also meant that he needed a fuck, so

I'd psyched myself, double-dosed the sexual vitamins, and done everything I could to make the night a success.

The reason for leaving early, the party wasn't due to start for another couple of hours, was that I had promised to drop in to my brother's place to deliver the final papers from his divorce which had come into effect that very day. The settlement had been pretty good but I had to go through some of the details with Ted so he knew where he stood financially. Because of a certain number of incriminating photos taken by a private detective which showed his church-loving conservative ex-spouse's adultery in glorious digital color which, it was hinted, would find their way onto the internet if she played hardball, she had settled quickly and amicably for the kids, plus a modest monthly allowance which Ted could easily afford. He'd kept the house and his lucrative construction business intact.

A dirty trick, but she'd led my brother by the dick into marriage and then made his life hell. She'd soured him enough that in the year since their separation, he'd made no effort to date again.

We could hear his celebration as soon as we turned into the street, the bass throbbing up through the asphalt. There were a number of cars parked outside the house which was ablaze with lights. I told Nat to stay in the car until I scoped out the terrain. I rang the bell a number of times before Ted, looking the worse for wear, answered the door. I could scarcely hear him over the din from inside. I had to shout in his ear. He put his arm around my shoulders, whether for support or to scoop me inside I wasn't sure, but he stopped when he saw my car.

"Who is that gorgeous creature you've got with you?" He staggered down to the footpath and knocked on the window. When Nat powered it down, Ted stuck his face inside the car, burping out an introduction. I hauled him out before he slobbered all over my boyfriend and explained the get-up.

"Holy fuck," Ted said to the delight of kids riding their bikes nearby, "If my wife looked like you I never woulda divorced her."

"Thank you, kind sir," Nat purred in a passable imitation of a woman who obviously smoked too much for her own good.

Ted turned to me in admiration. "She's good. Say, why don't you bring her inside to meet the mates while we finish up our business?" He turned to Nat. "No use sitting out here in the car playing with yourself. Unless you need some help."

Nat giggled coquettishly, slapping Ted on the shoulder. Yep, Nat definitely had a future as a transvestite hooker if all else failed.

"I don't think that's such a good idea, Ted," I demurred.

"Let's see how many of the guys are fooled." He was already opening the car door, offering his hand to Nat who took it and stepped demurely up the front path to the door attracting wolf whistles from some of the older boys in the street.

It was an all-male party. Wives and girlfriends were out corralling the kids around the streets or else at hens' parties having their own particular celebrations, probably with a male stripper or two. Ted's mates, however, were into beer, more beer, pornography, and beer. Men at their macho best were hanging out in the kitchen where the keg was flowing freely, in the living room in front of one of my brother's huge range of hetero DVDs, or outside on the back lawn where they lolled about in plastic chairs discussing the latest sports results and scratching their balls unselfconsciously.

We interrupted another argument over football scores. "Guys, most of you know my big bro Monty and this is Nat..."

One of the guys slapped me on the back. "So you finally given up being a fag, man?"

Most of them ignored me, their attention totally focused on Nat.

"What can I get you, Natalie," one of the bruisers asked, probably thinking his manner was the height of gallantry. "We've got beer, beer, and beer."

Nat hates the taste and smell of beer. It meant none of the guys with their boozy breath would get close enough to examine Nat's bona fides.

"Beer's okay for you big fellas but a li'l thing like me needs to watch her waistline. You got anything a lady likes to drink? A diet soda? Liquor goes straight to my head and straight to my butt." So saying she slapped her cheeks to the delight of the guys ogling her.

I whispered, "You keep this up and you'll be pregnant by the end of the night."

They were a younger bunch on the back lawn, including a young punk guy with piercings and ink enough that he scared the shit out of people in broad daylight let alone late at night in a dark alley. Whenever I'd had to visit Ted onsite, Ewan was obnoxious, scarcely concealing his antagonism. It must have been the 'gay thing.'

A couple of paper lanterns on a cable strung loosely from the house to the basketball hoop near the fence illuminated dimly the backyard. Dimly enough that Nat impressed them all. I suppose it was easy enough to fool a bunch of semi-drunken yobs who were pussy hungry. Suddenly, dropping in to Ted's place didn't seem like such a good idea after all. I whispered as much to my brother but he just smiled, telling me to relax.

"But how will they react when they start groping Nat and discover she's a he?" I whispered. "I think we should go and I'll drop the papers in to you at work on Monday."

Ted put his arm around my shoulder, steering me inside, leaving Nat to his or her fate. I looked back to see the guys moving in for the kill. It wouldn't be long before the shit hit the fan.

"Stop worrying, they're only having a bit of fun," Ted assured me as he got a beer for himself, brewing up a pot of coffee for me, before ushering me to his office at the back of the house. He unlocked the door. When he saw my querying look, he shrugged. "Old habit. After catching the ex where she shouldn't have been."

We sat in the old armchairs which he'd bought when he first set up his construction business, retaining them long after they should have been replaced. They were his good-luck chairs. He'd signed most of his lucrative deals while seated in one of them and had finally rid himself of his troublesome spouse when he'd come home unexpectedly and discovered her astride one of his principal tradesmen in that self-same chair. The grainy video he'd taken secretly on his mobile phone had been enough for him to hire a private investigator and, with his accumulated evidence, instigate divorce proceedings, thus ridding himself of the last impediment, or so he thought, to a rich and happy life.

Ted insisted on discussing family matters first although he knew I was impatient to get down to business in order to get to our own party. I was decidedly uncomfortable with the idea of Nat on his own with my brother's rough workmen. Normally it would not have mattered as he can take care of himself but I wasn't so sure when he looked good enough to eat in women's attire. I also wasn't sure how concerned Ted's men would be if they were sufficiently drunk and horny to overlook the fact the cute chick with the cock-sucking mouth and the fabulous ass had a cock concealed beneath a corset. Out of sight, out of mind.

It was the pressure on my bladder that made me pause mid-sentence in explaining a few of the intricacies of what Ted had to sign over to his ex-wife that made me aware we'd been at it for almost half an hour. I went to the bathroom and, after relieving myself, went in search of Nat. Everyone seemed to be outside so I headed for the backyard where there were the sounds of a rowdy party in progress.

Through the screen at the back door, I saw about ten men but no sign of my boyfriend. I had visions of the police digging up his slaughtered remains.

I called out from the doorway, "Has anyone seen Nat?"

Sexy dance music was playing but not loudly enough that I didn't hear someone whisper, "Shit!"

Nat's head bobbed up. He was wedged between two dancers grinding their hips against him like they were doing the lambada or one of those other suggestive Latin American dances. He loved dancing and I was pleased to see he was having a good time although I would have been happier if the chap behind him didn't seem so intent on grinding himself against Nat's ass.

"Are you okay, Nat?" I called.

"Having a ball," he responded.

The guys in the backyard laughed.

I was a little appalled when Ewan sang out, "We're looking after the little lady, so take your time."

Obviously, they still hadn't twigged to Nat's true gender. I decided it was better to get the business with Ted over and done with then we could get out of there rather than make a fuss now. I got the distinct impression Nat was slurring his speech although that was impossible on a diet soda and I knew he wouldn't drink beer. When the light from the paper lanterns swaying in the breeze caught his face, his lips and chin seemed to be shiny with some sort of slimy substance. He must have spilled his drink. I regretted now that his outfit seemed more revealing than absolutely necessary.

"I shouldn't be too much longer," I called then stood, unseen, a little way from the screen door watching the activity continue. Confident I'd gone, the partygoers seemed to visibly relax, especially the three dancers. Ewan pushed Nat's head down to crotch level while the guy in back pulled his skirt higher to reveal his plump muscular ass cheeks. As long as Nat confined their activities to a bit of bumping and grinding everything would be okay. I had no reason to doubt Nat's fidelity as our relationship was built on trust. Totally monogamous. Nat had insisted on it.

In the kitchen, I found a glass with lipstick on it and, what was more worrying, a three-quarters empty bottle of Johnnie Walker. The tumbler smelled of liquor. Someone had been spiking Nat's drinks and he had no head for spirits. I didn't like the odds: me against around a dozen burly construction workers. I didn't know whose side Ted would come down on but I suspected company loyalty would trump brotherly love.

I went back to Ted's office determined to get out of there in record time without making a fuss but, to my chagrin, Ted seemed to be particularly leaden-headed, forcing me to explain some really simple points two or three times before they sank in. It must have been the beer. I suggested adjourning the meeting so Ted could join his guests but he insisted I stay to complete the task as we were almost finished anyway.

About ten pages from the end he excused himself to go to the bathroom.

"Ted, there are only two or three points we have to cover. Can't it wait?"

"I'm bursting, man. Gotta go."

"I'll just check up on Nat while you're taking care of business."

"Nah, I'll only be a couple of seconds. You wait here, I'll be right back. Then you can head off to that party of yours."

It made sense, I suppose. So, I waited. I tapped my foot impatiently, and then paced the floor. After fifteen minutes, even my befuddled brain knew something was up. When I went to leave the room, the door was locked. Ted must have done that out of old habits. I sighed. There was no need to lock me in. I banged the door, yelling at the top of my lungs, but I guess no one heard me over the racket.

Rifling through Ted's desk drawers I finally found a spare key. After letting myself out, I went to the kitchen shocked to discover the whisky bottle empty and a large portion missing from an open vodka bottle beside it. I didn't know where Ted was or even if he would support me, but enough was enough. Surprise was my ally so I crept to the back door, keeping in shadow, until I could see what was left of the party, some of the men having left already.

I needn't have worried because Nat was perched on Ted's lap, his back to me, talking animatedly although I couldn't quite make out what he was saying as he sounded quite breathless. I sighed my relief, louder than I'd thought because eyes turned in my direction.

"There you are Monty," Ted called. "I think you're right, we should leave the rest of the paperwork until tomorrow. Come and join us."

Ewan thrust a glass in my hand before grabbing a chair, positioning it opposite Ted as Nat attempted to wriggle off his lap without success. He was held tight. I took a sip: it was unadulterated vodka. To be sociable and, if I'm perfectly honest, to steady my nerves I took a gulp, burning my throat. Too late, I remembered I hadn't eaten in hours and the alcohol would go straight to my head. I hoped I was sober enough to drive. If not, I could call a cab and pick up the car tomorrow. A warm glow washed through my body and I took another mouthful. It didn't hurt to be sociable and the half a dozen or so remaining guys seemed to be having a good time.

Although he appeared somewhat uncomfortable, wriggling wildly to get up, I knew Nat was safe while seated on Ted's lap.

Ewan gave Nat a drink, encouraging him to throw back another skinful of what could only have been vodka. Nat was gulping it like water, obviously feeling no pain. He turned his head to smile weakly at me. I raised my glass as a sign he should feel no guilt at drinking.

I was content to sit and listen as the conversation turned to the subject of wives and girlfriends but it inevitably led to my luck snaring Nat.

"I wish I could find me a slut like her," Neil, one of the guys said. "My wife can't suck dick for quids, never swallows my junk. Doesn't like it on her face or her tits."

There were moans of agreement. I was so buzzed by the grog, lulled into a place I thought was secure but which obviously wasn't, I didn't pick up on the language or the vibe. And there wasn't a peep from Nat who is normally the first to rail against any besmirching of his reputation.

When my brain woke up, I managed only a feeble, "Hey..."

"She sure is one fine piece of ass." Ewan smirked. "But then we all know that already. Ted is just finding out for himself. Right, Ted?"

Ted smiled. "Best piece of ass ever, I think."

I was so mellow I actually gloated over the fact they were acknowledging Nat's superiority to their wives and girlfriends. I looked at Nat who was still wriggling up and down attempting to get off Ted's lap, hopefully to sit on mine. But Ted held him firm by the waist although he was grunting from the exertion. Ewan grabbed Nat's face, squeezing his cheeks, forcing him to look around at me. "Monty's watching you, Nat. You think he knows what's going on? You think we should show him?"

Nat's eyes seemed glazed, dream-like, until Ewan slapped his face hard, telling him to look me in the eye or there would be more like that. I stood up to defend my boyfriend but Neil pushed me and I fell back unable to move, sedated from all the alcohol I'd gulped down.

Ewan lifted up the back of Nat's frock, revealing his delectable ass. "See what your little slut girlfriend was up to while Ted kept you busy. Now he's getting his turn." I was horrified to see my brother's cock embedded in my boyfriend's butthole. I attempted to stand again but managed to rise only a few inches before falling back into the chair. What I thought was Ted trying to stop Nat wriggling out of his lap was actually Ted thrusting his cock into my boyfriend's ass, the activity hidden by the black frock. Now that he didn't have to disguise his treachery, Ted began thrusting with more urgency, Nat slamming down to meet every upward surge.

"Like what you see?" Ewan smirked.

In my drunken state, I had to admit it looked pretty hot, really nasty. When Nat has cock in his ass it's like he's on another planet. You can do just about anything to him. I know because I have. Recriminations and accusations always followed when he remembered any of it. I wondered whether he'd remember any of this. He turned his head, staring directly at me defying me to intervene.

"You enjoying yourself, Nat?" Ewan asked.

"Fuck, yeah," he said dreamily.

I knew it was the grog talking, plus the cock stuffed up his gaping hole but that didn't stop it from ripping my heart out. It was too late to intervene and I couldn't anyway. I was too far gone and Neil, or one of the others, was ready to restrain me if I so much as made a move. I shrugged mentally. If Nat was having a good time there was nothing else for it but to sit back and enjoy the show. Besides, my cock was harder than it had been for months, something that was going to become all too obvious.

Ted sweated; groaning each time his prick sank into Nat's sweet red hole. I could see pearls of cum along Ted's prick every time he withdrew. I remembered Ewan had said it was Ted's turn. That meant some, or all, of the other guys had already fucked him.

"What you want us to do, Nat, to make this the most memorable party ever?"

Nat seemed to think it over.

"You wanna be our bitch?" Neil added helpfully.

"Fuck, yeah," Nat groaned. "How about you guys all doing me again? Or, how about a triple decker? I've always wanted to try that."

That was news to me.

"Show Monty how bad you want it, Nat," Ewan said.

I could tell by the way his face clouded that he'd fantasized about this for a long time and now it was out in the open. No way could you indulge when you're in a monogamous relationship so he must have suppressed it only to have it burst out now. Or else it was the outfit talking.

I wasn't sure what a triple decker was, my sex life being very vanilla and, now that I thought about it, probably rather dull.

"You like being a slut for us, Nat?"

"Fuck, yeah," he said, in a voice that sounded like it had been programmed to answer.

Ewan kept up the humiliation. "How's it make you feel that your boyfriend is watching you whore out that nasty hole of yours?"

"Slutty and wicked," Nat whispered.

"You want us to make cum soup in your ass?"

"Spunk soup is my favorite meal."

"Come on guys, you heard what he said." Ewan was directing the action. He got two of the men to support Ted as he pulled the chair from under him, laying him down on the grass, Nat still astride his cock, before one of the helpers stripped and plugged his cock in Nat's gob.

Neil was quick to get his shorts off, his cock already hard, and as Ewan pulled apart Nat's ass cheeks, the muscular construction worker kneeled and pushed against Nat's already full hole. There was much grunting and swearing as Neil attempted to slide his cock into Nat's ass alongside Ted's cock. Nat groaned in pain but perseverance paid off and with one almighty thrust Neil buried himself in the hot wet hole up to his balls.

I couldn't take my gaze from the double pounding Nat was copping, wanting to jerk my own cock that was oozing pre-cum. One by one, they lined up at Nat's willing mouth to dump a load, and one by one, they drifted away. I moved my chair to get a better view of cock in both Nat's holes, unnoticed by all but Ewan who kneeled to whisper in my ear.

"You could never satisfy a slut like Nat. You're not man enough where it counts." He grabbed my balls and squeezed. "Hope it hits you in the guts like it did me when Nat dumped me."

I must have looked surprised.

"So, he didn't tell you, huh? Your little boy slut was my secret fuck buddy until the day he met you. Said he was sick of having a secret boyfriend. Wanted a relationship. Wanted to be monogamous. You took him away from me. Now I'm taking him away from you."

If nothing else came out of this evening, at least I now knew the reason for Ewan's animosity, although it didn't help me cope with Nat's behavior any better.

Ted was wheezing his excitement, screaming a few choice expletives as he dumped his load in Nat's ass. The friction must have finally got to Neil who followed almost immediately. He pulled out, flicked the cum from the end of his prick, dressed and disappeared quickly. Ewan got two of the guys to lift Nat off Ted's withered cock to allow him to get up. It was finally all over. Or so I thought. Ewan immediately lay on the grass, holding his cock rigid so Nat could slide down onto it.

Ted apologized sheepishly. "Ewan told me how great Nat's ass is. Just once, I had to try it for myself. Sorry." He shuffled inside. "Let yourself out when you finish. Sorry."

The two guys who had helped Ewan seemed eager to be out of there. They didn't want to be the last man standing.

Ewan didn't care. He held Nat by the waist as he fucked his ass savagely. I stood awkwardly to remove my satyr costume, stroking my cock, hardened by all I had seen. Kneeling between Ewan's legs while Nat sucked a construction worker, I pushed against his well lubricated ass. I wasn't about to let my erection go to waste. They were too few and far between.

The first guy nutted in Nat's mouth as I slid into the warm ooze. Fuck, he was tight. I felt Ewan's throbbing dick slide against mine as I pushed the back of Nat's head forcing him to deep throat the second guy who now had his cock wedged in his throat. I didn't care whether Nat knew it was me inside him or not, I was more concerned with getting a load off my mind. With my spare hand I grabbed his nipples, pinching hard, wanting to hurt him for what he'd done to me.

Soon the second cock feeder had dumped and escaped leaving just Ewan and I working over Nat's ass. Neither of us was gentle, although he gave no indication it was hurting, merely panting his excitement. I pushed my hand under the cock corset freeing Nat's cock, slimy from a previous ejaculation by the feel of it. Wrapping my hand around his prick, I began to jerk him slowly. Not wanting to be left out, Ewan palmed Nat's balls, while the two of us kept up the rhythm, fucking his asshole.

All too soon, Nat let out a roar as he shot his bolt all over Ewan's chest and neck, the spasm of his ass muscles around our cocks enough to set off Ewan. I held on as long as I could then I, too, lost my load in his guts. Nat fell exhausted onto Ewan's chest as I clung to his back for support, the three of us sticky with sweat and spunk.

We lay there panting for the longest time, none of us wanting to be the first to speak. We all had so much to lose. I could tell the way Ewan was clutching Nat's arm he did not want to let him go. Neither did I.

Finally, it was Nat who broke the impasse. "I guess we really look the part for the Sluts & Satyrs party now," he giggled. "No need to wash up, just go as we are."

I felt Ewan tense.

"Hey, here's an idea," I said more cheerfully than I felt. "Why don't you come with us Ewan? Make it a threesome."

He was non-committal. "Well…"

"Nothing says 'slut' better than a threesome," Nat said helpfully.

I stood up helping the two of them to their feet.

Taking a deep breath, I plowed on. "Who knows, it may lead to a more permanent arrangement."

For the moment, the decision was taken out of his hands. Nat took our arms grinning like the luckiest slut in the world, dragging us toward the car as we attempted to make ourselves half-way decent.

"Woo hoo," he shouted joyfully. "I can hardly wait to see the theme of next year's party."

FRAMING THE PICTURE OF DORIAN GRAY

"Sherlock I beseech you. The scandal would ruin us."

It was early morning and Holmes smoked the dregs of his previous day's pipe, unable to find his tobacco which Mrs. Hudson hid regularly regarding it as the 'devil's weed.'

Isobel paced the far side of the room to be clear of the noxious fumes. She also paced in despair.

"My dear sister, if matters are as serious as you have explained then Inspector Bradstreet at Scotland Yard is the man to see. Especially if any laws have been broken." There was the trace of a smile around Holmes's lips.

I could not understand why he was so indifferent to his younger sister's plight. She turned abruptly, her anger flashing crimson across her cheeks. "You already know something of my predicament and you don't wish to tell me!"

Holmes smiled. He had often told me that although his sister's powers of deduction were far inferior to his own she had something that he wished he possessed: intuition.

"I knew it," she cried. "You have been baiting me. Why, I do believe you are already on the case."

I turned to Holmes for confirmation and the arrogant smile, close to a smirk, confirmed it.

"The devil, Holmes," I said. "I thought you had inured your heart to your family's distress."

"My dear Watson," he chuckled. "If I gave in to every request for help from my nearest and dearest I should never have a moment's peace. But when the matter is serious..." he placed his arm around Isobel's shoulder.

Isobel had contained her emotions up to this point but suddenly broke down in a flood of tears. Holmes was embarrassed, ushering his sister to the door where he called out, "Mrs. Hudson. Mrs. Hudson, here please. A nice cup of tea for Isobel in the kitchen. And perhaps some brandy." He closed the door on his sister gently as Mrs. Hudson led her away glaring at her employer as she did so.

"Holmes you simply must be more cognizant of Isobel's distress," I pleaded.

"Emotions get in the way of facts and clear thinking, Watson."

I could but agree with him although I did not like his cavalier treatment of his sibling. I was about to remonstrate with him but he put his index finger to his lips and quieted me. I knew better than to interrupt when he was thinking. He kept his finger to his lips until, satisfied, he turned to me and spoke.

"A very strange case, indeed, Watson."

"I thought you may have considered it beneath you, Holmes," I told him truthfully. "A missing nephew with a propensity for trouble, hardly the stuff of your more famous cases."

"There is no such thing as a small case, Watson, except that thinking makes it so."

I stood corrected, it seems, and not for the first time. I would hardly have called it a case. A missing person, perhaps, but even that was dubious. The young man in question was twenty-two and sometimes stayed away from home for weeks on end although he would normally get word to his parents of his whereabouts. Usually at one of his two clubs in London, or with one of his more disreputable social friends with whom he was often seen around town.

His father, Sir George Petherbridge, conservative MP for Stamford Valley, declared that 'marriage will set him straight', often encouraging him to find a 'filly with breeding prospects and get stuck into it.' Petherbridge was very much an old-school martinet and Holmes and I often wondered what Isobel saw in him, although they appeared to be a love match, and wondered little that his nephew, Bramwell, champed at the bit, especially as there was a 'touch of the artist' about him.

Holmes saw little of his sister because Petherbridge forbade her from contact, believing Holmes was, let me see if I can remember his exact turn of phrase, 'a bloodsucker on the rump of the body politic.' Consulting detective, he declared, is not an occupation, it's an insult to the police and all they stand for. His animosity only grew when Bramwell developed a severe case of hero worship of his uncle, even baiting his father to the extent of calling himself Bramwell Holmes and protesting an interest in criminology.

Petherbridge, of course, saw his son as the natural dynastic heir to his parliamentary seat even though his offspring revealed no aptitude for politics, barely even an interest in his own father's career.

It had taken a considerable force of personality for Isobel to go against her husband's explicit instructions that she was to have nothing to do with her erstwhile brothers. Not only did Petherbridge abhor Sherlock Holmes, forbidding that his name be mentioned in their family home, he also resented Sherlock's brother Mycroft, even though he worked for the government in a position of some authority.

"Come, Watson, there can be no more delay."

Fortunately, I was already dressed for the street because Holmes was halfway down the stairs before I had even folded my newspaper and was out of the comfortable old armchair. I raced after him, acutely aware asking our destination would do no good, he would reveal all in his own good time.

He hailed a hackney and I heard him give the driver an address near Russell Square, before sitting back in the worn leather seat, assuming that thoughtful position that attracts both index fingers to his lips. It was a beautiful spring day, so unlike the damp winter we had just endured during which the fogs made the streets impenetrable and dangerous to both body and purse. A series of heinous crimes had been perpetrated on the populace during the cold, grey months but Holmes had apprehended a number of perpetrators to the general plaudits of the populace, and the sneers of the constabulary.

We pulled up in front of an unprepossessing building of what appeared, on the surface, to be flats for impecunious students as London University was close by. Holmes checked the slip of paper on which Isobel had written the address then asked the cabbie to wait. He pushed his way through the door which had been so ill used it almost fell off its hinges, into a vestibule stinking of boiled cabbage and genteel poverty. The fading and peeling wallpaper had been augmented with juvenile artistic endeavors, whether to disguise the rotten state of the walls riddled with damp and mildew or as genuine artistic expression I was not sure.

Holmes's attention was not distracted by vulgar slogans scrawled crudely across the walls, most attacking the government although one particularly risible example of the failure of our once fine tertiary institutions was an attack on Her Majesty. If I ever discovered the perpetrator of this foul deed, I would horsewhip the vile miscreant. Holmes was reading the more mundane messages scribbled near the front door, a form of telegraph for the occupants of the building.

He strode to the stairs and I hurried to keep up with him. "We have the right address, Watson."

The number we were looking for was on the third floor, tucked at the end of a shabby corridor most of whose gaslights had been sealed thrusting the landing into a soupy gloom. Holmes, whose eyesight has always been razor sharp, found the number he was seeking and rapped sharply at the door with his cane. A languid voice, raised barely loudly enough to be heard even in the quiet recesses of the creaking old establishment, called "Come in."

We entered a sitting room that had all the outward appearance of a Middle Eastern harem decorated as it was with swathes of diaphanous fabric that hung from the ceiling in huge swirls, gathered like giant curtains or else floating limpid-like to a floor liberally littered with a number of outsize cushions. Save for the pictures that adorned the walls, that was the total decoration.

Pushing aside the tulle drapes to find the issuer of the invitation to enter, Holmes almost stepped on a young lad dressed only in harem pants transparent enough that his manhood could be easily seen, although the lad himself seemed to be unconscious.

"Just push poor Toby to one side," the languid voice instructed. "Nothing will wake him after he's been kissed by the green fairy."

Holmes did as instructed with his boot and continued into the folds of the room. I quickly examined the comely young lad to discover he was merely sleeping off a drunk, obviously from absinthe. I positioned him more comfortably to also allow visitors easier access into and out of the room. By the time I had caught up to Holmes he was seated on a very large aquamarine cushion opposite an effete young man, also dressed in harem pants, again diaphanous enough to reveal his masculinity, who was posing lethargically while sucking on a narghile.

I was familiar enough with these Persian hookahs used for the smoking of marihuana in the Middle East. It was a habit that many young Londoners affected in an effort to be seen as modern. The young man offered the flexible stem to Holmes who took it, drawing the smoke into his lungs as the contraption bubbled, before handing it to me. He cast me a look which brooked no argument. I inhaled the bare minimum I believed I could get away with to establish my bona fides, for that was what I believed Holmes was doing.

"Welcome, gentlemen," the languid youth greeted us. "What is your pleasure?"

"Bramwell Petherbridge," Holmes said.

The languid youth examined us more closely, then lay back among the pillows. "Ah, a splendid choice, but I hate to disappoint. He is unavailable." He looked about as if he were about to impart a major secret. "Just a word of advice, he has taken Holmes as his family name. He wishes to be addressed thus."

"Because of his admiration for his uncle or to irritate his father?" Holmes asked.

"A little of both, I would hazard."

I felt something crawling on the back of my neck. I brushed at it to dislodge it from my person only to have my hand gripped by another. I half turned to be confronted by a smiling Toby attempting to kiss me. I moved my head quickly to one side and Toby fell face down, unconscious into my lap.

"Pay him no heed, although he does admire older gentlemen such as yourself and there's no finer sodomite in all of London than young Toby. He has earned and spent a fortune from the gentlemen that use his arse for their pleasure," the languid youth informed us, not a hint of condemnation to his voice.

I took an opportunity to examine Toby's plump backside and could immediately see why he would be so popular. There was a promise of paradise nestled between those cheeks.

"On the other hand, Bramwell, is more your rough trade admirer. Working class lads, soldiers, sailors, that sort of thing, so I don't think you gentlemen would have much of a chance there."

"You mean he's not for sale?" Holmes asked. I could see he dreaded the answer.

"Good lord, no. He's not like those post office boys or members of the Horse Guard. He does it for pleasure."

Holmes visibly relaxed. It came as no surprise that Bramwell was queer, we'd heard rumors of his lack of interest in female company. Unfortunately, if it had reached our ears it had also reached his father's which might explain his antipathy to his son and his recommendation to marry as quickly as possible.

Holmes sucked at the hookah again. I refused, so he passed it back to the youth who looked at us quizzically.

"You are not sent here on behalf of his father. No. You would not have partaken if that were the case. Who are you?"

"I am Sherlock Holmes and this is Dr. Watson."

"Ahhhh. The famous uncle." He turned to me. "And his catamite?"

I went red in the face and Holmes sidestepped the question.

"Where is the miscreant now?"

The young man seemed to be wrestling with his conscience, for he took such an inordinate amount of time to reply, Holmes interrupted the silence.

"We are not here to return him to the family fold. We are concerned for his wellbeing."

The youth smiled. "Does that encompass his friendship with myself?"

"Not at all, Mr. …"

"Do call me Bryden." He sat up, more attentive now, holding out a limp hand which I was unsure whether to kiss or shake. In the end, Holmes fingered it briefly and I imitated his action which seemed to be enough in the way of respect for the young man.

"I admit, Mr. Holmes, his friends have been concerned about him. He just up and disappeared. We were unsure whether his father had kidnapped him and taken him back to the country in an effort to force him to marry." Bryden laughed. "As if that would cure him."

"Can you think of any reason he might vanish?" I asked.

Bryden, who had pretty much ignored me until now, turned the full force of his charm toward me. "Apart from the threat from his odious father? Well, he had gone slightly wobbly since he changed his family name to Holmes. He was looking into changing it legally and was wondering about your likelihood of adopting him, Mr. Holmes. He whispered about a 'case' he was working on. Something mysterious, he intimated. Something so bizarre it would be written up in the annals of crime for hundreds of years to come."

"It didn't pique your interest?" I asked.

"Of course it did, but he was reticent about the entire enterprise. No amount of begging would get him to reveal anything. He told us we would have to wait. In the end, we got tired of the secrecy and forgot all about it. Except…"

Holmes prodded. "It may be important."

"Now that I think about it, it was the last time any of us saw him."

"It being?" Holmes asked.

"The Pandemonium Club."

Holmes and I had both heard of the establishment. Unlike the gentlemen's clubs on Pall Mall, this one was in the back streets of Soho, the far from salubrious area of bars and brothels where, if rumor were to be believed, it fit right in with its neighbors. The club had a reputation the envy of pickpockets, thieves and other low-life. It was a club for all manner of perversion.

I had to ask. "Is opium one of young Bramwell's habits?"

Bryden appeared shocked that I would even ask. "Good heavens, Dr. Watson. We merely play act at degeneracy. At being the aesthete. It is fashionable in our circle. A little absinthe, a little puff of the hookah, even a mild cocaine, which I hear even Mr. Holmes dabbles in from time to time. But that's the limit. Most of us will go on to be reputable members of society and join the judiciary, the parliament, or else live off our land. Bramwell, unfortunately, had fewer prospects than most of us because he simply could not bring himself to succumb to pressure, to play the game."

"Did he have a special friend?" Holmes enquired.

"Not as such, his tastes were specific but he liked variety. In those last weeks before he disappeared, he did mention a young man that he was seeing on a semi-regular basis. What was his name?"

We kept silent as he racked his brain. He threw out a few names, retracting them almost as soon as they were out of his mouth. "Bert...no. Charlie...no. What was it now? Ah, Toby would know."

I attempted to rouse the young man but to no avail.

"Jack. Yes, that's it. Jack. Did some sort of manual work, which always appealed to Bram. He was going to meet him at the club. Said it would bust the case wide open. Or some such other rot. I'm afraid I didn't take him seriously."

"How can we get inside the club?" Holmes asked. I was both pleased, as well as chagrined, that there were some things beyond even his knowledge.

"Oh, it's quite easy if all you require is a room, it's a matter of picking up one of the women or even a boy on the street and hiring a bed for the evening. Or for an hour if that's all you require. If you want to get inside the club proper, I hear it's a great deal more difficult but the rewards are that much more delicious."

"What does this Jack do for a living?" I asked.

"Bram did tell me what sort of work he was engaged in, but I've long since forgotten. He did mention Jack was frightened. Must have got himself involved in something particularly nasty. He brought him home here once but none of us took to him. Had some sort of stains all over his fingers. Not dirt or anything unclean, something to do with his job.

Bram told me he spends most nights at the club, looking for pickups. Seems gentlemen of a certain persuasion find the lad very attractive."

"Does he expect payment?"

"He doesn't turn down a gratuity, if offered, but he is like Bram in that respect, he does it for pleasure. If a hot meal or a feather bed is thrown in for good measure he's not one to turn it down."

Holmes had allowed me to do much of the questioning but now he sprang to his feet. "Thank you, young man, you have been most helpful. We are one step closer to finding your friend. Watson, I think it's time we paid a visit to the Pandemonium Club. To make enquiries about membership and to see if we can find this Jack."

I eased Toby so that he lay supine on the cushions and Bryden had already dismissed us from his mind, going back to the soporific joys of the hookah.

The cab dropped us off in Shaftesbury Avenue in the West End, near Dean Street one of the city's most unsavory areas. It was not difficult to find the establishment. It was in Greek Street which brought a smile to my face and I would have pointed out the irony of the sexual predilection we British call Greek but Holmes was engrossed in his own counsel.

The club doorway was marked with its name spelled out in three colors. The emphasis was on Pan and demon, both picked out in variations of crimson, the 'ium' almost invisible in the fading light because of its black paint. A sort of calligraphic afterthought. In case passers-by were too stupid to pick up on the coloured typography, a well-meaning management had painted a red horn on either side of the 'P'.

We stood and watched the door as a number of reputable types came and went without so much as a backward glance, sometimes accompanied by the disreputable. We lounged against the wall just down the road from the entrance for so long I was afraid we would be arrested for loitering but the police seemed conspicuous by their absence so transactions were conducted openly on the footpath.

"Come, Watson, I have seen enough."

I followed him toward that gaping doorway to hell, dreading discovery by any of my medical colleagues, their own proximity to such degradation little comfort to me.

The stairs were steep and narrow, barely enough room for those ascending to pass those descending, a challenge to the inebriated who were likely to fall and crack open their skull. At the top, a small foyer area welcomed the intrepid seeker after pleasure, a counter behind which stood a harridan who cast a suspicious eye over our arrival.

Holmes greeted the gorgon at the gate with good cheer. "Hetty Lambeth, as I live and breathe. Although after the climb up those mountainous stairs of yours I'm not convinced I am doing either."

She slapped him on the back, "Sherlock 'olmes, you old bastard! What brings you 'ere?" She smiled slyly. "You 'aven't changed sides, 'ave you?"

Holmes chuckled. "Which side are you talking about, Hetty? Side of the law? Or preference side?"

Her eyes sparkled at Holmes's good humor. "Either."

"When it comes to the law, I bat for the same side as Scotland Yard, although I am not so wedded to the concept of behavior being just black or white. There are a number of shades of grey. I believe, Mrs. Lambeth, in justice rather than law. As to the other, well, that particular box has many sides as this establishment no doubt proves daily, so I would be foolish to restrict my pleasure without sampling what is on offer."

"And is sampling what brought you 'ere?"

"Not a bit of it although I remain intrigued. Is the club a front for blackmail? It must be quite a temptation knowing what some of the good folk get up to on the premises. Plenty of scope for two-way mirrors, photographs."

"Mr. 'olmes, 'ow could you say such a thing. We are the 'eight of respectability, we are. Would you like a happlication for yourself and Dr. Watson. You'll find many a 'olesome wench to make you 'appy. Or a comely young lad hif that is more to your taste."

She leered at us as if expecting our concurrence with her speculation. When it was not forthcoming, she soldiered on.

"Per'aps, it's a touch of the lash that excites you, give or take, or—"

Holmes stopped her before she could go through a litany of perversions to which the club catered.

"Good Mrs. Lambeth, as tempting as they all sound, we are here on business. We are looking for a young lad—"

"Aha, I knew it," she crowed in triumph.

How Holmes kept his temper in the face of such flagrant disrespect I do not know.

"Mrs. Lambeth; that is not the sort of business I had in mind. I am seeking my nephew who has gone missing and he is known to visit this club on a fairly regular basis."

"I 'ope you are not hinsinuating' we sold 'im into white slavery or some such."

"No, we don't believe the club has anything to do with the case, we are merely attempting to track down a young man who may know something about my nephew's whereabouts."

"Why didn't you say so? I'm glad to do a favour for the great Sherlock 'olmes. And, per'aps, he may someday return that favour."

"Ah, now we are of like mind, Mrs. Lambeth."

"So, who is this young lad you is seekin'?"

"All we know is that his name is Jack, a working class lad whose job entails something that leaves a stain on his fingers."

"Oh, you means little Jack Woodward. Nice kind of lad. Means no one no 'arm. Defenseless, though. 'e'll have a bad time of it as 'e gets older."

"Meaning?" I asked.

She was matter-of-fact. "Well, 'e's obvious, that's what I means. Can't disguise what 'e is. No chance of 'im being the marryin' kind. Poor sod gives it away when there's plenty willin' to buy."

"Has he been in recently?" I asked, tired of her chattering.

"'e's 'ere now, as a matter of fact. In the Gentlemen's Lounge."

"I suspect we will find it rather short of gentle men, Hetty," Holmes said. She snickered. "Point us in its direction."

"Through that door, Mr. 'olmes," she said, scarcely concealing her delight that he meant to enter the premises.

He strode over and pushed the door but it refused to budge.

"Mr. 'olmes," she called.

He turned. She rubbed her thumb against her index finger.

Exasperated, Holmes barked, "Pay her, Watson."

I handed across several notes until she was satisfied, folding them before tucking them between her ample breasts.

"No trouble, please, gentlemen, or I will 'ave to ask you to leave," she said without rancor.

Holmes snorted. She released the door and we entered an ornately decorated bar, subtlety lighted with polished brass gas fixtures that flattered the red velvet plush and the mirrored walls. No one could enter or exit without being immediately obvious to everyone. I didn't think for a moment it was solely for security, it also gave members a chance to give new arrivals the once over.

And so we were. The bar had a number of groups seated, talking quietly. There was a constant buzz of conversation, just soft enough it was impossible to make out what was being said, but I could tell from the surreptitious looks we were getting that a number of conversations were about us.

The barmaid was a cheerful lass whose breasts had been thrust upward against the forces of gravity and whose nipples were a scant hair's breadth from being revealed in her tight bodice. For gentlemen of a different persuasion, there was a man, bare to the waist, whose chest and arms showed the musculature of hard physical labor. We learned, much later, that they were husband and wife although both or either was available for hire by the hour if the price was right. And they did not differentiate between the sexes. Once a week, in the early hours of Sunday morning, they gave a live act in the downstairs theatre. The show was very well patronized and amply stimulating that it was known to have excited the ninety-one-year-old Duke of Smethwick sufficiently that he managed to impregnate his twenty-three year old bride and thus ensure the continuation of his line.

Holmes got directions to the Gentlemen's Lounge and we pushed our way through the curtain to descend the stairs which were dark and intimidating as we had no idea into what we were stumbling. At the bottom there was a door, barred to our entrance until a peephole was opened and a brutal scarred face gave us the once over before unlocking it.

The guard whispered, "The show has already begun, gents, but the best part is yet to come. Follow me."

He led us through the darkened basement which had been set up for all sorts of sexual predilections as I saw paddles and riding crops, stocks, chains, and other paraphernalia I could not identify and for which I could think of no possible use. There were, of course, various wooden phalluses of regular to enormous sizes which I would have thought a danger to man or beast.

We heard the groans before the guard had even opened the door. When he did so, the sound of flailing rent the air and the screams of pain of a young man intermingled with the groans of excitement. We stood at the back of the small, makeshift theatre until our eyes became accustomed to the darkness.

I was shocked by the audience, a number of whom had loosened their britches and were openly stroking their erections. One was pushing the head of an obvious street urchin down on his weapon, choking the lad. My shock was not at the behavior but rather that at least half a dozen of these men were my patients.

Holmes dragged me closer to the performance although I was very reluctant to be seen and stayed well back in the shadow.

On stage, a young lad, trussed over a wooden horse of some kind was being thrashed with a riding crop. His cheeks were already crimson and a slight trickle of blood oozed over his thigh. A hirsute brute towered over him. There had been a superficial attempt to make the man with the whip approximate a pirate. He wore an eye patch and a bandana around his waist, but little else. His manhood swung pendulously every time he raised his arm to whip his victim into submission.

Holmes nudged me. The lad's hands, bound to the legs of the wooden horse, were stained the color of varnish. I closed my eyes to the sadism that was being performed for the supposed enjoyment of the people watching, disgusted that Holmes sat forward in his seat, enthralled by the action on the stage. The brute had begun laying stripes across the lad's back and former scars, not yet totally healed, opened up. The whip master rubbed the blood into his prick using it as lubrication before inserting it into the boy's hole, the audience groaning their appreciation.

The young lad screamed that he could take no more; that the brute's prick was too large and it was splitting him open.

I was hoping Holmes would intervene. When he did not I intended to remonstrate with him at the earliest possible moment. Perhaps the screams and the groans from the stage were more histrionic than real, but I was too innocent to tell, having only coupled myself in total silence.

Eventually, with a roar, the brute withdrew his blood covered weapon and moved quickly to the lad's face whereupon he squirted his seed until it dripped on to the stage.

The performance over the ejaculator invited any member of the audience who so wished to share the pleasure of the young lad's posterior. Holmes was on his feet so quickly no one in the audience had a chance to move. He spoke to the brute, thrust cash into his hands and turned to the audience whom he addressed convivially.

"I'm sorry gentlemen, but I have need of this young man and I have paid a high price for him exclusively. He will be available again later in the week. To assuage your disappointment, I invite you all to the bar at my expense for whatever libation you feel may leaven your disappointment." So saying, to a fair amount of grumbling, Holmes untied the lad.

I skulked in the shadows as the audience filed out, having put their manhood back in their trousers. Holmes whispered to the young man who appeared frightened they might be overheard. As I joined them, Holmes hoisted Jack to his feet and squeezed him affectionately on the shoulder, instructing him to go and change into his street clothes.

"Go with him, Watson, and do not let him out of your sight for even one moment. I will see you upstairs in the bar when he is clothed."

I followed Jack into the stinking latrine that doubled as a dressing room, preventing him from closing the door by slamming my foot against it. When Jack pressed one of the loose bricks in the wall, and it swung back to reveal a secret room, I knew Holmes was right to be wary. I grabbed his arm before he disappeared and dragged him back.

"We're your friends," I said. "We only want to ask you a few questions."

"Questions can get you killed around here."

"How so?" I asked.

"Never you mind," he replied. "Who was the gent who paid for me, eh? Where did he go?"

"He's upstairs, waiting for us."

"So, there's to be two of you?"

I was disgusted. "Nothing like that. Holmes wants to ask you—"

"Is that geezer Sherlock Holmes?"

I confirmed it.

"Why didn't ya say?"

I shook my head. I thought Holmes would have introduced himself but Jack was already half way through the theatre before I caught up. Back in the bar, the introductions were made, officially this time. We sat in a quiet corner, Jack with a pint of ale, Holmes with whiskey and myself with a gin and soda. As I went to raise my glass, Holmes laid his hand gently on my wrist. I understood.

Whatever it was, it was very fast acting, for Jack had only taken a few mouthfuls of his ale before his head flopped forward on to the table.

In the mirror, the husband and wife behind the counter were watching us carefully. "Never could hold his grog, our Jack," she called. "I'll get one of the boys to take care of him for you."

Holmes was out of his seat, dragging Jack by the arm, "Not necessary. We paid for him and our time is not up. We'll just take him out and sober him up."

The husband came from behind the counter, smacking a large wooden club against his open hand in a threatening manner. "I'm afraid rules of the house forbid that, sir. We wouldn't want to go breaking the rules, would we? Now, if you just leave quietly, no one will get hurt."

"Oh, we fully intend leaving quietly. It's entirely up to you whether we hurt you or not."

The wife guffawed.

"Watson," Holmes instructed me. I took the pistol from my pocket.

The other men in the bar, who up until then had been snickering while watching the drama unfold, rapidly moved out of range. I moved to the door to open it while keeping my eye on the bar. Homes shucked the young man over his shoulder, carrying him to the foyer.

"I knew you'd be trouble the moment I laid eyes on you, Mr. 'olmes," Hetty said.

Holmes grinned. "Ah, a woman with the powers to foretell the future. Perhaps those powers may also reveal the owner of this establishment."

"Poor 'etty is but a 'umble worker. No idea 'oo the owner be."

"No mind," Holmes said cheerfully. "We will find out." He turned to go. "Oh, Hetty. If they ever try to serve you with a drink that seems to have a very faint blue tinge under the gas light. Be sure not to drink it."

"Is that what they done to little Jack? Bastards!" She hesitated for a moment then she said. "Mr. 'olmes, they'll be waiting for you at the bottom of the stairs."

"Is there another way out?"

Hetty pulled aside a curtain behind her concierge desk.

"In case of a raid," she said.

Holmes disappeared through the gap before anyone could witness our escape. I followed, gun drawn in case it was a trap. Hetty slammed the door behind us condemning us to pitch darkness so we had to feel our way via the railing until we reached the ground floor. We stumbled through puddles and spider webs the length of a long corridor until we saw a sliver of light which proved to be coming from beneath the exit.

I pushed but it refused budge. "Try pulling it toward us," Holmes suggested.

I felt it give slightly but the damp had swollen the door and rusted its hinges so that it stuck fast. Holmes cursed. I heard him thumping the wall until he cried out in triumph, "Try it now."

The door swung toward us effortlessly.

I was flabbergasted.

"No use as an escape route when every second counts unless there was an easy way to get free," Holmes said.

We found ourselves in the middle of the footpath on Charing Cross Road. A passing cab stopped for us and we were soon on our way back to Baker Street. Now that we were alone I had a chance to remonstrate. "Holmes…"

"I didn't intervene because up to a point he was enjoying himself, Watson."

The man was a mind reader.

"If you'd noticed, young Jack was tumescent all through the display. It may have seemed cruel but for better or worse, some men find pleasure in pain. Although, in Jack's case, I suspect there may be more to it. We'll find out after he sleeps off the drug they put in his ale."

"Should we report it to Bradstreet?"

"He must know what goes on there. I'm certain I saw one of his men drinking in the bar and, unless I'm mistaken, they know he's a plant. I'll get a note off to him warning him the chap's life is in danger. I don't want to bring Bradstreet into our escapade as yet. He could ruin it all."

"Then you know what's going on, Holmes?"

"I know my nephew's life is in mortal danger. Jack, here, is the key to it all."

It was some time before Jack regained consciousness, no thanks initially to Mrs. Hudson whose strong Christian convictions led her to believe that Jack was the devil's spawn. Only after I'd stripped off his shirt, she gasping at the wounds on his back, did the poor woman relent, tears in her eyes as she begged God's forgiveness for her lack of charity.

Holmes left Jack in my hands while he went to his sitting room where I found him going through his archive copies of the city's newspapers. He had a few pages strewn about.

"How is he, Watson?"

"He'll be out for a few hours, but no permanent damage."

"We're dealing with a fiend. He has to be stopped. And stopped quickly. Aha." Holmes tapped his finger at an item on the social pages, then hurriedly turned back to other items he had spread before him. "I think we have cracked the case, Watson. All I need now is confirmation. There may yet be time to save my nephew."

"Holmes, you don't mean—"

"Yes, Watson, I feared the worst. Young Jack gives me hope. But we are running out of time. If there is anything you can do to expedite his recovery, please do so."

I went back to my patient but he was still comatose. I'm afraid I paced but it did not bring Jack back to consciousness any sooner. Fortunately, he had drunk only a small portion of the drugged ale, so that it wore off within two hours of his arrival at Baker Street. As soon as he was able, I marched him in to Holmes.

"What happened?" he asked, flopping sheepishly in a large armchair, holding his head which was obviously throbbing from the after effects of the drug. I prepared a headache draft for him which he gulped down quickly. Holmes rang and requested a light snack for all of us, including our guest.

"It seems our friends at the bar drugged you. They tried the same trick on Watson and myself but we realized in time. They obviously wanted us out of the way for some big event or other."

Jack groaned. "They intend to kill Bram. You ruined everything," he wailed. "I could have saved him. Now they know we're on to them."

Holmes was impatient, treating the boy more harshly than he deserved. "Putting aside, for a moment, the fact that you would also have ended up dead if you had attempted any such foolishness, why did you not go to Scotland Yard?"

"Because no one would believe me. Bram only took me seriously to impress you."

Holmes was amused. "Impress me?"

"Bram looks up to you, Mr. Holmes. He wants to be like you and he thinks the only way to do that is impress you. With his powers of deduction."

"And he's found himself in over his head, has he?"

"I warned him. But once he started he was like a dog with a bone, he just wouldn't let go. I begged him to come and see you but he was too proud. He wanted to show you what he was made of. He walked straight into their trap."

"Perhaps if you begin at the beginning," I suggested.

The lad wolfed down the sandwiches that Mrs. Hudson brought him, and gulped the strong black tea before launching into one of the most extraordinary stories I have ever heard, more bizarre even than any case on which Holmes had worked. Frankly, I was prepared to scoff, but Holmes quelled me with the raising of an eyebrow.

I have transcribed Jack's story as near as I can recall. I took notes at the time but I was so sceptical that I believed the lad mad.

"I work for Melville and Mapplethorpe, the picture framers in Covent Garden. A lot of the big houses use us. We're respected for our work. Top quality it is. So, one day, this gent brings in a painting, and the boss, Mr. Melville brings it into the workshop. It's a portrait of this young man. There's something about it, it's so lifelike it's like the gent himself is in the room. Of course, I recognized him at once. It was a picture of Mr. Gray. He's always at the Pandemonium Club. One of their best customers. Not a nice person in the flesh but in the picture, an angel.

"I was told it was priority, to drop everything else I was doing. Mr. Gray needed the portrait back within a matter of days and I was to stay back at night to get it finished if I had to. He was paying through the nose for the service, granted not much of it would make its way into my pocket.

"The frame had been damaged and he wanted it repaired, but it had a special varnish on it which had to be specially mixed. An almost impossible task. That's why I have these." He held his hands up to show us the stain which gave his hands the appearance of brown gloves. "It'll take weeks to wash off. Not that Melville and Mapplethorpe care. An extra shilling for my trouble and they can forget about it.

"As it happened, I did need to work one night to get it finished. The boss did not want me wasting his precious gas so I worked almost in the dark. Just enough light around my work bench, so the first time it happened, I thought it was a trick of the shadows. But then it happened again. I stopped my work and just watched the picture. For about twenty minutes, I watched it. It fair made my blood run cold, Mr. Holmes."

"What was it?" Holmes asked patiently.

"The picture moved. Ever so slightly, but it moved. Oh, I don't mean the actual canvas, I mean the figure on the canvas."

I was about to interrupt but Holmes stilled me.

"Like this?" Holmes waved his arm about.

Jack was adamant. "No, sir. It was small things, mainly in the face. His eyebrow moved. His lips curled. If I may be vulgar, sir. His manhood seemed to harden in his trousers."

He paused to let us take in his words.

Holmes's brow clouded. "The portrait's mood changed, almost as if it could have been reflecting the current mood of the subject."

Jack smiled. "That's it exactly, sir. That's what I thought."

"What did you do, Jack? Think carefully. Don't leave anything out. We're not here to judge you. It's very important you tell us everything."

The lad went crimson with embarrassment.

"I'm ashamed to say, sir, I felt him."

"Felt him?" I said.

"I think, Jack means he touched the bulge in Mr. Gray's painted trouser leg. Am I correct?"

"Yes, Mr. Holmes."

He hung his head. Holmes lifted his chin. "Mr. Gray is very pleasant on the eye, is he not?"

"Yes. But he would never give me a tumble."

"Did he feel good?" Holmes smiled encouragement.

"Mmmm, better than good. I played with him a while and he smiled. That scared me, I can tell you. Especially when a little wet spot formed on his trousers. I couldn't concentrate. I went out to get a bite to eat. Have a drink. Clear me head. I found myself wandering toward the club. It weren't that far. They let me in because working lads is popular with some of the gents. I went downstairs and Mr. Gray was there. When I saw he had a wet patch on his trousers in exactly the same spot as the painting, well, I could hardly breathe. I guess I had a look of horror on my face. Anyway, Mr. Gray saw me. He smiled. He'd never spoke to me before but he came over to me as friendly as anything. He grabbed my wrist and held it against his prick. It was hard as hard can be.

"He smiled at me and said, 'Are you responsible for this?' I stuttered that I didn't know what he was talking about. 'I'm sure you do, boy. Aren't you working on the frame around my portrait?' I told him I was and that I'd just ducked out for a meal. "Perhaps you could make a meal of this,' he said and unbuttoned his britches, forced me down on my knees and rammed his prick into my mouth. He didn't let me breathe until he'd loosed his spunk in my mouth, sir. Then he laughed and told me to swallow because it was the most expensive meal I would ever have. Then he and his friends left me there.

"That's how I met Bram. I must have been so shocked by the way he treated me, I was just kneeling there when Bram came along. He took me back upstairs for a cup of tea. I'd seen him around but it's against club rules for a lad like me to approach a toff. He was nice. I liked him. He spoke gently, asked if he could see me special like one day because I told him I had to get back to work.

"He told me all about himself and I felt myself getting to like him more. I suppose that's why I did what I did. I told him about the picture. I never seen anyone's eyes light up like his did. 'A real mystery,' he says and chuckles. 'A mystery that would do the great Sherlock Holmes proud.' He had explained you was his uncle and that he wanted nothing better than to be your apprentice…"

Sherlock laughed loudly. "Indeed. The young scoundrel."

"He came back to the workshop with me though it's strictly against company rules. We watched the painting for a while but nothing happened. I felt an idiot but Bram said it had been worth it just to get to know me better. Then he did something so unexpected, well, it turned my world upside down, Mr. Holmes. It may not be much to a gent such as yourself but…he kissed me. There's not many gentlemen would kiss the likes of me, sir. They'll use my body. My cock, sir. Or my arse. They'll use my lips to unload. But it's rare they kiss me, sir."

Holmes and I were reluctant to intrude on something so personal.

"I'm sorry, sir, if it offends being that Mr. Bramwell is your nephew and that I kissed him back."

"It does not offend me, Jack. Go on with your story."

"The next day, Mr. Melville comes down to the workshop and says I have to finish off the framing of Mr. Gray's picture within the hour because he is coming to pick it up. I tells him I'm supposed to have another day to finish it off proper like but he tells me there's no time and to do the best I can. Well, I work double quick and it's all but finished by the time Mr. Gray comes to collect it himself. I tell him to mind the varnish because it hasn't had a chance to dry proper. He pats me on the head and winks at me when no one else is looking. Then he whispers, 'This picture will be our little secret, right?' It seems a pity because it's so beautiful, and I tell him so. That must have been the right thing to say because he calls me his 'good boy' again and gives me a florin coin. He has his man carry it out and I hear him tell Mr. Melville how impressed he is with my work. I'm sure he said it loud enough on purpose so I would hear and think him nicer than he is.

"I met Bram for a cup of tea for lunch at the Garden and I tells him everything that happened. 'Bloody mysterious,' he says. He intends visiting the artist who painted the picture to get to the bottom of it. And he'll meet me after work.

"But he didn't return, Mr. Holmes. I waited and waited for him but he didn't show up. I went to the club to see if he was there, but again no luck. I liked him, Mr. Holmes. More than anyone I've ever met before. I thought he liked me. We'd done it there on the workshop floor. Not just rough and ready, you understand. We made love, taking turns, until we couldn't do it no more. And he told me he wanted to do it again with me in a proper bed. So when he didn't turn up, I thought he was like everybody else. Part of me didn't believe it.

"Then I heard that the man what painted the portrait had disappeared. I got suspicious. Even if Bram was avoiding me at the club, he would still turn up eventually because I wasn't allowed to talk to him and if he didn't wish to talk to me there was nothing I could do about it.

"One day I heard Lord Wotton discussing a private party at Mr. Gray's house where they had a perfect angel they were all going to 'break in.' I knew it must be Bram. The way they talked about what they were gonna do to him was disgusting.

He'd been confined to Mr. Gray's basement until... They were all going to take turns until he went mad or..."

I glanced at the newspapers at Holmes's feet. On top of the pile were the reports of the unveiling of Dorian Gray's portrait a few years back at his residence in Regent's Park. More sinister were the reports of the disappearance of the portrait's painter, Basil Hallward, about twelve month's after the unveiling. He had not been seen since.

"Watson, there's not a moment to lose. Bring your gun."

"Mr. Holmes," Jack called. "Can I come with you? I'm sure I could help in some way."

"Yes, lad. The more fists the more I like the odds."

We hailed a cab and headed as fast as the cabbie could gee up the poor horse toward the palatial mansion that Dorian Gray called home.

"That whipping, not your first?" Holmes enquired of Jack.

"No, Mr. Holmes, it was part of my plan to rescue Bram."

"By allowing yourself to be degraded, you hoped to inveigle an invitation to the party. Was that your plan?"

"Yes, Mr. Holmes."

"Then what?"

"I would decide at the moment. We would either escape. Or we would perish together."

Holmes put his arm around the young man. "You're a brave lad. Bramwell is a very lucky man."

Jack basked in Holmes's praise but it would be no defense against whatever Gray had in his armory. There were a large number of hacks in the driveway so it was easy to gain entrance to the property. We stopped to let Jack off near some bushes because he would not be allowed into the house. He was going to reconnoiter for us. Holmes and I alighted at the front door, dismissing the cabbie. It would be easy enough to find another and we had no idea how long we would be, nor what sort of reception we would get.

The butler refused us entry as we did not have an invitation. Holmes demanded to see Gray but only after the threat to call on Scotland Yard did the butler condescend to call for an underling to deliver our message. We were shown to the library but a servant was placed at the door to ensure we did not attempt to mingle with the guests. It was a matter of minutes before Gray burst through the door in an effusive manner, hand outstretched to shake Holmes's hand.

"Sherlock Holmes. I have never had the immense pleasure," he gushed before turning to me. "And you are the inestimable Dr. Watson, I presume. How very good to meet you both. Whatever can I do for you? Not an official visit, I hope."

Holmes was steely. "We have come to take my nephew home."

"Your nephew. I'm not sure I understand."

"Young Bramwell Petherbridge," Holmes said.

Gray frowned. "I'm almost positive he's not on the invitation list tonight. I only know him in passing. His father is one of those old-fashioned titled gentlemen who has no time for pleasures of the flesh, something to which I have devoted my entire life."

Just then, there was the sound of voices raised in anger and I put my hand to my pistol. The doors to the library were pushed open and a bloodied Jack was pushed forward. Two men closed the door behind them so none of the guests could see what was going on.

"We found him snooping around the house, Mr. Gray," one of the men said.

"You abuse my hospitality, Mr. Holmes." Gray turned to the two men. "Did he…"

"Yes, sir. We found him near the cellar."

"So, Mr. Holmes, you already knew that your nephew was not a guest, but did you know he is tonight's entertainment? We brought our little pleasure party forward once we'd heard that you and Dr. Watson had been at the Pandemonium Club. I had high hopes that you'd come to see for yourself the pleasures available to the man of discernment. I had hoped that you and Dr. Watson may have shared a few of my proclivities."

"Not bloody likely," I spat.

"Yes, I guessed that when I was informed that you had both escaped with young Jack here. No matter. We are all together now. Perhaps you would care to watch our little entertainment. We have a very muscular, extremely well endowed negro that I personally selected to perform with your nephew. I'm sure we will all enjoy watching Bramwell's ravishment, although I'm not so sure he will."

"Bastard," I yelled.

"It's no use offering you a lifetime membership to the Pandemonium Club, gentlemen, to overlook tonight's pleasures? No, I thought not. What if I allowed you to join in with the other guests after our African guest has had his way?"

Holmes covered the space between them in the blink of an eye and struck Gray forcefully across the cheek with his cane. It drew blood.

"Most unwise, Mr. Holmes."

We were both in the grip of the two men who had cast Jack on the floor. My gun was lifted from my pocket and handed to Gray before I had a chance to use it.

"Take them downstairs," Gray commanded, dabbing the blood from his cheek with an overly perfumed handkerchief. "There are probably a few guests here tonight who would enjoy watching the great Sherlock Holmes buggered by a negro cock. Like nephew, like uncle. And tie this piece of street refuse to the same beam as Petherbridge. Face to face, so they can watch each other as their arses are split open and their lights go out. But not close enough that they can touch. Gag them too, so they can't converse."

Holmes and I were manhandled to the cellar where men stood about in groups, drinking, a few of them with phials of drugs that they were inhaling or swallowing. The atmosphere was charged. Gray instructed we were to be given free movement because it was impossible to escape and, being gentlemen, he hoped we might change our minds after we'd witnessed the entertainment. Jack was stripped and tied to the wooden horse. Bramwell struggled when he saw Jack's bloodied face opposite him. Holmes made no effort to go to their aid. It would have been futile as the two men stood guard over the prisoners. Instead, he turned his attention to the room in which we found ourselves.

The gaslights were lowered, a signal to the gathered assembly to take one of the chairs that had been arranged in a semicircle around the platform upon which the two youths were tied. Holmes took a seat right at the end of the row and I sat beside him. Gray gave a short speech welcoming everyone to the night's entertainment then brought out the man about whom he had been boasting.

London had seen any number of Africans, including those from the Americas, but this man was without peer. His oiled body glistened under the gaslight, his muscles standing out so that he seemed to have the strength of ten men. But what impressed the audience most was the size of his manhood. In all my years of examining men, I had never seen anything like it. I estimated it at ten inches long and thick as a young boy's wrist. I admit I flinched at the thought of the damage it would wreak.

Gray proudly paraded him around the audience, allowing the guests to fondle and frig his prick. He offered the same opportunity to us but I declined, politely so as not to give offence, while Holmes ignored him. Gray poured oil from a glass bottle, liberally coating Bram's arse crack before doing the same to Jack. The negro took up his position behind Petherbridge, parted his cheeks and, with a smile to the audience, speared himself into the sensitive hole. Petherbridge screamed. Even through the gag, we could tell he was in incredible pain.

A tear gleamed in Jack's eye as he watched his friend's rape helpless to intervene. The black man pulled out slowly before plunging back even more powerfully. Those watching applauded as Petherbridge screamed again. I feared for the young lad's sanity. A few more thrusts and the screams began to subside, so Gray insisted it was Jack's turn.

Jack was obviously more experienced and managed to take the huge prick with less discomfort for the look of pain that crossed his face was fleeting, and the black man began to thrust in earnest as if Jack were doing something with his sphincter to encourage him to spill his seed. I noticed too, that Jack was erect. He was willing himself to enjoy the experience, I guessed so that he might milk the powerful black man's weapon and thus save Petherbridge from further pain.

It was a useless exercise because the audience was going to be let loose on the unfortunate pair as soon as the black man had widened their holes. Gray must have realized what Jack was doing for he motioned for the negro to position himself back behind Petherbridge. That's what the audience had come to see. Sir George Petherbridge's heir buggered to death.

The negro plunged back into the young man, withdrawing, only to repeat the process. Gray invited the audience, by now in the throes of passion themselves, to investigate the gaping hole left when the black man withdrew his prick. A few men fingered the passage, one even attempting to push all four fingers inside but Gray told him he could do that later after everyone else had taken a turn.

Gray seemed impatient with our intransigence as we had not moved from our seats. He pointed the gun at us, insisting we join the crowd around Holmes's nephew.

"Where is the famous portrait?" Holmes asked. I thought this was a very inopportune time for such a question. "Surely you are vain enough that you would wish to see what effect tonight's evil would have upon your soul."

"Ah, Holmes." Gray sounded almost admiring. "You read me too well."

"It would have to be somewhere in this playroom. You would want to watch it while you indulge your senses. You would want it hidden initially this evening but later when you join the rabble on my nephew, you will want to watch the evil flood your portrait. It excites you! That's the secret, isn't it? It makes you harder than you've ever been before."

I did wish Holmes would hurry with his plan, whatever it involved, as I feared for Petherbridge who was as limp as a rag doll as he was penetrated incessantly.

Holmes strode around the cellar, Gray's laughter ringing in his ears, mocking him as he searched the walls, interfering with his concentration. "Why are you doing this to young Petherbridge?" I asked to distract Gray's attention.

"He came to my house to offer himself to me. He stood in the library while speaking in the most lascivious manner until I felt myself harden. He was offering his arse to me. He'd always avoided me at the club which made him all the more desirable. He saw the bulge of my prick in my trousers and even ran his fingers along it. Then he turned triumphantly to the portrait, the outline of my excitement quite obvious there as well. He laughed at me, called me evil, and said the painting was the work of the devil, that it should be burned. That it was his ambition to destroy a work of evil incarnate. Naturally, I could not allow him to do that. When money would not change his mind, I tried other bribes but he was impervious to all of them. I have to destroy him or he will destroy me."

I heard Holmes's note of triumph. He turned a metal wheel embedded in the wall behind the platform and two sections of the stone wall slid apart to reveal the magnificent painting. Those engaged in sex, one of the men had slipped his cock into Jack while the black man raped Petherbridge, while others were handling their stiff manhood ready to spill their seed over the naked bodies, ignored the unveiling. They missed the red streak on the cheek of Gray's likeness, the result of Holmes striking the subject.

"The game is over, Gray. Tell your party to go home."

Gray raised the gun. He could not miss. The men on stage scattered as soon as they saw the weapon. Gray must have realized he could not shoot at Holmes for fear he might miss and put a bullet into the portrait. He aimed the gun at poor Petherbridge. The black man who must have been near spending his seed withdrew abruptly and his spunk shot over Bramwell's back. He fled still dripping.

"Move away, Dr. Watson. I would hate to shoot you when I have a fate much more terrible lined up for you. Mr. Holmes, I will give you to the count of three to move away from the portrait or I will shoot Jack through the head."

"Better fate than what you have in store for him," Holmes said calmly.

"Then I will shoot your nephew in the balls."

"It's all over, Gray. Surrender now and you may spend the remainder of your life in Bedlam. Continue this charade and you will surely die."

Gray's laugh echoed around the cellar. It made my blood curdle.

Holmes shrugged. "I gave you the opportunity." He raised his cane and struck the portrait on the arm.

Gray screamed in pain and dropped the gun. We both scrambled for it. Holmes must have struck the portrait again as Gray no longer fought me, instead he doubled up clutching his groin looking decidedly ill. Holmes had the cane wedged against the portrait's crotch.

"Keep him covered, Watson, while I unfasten the lads. And Gray, one false move from you…" Holmes unscrewed the top of his cane and withdrew the blade that is hidden inside. He nicked the portrait on the throat and blood flowed down Gray's own neck. "I will not hesitate to drive this through your portrait."

Gray gasped.

Holmes cut the ropes binding Jack, who seemed not too much the worse from his experience. Then the ropes holding Petherbridge down were severed and he would have fallen to the floor had Jack not caught him.

"Jack, we are still not in the clear. Do you think you can help Bram?"

To demonstrate, Jack lifted Petherbridge into his arms.

"Now, Gray, you will lead us out of here and tell your guards to back away."

"Why would I do that?" Gray's bravado was frightening.

Without answering, Holmes waved his blade in the air and slashed the portrait from its frame. It crumpled into his hands.

"If you allow us to leave unharmed, I will do no damage to this painting. If you attempt to stop us, you will surely die. I will not hesitate to put my blade through it."

"If I allow you to leave?"

"I will give you forty-eight hours to wind up your business in London and leave this country forever. If I ever hear of your return to these shores, I will destroy you. Come Watson, bring him with you."

We made our way upstairs where we were met by Gray's guards who formed a phalanx against our departure.

"Where are the guests?" I asked.

Gray nodded that they could answer.

One of the men stepped forward. "They've all departed."

"Right, what is your name?" Holmes asked.

"Hay, sir."

"Right, Hay. You will lock the rest of the staff in the cellar."

Hay looked at Gray for permission. He nodded agreement.

"Now, Hay."

He rounded up those members of the staff still in the house, a few having absconded with the departing guests, herding them to the cellar to imprison them.

"Now, Hay, you will go out into the street, hail two cabs and bring them to the front door. Go with him, Watson. No, take the gun with you. I have all the security I need here."

The staff locked in the cellar had begun to clamor to be allowed out as I left with Hay. He was surly and uncooperative but grudgingly did as he was told. I made him walk a few paces in front of me, acutely aware that there may be other staff lying in wait. We reached the front gate with no trouble and within fifteen minutes, two cabs were at the front door. I had hidden the gun in my coat pocket but let Hay know that I would not hesitate to shoot if he attempted anything foolish.

The two lads came out first but I had forewarned the cabbie's that there had been an accident and that I was a doctor. I helped them into the cab, Holmes insisting I go with them to tend to their medical needs. He knew we could not go to a hospital so Baker Street was our destination.

"Make up some excuse for Mrs. Hudson as to their injuries. Put them in the same room and make sure the door can be locked from the inside."

I understood what he was asking and I noticed Jack smile. Petherbridge kissed Jack's chest, laying his head against his shoulder.

"I'll be along shortly," Holmes said before reiterating his offer to Gray. Then he turned to the servant. "Hay, your master is going away. Unlock the cellar door and tell all the staff to evacuate the premises. I will give you all twenty-four hours. If you are still here after that time, you will die as surely as my name is Sherlock Holmes."

For the next two days, I scarcely saw anything of Holmes. He was preoccupied and I thought it better to leave him to his fancies. The second night after our return I left him pacing, staring at the portrait he had spread out on the floor, muttering about how Dorian Gray would rue the day he defied

Sherlock Holmes. I gathered he had not wound up his affairs and left the country. I looked in on the two lads who were still recovering from their injuries but they were young. They were also very much taken with each other and held hands as they spoke to me. I wondered whether they had the strength of character for what they had planned for their future.

I wished them good night and went to my room. I slept soundly and awoke to the welcome arrival of Mrs. Hudson with my breakfast on a tray and the morning newspaper.

"Terrible. Simply terrible," she tutted as she poked her finger at the late item which told of an immense house fire in Regent Street. The premises had been gutted even though the fire brigade had arrived promptly. A man's body was discovered among the ashes.

I jumped out of bed to tell Holmes the awful news but he was not up as yet, unusual behavior for him. I was surprised to discover that he had lit a fire in the grate, as the previous evening had been so balmy. When I looked more closely I noticed an edge of painted canvas which had obviously been the fuel for the conflagration. When I stooped to examine it more closely, I noticed it was signed Hallward.

Fuck Buddy

Hi, my name is Buddy and I'm a slut.

This is where you're supposed to say, "Hi, Buddy."

Just like a real meeting of Sex Sluts Anonymous.

Why else would you be reading this book if you weren't a slut, or addicted to sex in some way? Crave it every waking minute? Seek opportunities for sex in all the right and wrong places?

So, let's try that again.

Hi, my name is Buddy and I'm a slut.

I left a space for your response; please feel free to fill it in as appropriate.

As with all these sorts of things, you want to know how it started. It's a cliché, but it started with a dreary relationship. Not a bad one, not a good one, but one of those relationships that went from boiling, to hot, to tepid, to lukewarm, to dreary. Of course, dreary is not a temperature, it's a state of mind.

George was my mate du jour, or rather mate of three years. I've always heard that apart from the seven year itch there's also one at eighteen months and another around three years. Well, if this was our three-year moment, I was in dire need of calamine lotion.

To make it worse we were headed to the bush for our annual holiday, ten days in pristine bushland by Lake Legacy. The expanse of water, wide and deep enough for diving, skiing, fishing and most water sports, within walking distance of the small town after which the lake was named, had been discovered by gay men back in the 1990s who descended like Glinda the Good Witch and settled a layer of glitter over the area.

In the beginning, gay men were not always welcome; the mayor of the district in particular had opposed the influx of 'perverts' and the gentrification that would follow. Inevitably, the prospect of a revitalised economy as well as the discovery that the men who flooded the town were not predatory animals about to corrupt and ravish every male for miles, changed many attitudes. The financial lifeline alone led to the mayor being ousted from his position of power and the welcome mat being thrown down to the extent that the local bar 'went gay' late Friday and Saturday nights.

Mind you, a few of the local men did stray, but it was at their own instigation and it was always very discreet. The visitors didn't wish to rock the boat and, in exchange, they were accepted as part of the town fabric to the extent men could walk through the main street holding hands and the only pharmacy stocked plentiful supplies of lubrication and other gay necessaries for those last-minute needs.

It was a nice place to visit – once. But this would make our fourth trip. We'd made our first when George was contemplating asking me to become a permanent fixture in his life. He wanted time alone with me to see if he thought it would work.

Time alone is the last thing you get at Lake Legacy. Most of the cabins that dot the water's edge are time share. They once belonged to families who commuted from the city in summer, usually dragged there by the alpha male dad who did a spot of fishing while leaving the rest of the family to fend for themselves. An ambitious gay entrepreneur, sniffing long-term gain, snapped up the neglected cabins for a song, renovated them, and sensing gay men's predilection for group activity both in and out of the bedroom, had sold time shares in the large bedrooms each with its own accompanying bathroom and toilet, in a pseudo-log cabin with sleeping quarters on the floor above the communal living/dining/entertaining area.

We were the first to arrive, carting our bags up to our reserved room which had clean sheets and towels, plus a number of welcoming biscuits and chocolates laid out on the bed. After a long and exhausting drive from the city, all I wanted to do was crash. George, my other half, had other ideas. The country air always made him frisky.

He tackled me to the bed, clamping his mouth over mine, sucking the breath out of me. Normally, I would have appreciated his attention as it was happening less and less regularly but not when I felt dusty, sweaty, and in need of a shower. The place was eerily quiet, our whoops and hollers echoing through the deserted corridors.

In the end, I made a deal with George: if he allowed me to shower, he could have his wicked way with me. After he'd come in all-too-close contact with my armpit he readily agreed, although I was hard pressed to clean myself as he joined me in the bathroom, pressing his rampant cock between the cheeks of my ass. I loved playful George; it was just a pity it took an annual holiday to bring him out in the open.

I soaped my body paying particular attention to the bud snuggled between my butt. I pretended to drop the soap and bent from the waist to retrieve it. That was all the opportunity George needed and I felt his prick nudge my opening before slamming through. I spread my legs as I stood up, my hands against the tiles to support me. Gripping my waist, he thrust his cock up and into me with an urgency I found endearing. But there's just so much water I can take before I begin to prune or else feel like I'm drowning and I begged off, asking to take the action to the bedroom.

George must have been equally as soggy because he agreed readily. A quick towel down and we assumed our positions on the beautiful quilted bedspread, me flat on my back resting my legs on George's shoulders while he plugged my butt with his admirable cock. On occasions, he lasted for hours and I was hoping this was one of those. I relaxed into the tempo of his thrusts that were neither too rough nor too feeble. They were just right, doing things to my body and my brain.

I guess somewhere I registered the sounds of activity downstairs, undoubtedly the new arrivals, but as it didn't concern me I grabbed George's thighs, eager for him to drill me harder because I was getting perilously close to the finishing line. My almost imperceptible sounds of excitement died as the door to our bedroom opened and Dean stood there staring at our naked bodies in the throes of fucking.

George couldn't see who it was and in all likelihood hadn't heard the intrusion, but I saw the smirk on Dean's face as he zeroed in on my butt copping a bloody good rogering.

"Piss off, Dean," I shouted.

"Whoa, sorry," he said, backing out of the room, "I didn't think you'd be here again, especially after what happened last year..."

George looked puzzled. "What happened last year?"

"My mistake. Sorry." He turned his beaming smile on me. "Good to see you again, Buddy. Hope we get a chance to catch up during your stay."

He closed the door but we could hear him swearing vehemently on the other side.

George looked at me strangely. "What was he talking about? What happened last year?"

I shrugged my shoulders as best I could. "No idea. Unless he meant about how annoyed you got over his constant parties and the noise."

It was true. Dean was a spoiled rich kid, indulged by his wealthy family who believed they could pay their way out of any unwelcome developments. His friends also played to his ego in exchange for drugs, booze, and good times so they didn't have to work in any conventional sense. Easily done, as the guy was vain. He was also good looking, well built, and hung. Everyone who holidayed at the cabin was privy to his not-so-private privates because he spent as much time naked, and erect, as he could. He reckoned it saved him time undressing when he had an ass that he fancied in front of him. I was careful to keep mine out of his line of sight.

Not that he didn't go out of his way to seek it. That was the other problem from the previous year. And the years before.

"And what was that smart remark about catching up?" George was the jealous type.

"You know what a sleazy bastard he is, always trying to chat me up."

I wasn't a patch on Dean in the looks department, hell, any department but many a man looked upon me with favor before George, and quite a number since. In all modesty, it's the combination of looks and body, plus personality. Totally different combination to Dean's looks and body, plus wealth.

"You wouldn't, would you?" George asked hopefully.

"Wouldn't what?"

"You know, do it with him?"

That was one of the problems with George: his reticence. His modesty. He avoided four-letter words, preferring euphemisms wherever possible which meant our sex life was conducted in an eerie verbal silence over the slap of greased and sweaty bodies, the grunts of exertion and excitement and the inevitable 'ungs' of ejaculation. I have a rather spicy tongue when someone's fucking me but I've curtailed it for the years I've been with George. Occasionally, during a particularly vigorous fuck, I've exploded with porn movie expletives but the look of disapproval on George's face is enough to silence me.

"Would I consider succumbing to Dean's obvious charms? Not a chance," I said.

I did once. Consider, not succumb, when I first met him. The guy is the antithesis of George. Charismatic, charming, hot, hung, and dangerous. George is dependable, attractive in an unassuming way, average body, self-deprecating humor, comfortable. And an average cock. So the first time I saw Dean in all his rampant glory, I couldn't help but salivate. Unfortunately, he saw me. He grabbed his cock and swung it in my direction. "See something you like? I can see you do, you're drooling."

I sucked the spit back into my mouth.

"Come and get it, cutie. I like the look of your ass, I think the two of us would fit together just fine."

I'm not sure what I would have done had George and other members of our cabin not come in from swimming in the lake at that moment. All eyes were riveted on Dean's prick, giving me enough time to compose myself.

"Oh, man, put it away," Simon, one of the longer residents moaned. "Don't take any notice of Dean, guys, he's always flashing his tackle. It scares the newbies but it gets tired real quick. Been there, seen that."

When George got me back to our room, he turned on me. "What were you doing with that guy?"

It wasn't the first time he'd interrogated me. "I wasn't doing anything with him. I was actually coming to join you for a swim. If you noticed, I was on the other side of the room."

George huffed. "I also noticed your cock was so hard you could hardly contain it in your Speedos."

Oops, I'd forgotten that part of it. But there in a nutshell was my relationship with George. He had trust issues, as well as a problem with my wearing Speedos which revealed a great deal more of my body than was comfortable – to him. He preferred, and wore, board shorts even though the closest he'd ever been to a surfboard was watching on old *Beach Party* movie on TV.

I took a gamble with my response. "And your cock wasn't."

I knew by the way his face flushed I'd hit a bullseye.

"Let's say no more about it," he insisted.

I wasn't about to let it go without putting his mind at rest. "Just so you know, I did nothing with him and I have no intention of doing anything with him." Okay, the last bit was a bit of a lie as I don't know what would have happened if they hadn't interrupted, but it became my mantra from that moment on. I didn't want to jeopardize my relationship with George for a quick emotionless fuck with an egotistical rich boy.

That didn't stop Dean who tried to maneuver his way into my good books, and my ass, every day for the remainder of our stay. And every one since. Attractive as he was, I've had better, and the danger signal always lit up when he was in the vicinity. I doubt he ever gave me a moment's thought when I wasn't around because steamy young men who were more than willing to sacrifice their posteriors for his friendship always surrounded him. No, not for his friendship, I guess the correct word is acquaintanceship.

At twenty-four I still had a few good years left but I had few skills, even less education, and the prospect of becoming an unpartnered old gay man who trawled beats and bars on the lookout for a guy who wanted a grand-daddy for sex did not appeal. Safer to stick to George.

I expected George would lose his enthusiasm for buggering my ass after the inopportune distraction of Dean. On the contrary, he went back to the attack with renewed vigor, whether to prove he was Dean's equal or because he fantasized Dean getting his cock into me, I couldn't tell, but he nailed me to the mattress like never before, until he blew a huge load with an uncharacteristic yell of triumph. Perhaps that was his way of verbally staking his territory because the entire cabin must have heard him.

It was also one of the few occasions on which I came without touching myself. We both fell asleep in a mangle of sweat and sperm. Long live coitus interruptus.

The sound of late arrivals dragging their bags upstairs and past our room together with loud greetings and laughter woke me up. There would be no chance of getting back to sleep until the house was silent. George could sleep through anything but I got up because my mouth tasted like dried sperm and I needed a drink. Scratching my balls through my boxer shorts, I went downstairs into the thick of activity. I was barely awake, but even I could see there were more people than normal and a hell of a lot of baggage cluttering up the floor.

"Hey, Sleeping Beauty honors us with his presence," Dean shouted.

I heard Brent whisper loudly, "I thought you said they wouldn't turn up this year."

There was good reason for Brent to be concerned. He'd been George's best friend until about a year ago when he stopped visiting us at home and even phone calls to him and his boyfriend, Cameron, went unreturned. George had been heartbroken by the split from his old friend, especially as he had no idea what had caused the rift.

"Good to see you, too, Brent," I said. "Cameron."

I begged George not to come back to Lake Legacy, telling him it bored me, that I found Dean's attentions odious and a change of scene would do us good. George would hear no argument against it, not even that it would be awkward mixing socially with his old friend, which I suspect he saw as an opportunity to discover what the problem was.

"Is *he* here, too?" Cameron asked.

I bridled that Cameron couldn't even bring himself to mention George by name.

"Caught them fucking when I burst into their room earlier," Dean smirked. He grabbed for my ass as I passed him on my way to the kitchen, bending me over and pulling down my boxers. I didn't bother to struggle; it would have just given him more pleasure in his attempt to humiliate me. "See how moist his tight little ass is?" I heard a few sighs from the audience. "Anyone for sloppy seconds?"

I wrenched myself out of Dean's grip, grateful I was wearing boxers as I tugged them up otherwise my stiffening cock would have been a dead giveaway on my way to the kitchen. "In your dreams!"

Splashing my face with cold water before retrieving a carton of juice from the fridge, I wandered back into the living area. "What's with all the gear?" I asked, swallowing a mouthful of cold orange and mango.

They looked like they were all hiding a guilty secret. Smiling broadly, Dean attempted to put his arm around my shoulders but I shrugged it off.

"We're making a porno."

"Who's we?" I asked.

"All of us."

"Except for me and George."

"Ah, yeah, you two are a distraction we didn't take into account, because we didn't think you'd be here after last year. You haven't told him then?"

"Maybe he's the accepting type," I replied.

Brent laughed.

I brought their attention back to the subject. "The movie?"

"We thought you'd both be no shows, whether because you'd split up or because you were too embarrassed..." Dean shrugged. "You've got balls, mate."

"And a licensed glock pistol in my luggage upstairs," I added.

They didn't know whether to take it as a joke or whether I was serious. I wasn't about to enlighten them.

"No need to be like that," Brent said.

"Anyway, short story is we all enjoyed last year so much we thought we'd go the whole hog and film the weekend for the memories. Keep it on DVD."

"So this is DVD equipment?"

Dean nodded.

"Let me guess. Our bedroom has been rented out to the film crew, hasn't it?"

"Fraid so," Dean smirked.

"Fraid they'll have to look for other accommodation because we ain't going nowhere."

"Shit!" Cameron cursed.

"I'm guessing you lured some young twink down here for a free holiday in exchange for free board and body. You obviously weren't going to fuck each other, that's for sure. You can barely stand your own boyfriends let alone one another."

The way they shifted uncomfortably confirmed my suspicion.

"Which of you is familiar enough with photography and lighting that the whole enterprise won't look as amateur as a wedding video?"

Cameron took the high ground. "One of the best in the porn industry. And, by the way, the twink you were so disparaging about is Darren Stonewall, just the hottest guy in the biz."

I whistled my appreciation.

"He has one hot ass," I concurred.

"There's still time to buy your way in," Dean said. "In fact, I'll pay your share if you let me at that ass of yours this holiday."

"What about George?"

"He can pay his own share."

"When's it all happening?"

"They arrive tomorrow around lunch time."

"Have fun," I said making my way to the stairs, pausing half-way. "Brent, if I were you, I'd rehearse some sort of excuse on why you cut George out of your life this last year because he's gonna be demanding answers and, between you and me, I don't think the truth will hack it."

I was chuckling to myself when I clambered back into bed, kissing George on the cheek. I was asleep in moments. When I woke up the next morning George was spooning me, attempting to shove his morning woodie into my ass.

"Morning, gorgeous. What's got into you?"

"It's the air here, gets me in the groin."

"And I get you in the butt," I smiled as I eased his cock into my asshole, still lubricated with the previous night's spunk.

It wasn't a passionate fuck, more George relieving himself in my ass. I didn't come so I played with myself while he showered with the bathroom door open so I could tell him what I'd learned last night. His gobsmacked reaction was apparent even over the sound of running water. As was his excitement when he emerged from the bathroom.

"Hmm, methinks George wants in on the action," I said.

"It's Darren Stonewall. You don't?"

"How soon our vows of monogamy fly out the window." I was smiling as I said it.

"You don't mind?" I'd never heard so much pleading wedged into three words.

"Go for it, stud. Give my ass a rest."

It surprised me how little I cared that George wanted to be part of a gang fuck of some twink porn star. When he pounced on me, plowing my ass with as much passion as he had the previous night, I thought maybe this experience might reinvigorate the old George, for the most recent version had become just a little boring. Of course, I didn't really mean I wanted him to give my ass a rest because it's the one thing I live for, cock in my hole, and it looked as if George was going to reward my loosening of the chains of monogamy with more than his irregular lackluster fuck.

It was already mid-morning, yet I'd not heard anyone else stirring in the cabin. It was an ideal opportunity for me to slip on my Speedos and head to the lake for a lazy sunbake on the pontoon. I like an all-over tan so after I swam out, I slid my swimming togs off, keeping them within reach in case I got unexpected company. I tan easily, so about midday I was ready to head back to the cabin because I'd seen Simon and his German boyfriend Rutger pull up earlier, the last of our group to arrive. An ostentatious limo followed which I thought was the star of the show arriving for his close-up. However, a rather portly gentleman with the worst comb-over ever, but who was wearing expensive casual clothes and shoes, got out of the car. Julian Clench was recognizable anywhere. Those in the industry called him Junior because his father of the same name had been a famed movie director in the seventies and eighties. Junior had inherited his father's talent but shoehorned it in a different direction, preferring his action to be male-on-male ballbusters rather than his dad's Hollywood action blockbusters.

I swam back, dried myself on the beach, wrapping the towel around my waist before I scrunched up the beach to the house. I could hear raised voices even at this distance and, worried that George had already lost his temper with one of the other guests, hurried through the door. I needn't have concerned myself because George was in conference with Dean in one of the corners, obviously working out an arrangement whereby he could join the weekend's activities, Cameron was rinsing mugs in the galley kitchen while the others sat about nursing morning coffees attempting not to listen to Junior spill his guts, the limo driver awaiting instructions on what to do with the bags.

"Listen, Larry, if you can't bring a picture in on budget and on time then you shouldn't be in the business. They're just porno for fuck's sake, they're not Kubrick." He paused to listen. "Kubrick. Stanley Kubrick. Used to spend years making one boring load of old cobblers. For fuck's sake, you're making pulp fuckin' films."

I snickered at his turn of phrase and received a silencing glare in return.

"Right, I need him up here this afternoon or the deal's off. Get it? For Christ's sake, Larry, this is easy money, big money, and all he has to do is lie on his back for a few hours. Give me a break, his ass is so elastic you could sew it in the band of your underpants and they'd still stay up. Screw you, motherfucker." He flung the phone across the room.

The limo driver must have been used to such behavior, diving for it like a cricket mid-fielder, catching it in his outstretched hand.

"Um…Problem, guys." Junior had our undivided attention. "Darren Stonewall is still on the set of his, and I quote here, his 'major new motion picture porn epic about the sex life of Alexander the Great' end quote, in which his sphincter will be speared by no less than a Roman Legion."

I put in my tuppence worth, "What's the name of the movie, *Alexander the Gape*?"

There was general laughter but you could see everyone was disappointed.

"Can't we get someone else?" Dean was practically begging.

"I doubt we can organize anyone and get them down here in time. I'm due back in town by this time tomorrow. It was always going to be a tight squeeze. But I'll try." Junior scribbled a number of names on a magazine he found on the coffee table, handing it to the limo driver whose name turned out to be Harry, telling him to dial those people and see if they were available for a quick shoot. "Their numbers are in the phone," he called as Harry went outside to ring.

"If that doesn't work?" Cameron asked.

"I guess I refund your money minus my very substantial fee for my wasted time and effort and we call it a day."

"There must be some other way," Dean said.

"Well…" Junior pushed his dark glasses onto the top of his head and looked around the room. He zoomed in on Cameron but Brent was ready with, "Don't even think about it."

It was inevitable, wasn't it?

Most of the guys in the room were in their early thirties, except for Cameron who was about five or six years older than me. Why be modest? I was superior in looks and body to all the others. Junior looked at me, really looked at me. He studied me like I was some form of insect or alien life form.

"Drop the towel," he instructed in such a manner that it brooked no argument. The towel fell to the floor. "Turn around."

I did as instructed, amused at the slobbering expressions on the guys' faces. All except George who I got onside by winking at him to show I was teasing.

"How old are you?"

"Twenty-four."

"Top or bottom?"

"Versatile, but I prefer to bottom."

"Show us what you've got."

I dropped my Speedos, standing naked and semi tumescent in front of my boyfriend and the other guys in the cabin.

"Bend over, spread 'em."

I bent over, pulling my ass cheeks apart for him to run his pudgy hand over my buns and finger my asshole.

"Sweet," he complimented. "What's your name, boy?"

I laughed at the fact my name was the least important fact about me.

"Buddy."

I retrieved my swimming costume and was putting it on when he said, "Okay, you'll do."

I laughed. "I don't do promiscuous. I have a boyfriend."

Junior turned to Dean with a puzzled look. "Isn't this the boy you had last year…?"

Dean frantically shook his head to get Junior to be quiet.

With everyone in the room holding their breath and looking at him, Dean added, "I might have exaggerated a little."

Junior looked Dean in the eye, demanding, "Which part of you drugged the boyfriend and, while he was out cold, fucked the slut one after the other in his bed until he was begging for more, is exaggerated a little."

All of it was the truth, but I have to hand it to Dean he made a small effort to save my reputation which now lay in tatters. "I guess the bit about him begging for more." Nope I was screaming for it by the end. "And we had to force him." Border line. I put up minor resistance when Dean crept into our room to slide his cock into my sleeping mouth waking me when I couldn't breathe, but my resistance was more in fear that he might wake George who was in the bed beside me. I relaxed once he told me they'd drugged him and he'd sleep until morning. I shook George, shouting his name to confirm he really was out of it. When I was satisfied, I went back to sucking Dean's cock with the ferocity of a starving baby. Later he'd turned me over and fucked me hard and long, George's snores somehow adding to the frisson of danger.

After Dean had finished they each took a turn, sometimes a second, until I fell asleep from exhaustion. The next morning, when George and I awoke, they had all left the cabin, some of them like Brent obviously guilty at what they had done. That would explain his peculiar behavior in suddenly dropping George's friendship.

"You drugged me so you could fuck my boyfriend," he snarled. "You low-life piece of shit."

Before anyone could stop him, George was on top of Dean, felling him with one blow to the jaw. While the others went to separate them, Junior ushered me outside as, during the melee, Harry appeared at the door shaking his head.

Junior helped me into the plush black leather seats of the limo, turned on the air conditioning and invited me to take my pick from the well-stocked bar, as well as offering me various packaged sandwiches and other goodies. I didn't trust alcohol so I stuck with a soft drink but I did hoe into a sandwich while he explained a few pertinent facts, foremost among which was the likelihood that I could have a very lucrative career in gay porn as a bottom.

"With that ass of yours you could be as big as Darren Stonewall," he enthused.

"You mean my asshole will look like the Grand Canyon?"

Junior snorted, almost losing his Vodka and bitter lemon.

"You obviously didn't tell your boyfriend what happened last year."

"I didn't think that would be conducive to a happy relationship," I admitted.

I warmed to Junior even with his flabby body and his awful attempt to disguise his baldness. In the end, he left me with a couple of decisions, the one that occupied my mind most being my future in retail versus my future as a porn star. It didn't occur to me that I wasn't taking George's opinion into account until there was a tap on the limo's tinted window which Junior powered down to reveal George's scowling face.

"Hop in," Junior invited, opening the door for him. "We're having a confab which you should really be a part of. Do help yourself to the sandwiches, there's smoked salmon, ham, egg and cress, as well as peanut butter. Harry does love his peanut butter sandwiches. And, of course, there's any variety of wine or spirits. Whatever tickles your fancy."

Once George had ascertained we were both fully clothed or, in my case, costumed, and that neither of us had our dick out, he availed himself of the hospitality.

"Great right hook you have there. I suspect Dean will be feeling rather sorry for himself for the next few days," Junior added. "Anyway, I think you two have a lot to discuss so I'll leave you to it."

Junior left us in cool privacy.

George looked me in the eye. "Why didn't you tell me?"

"What good would it have served?"

"I would have taken your advice and not come here this year."

"Ah, but then you wouldn't have had the satisfaction of thumping Dean and making the others feel even more guilty than they already do."

"Did they hurt you?"

"Nah, I'm a big boy, I can take it."

He hesitated. I knew what was coming and I was determined not to lie. "Did you like it?"

I took a deep breath. "It's not what I would have chosen but, in the beginning, yes, I did. By the time they finished they were using me as a piece of meat and I was very glad when it was over. Sorry you won't get to pork Darren Stonewall."

"The fantasy is probably better. So what did Junior want?"

"Me to sub for Darren."

I thought George would explode.

"What, it was all right for you to fuck a porn star but it's not all right for me to be one?" I asked.

"Even you must see there's a difference."

Of course, I did, but it was interesting to see George's reaction.

Junior returned with what he believed was good news. "The guys have talked it over and find you a more than satisfactory substitute," he announced.

"That's flattering," I said, "But I don't remember agreeing to it."

He cut to the chase. "How much do you want?"

"How much was Darren Stonewall getting?" I asked as a joke.

He quoted a price that made even George gasp.

"That's what the big boys get," Junior said, smiling at our reaction.

I'd heard, of course, that bottom boys were a dime a dozen in Porntown and got paid in sperm. It was good tops who earned a premium.

"I couldn't possibly sacrifice my ass and my relationship for less than Darren."

"You're not a big star yet, kiddo," Junior snapped. "Look, I'm trying to save this situation so everyone gets what they want. I don't like to see people disappointed. George, would you mind going back inside while I talk to Buddy a bit?"

"Sure, but you won't get him to change his mind."

When George left, Junior turned to me. "No bullshit this time. How much do you want to do this? The guys are so hot for you they'll offer just about anything."

"What's your cut?"

"I usually take twenty five per cent."

"I'll give to ten per cent."

"Done," he said. I knew he'd already received his fee and had no intention of returning it. An extra ten would be like sperm on the icing.

"What are they offering?"

"As little as possible, of course. I suggest you hang out for five grand."

I knew if that was the initial offer then I could probably double it.

We haggled back and forth, Junior finally tired of acting as go-between brought Dean out to the limo.

"You bullshitting or really gonna go through with this?" he asked.

"Depends on the offer," I said.

It started as a joke but as the dollars mounted so did my prospects of being mounted as well. The idea was turning me on, even with a less than enthusiastic boyfriend looking on. It was my life, and maybe it was time for a change of career. I didn't know if George would accept it, but there must be other boyfriends out there who would.

"This my final offer," Dean said, slipping a piece of paper into my hand. It was substantial although I knew it would hardly dent his daddy's bank account.

Okay, top movie stars probably make that much in a minute of screen time but I wasn't a star and it would take me two months to earn that sort of money in retail. Admittedly, it was my ass on the line, but I enjoyed being fucked, had not been gang banged since before I met George, if you exclude last year's dubious consent, and...

I realized I was coming up with all the reasons for doing it and none against. The only one on the negative side of the ledger was George's reaction and I was prepared to weather that.

"You've got a deal," I told Dean who was about to jump from the car to spread his good news.

"I'll be ready to party as soon as I see the money in my account."

That took the wind out of his enthusiasm.

Eventually, though, when I wouldn't budge in my demands, accept a cheque or a promise of cash in hand at the end of the holiday, he dragged his laptop to the car, and I watched as he put half the amount in my bank account and half in George's.

There was loud applause when I walked back into the cabin, before George grabbed me by the elbow, hustling me into our bedroom.

"What do you think you're doing?" he demanded.

"I'm making a porn movie with the guys in the cabin, you included if you want to be in it. And, in return, Dean has deposited a rather substantial amount of money in both our bank accounts."

"I told you I don't want you doing it."

"You don't own me, George."

"I thought I owned your affection."

"You do. Nothing I'm about to do will change that."

"I don't know how I'll react," he said.

"Just be yourself. We'll worry about it later," I suggested as I stripped to take a shower.

"If there is a later," he mumbled.

Junior came up to discuss logistics with me while I showered, George affronted that I let him see me naked.

"For god's sake, George, he's going to see me with a cock up my ass in a minute."

"We need to discuss a brief outline for a story, makes it more interesting, I think," Junior said.

"I might have an idea," I smiled, spelling out the plot to which Junior clapped his hands enthusiastically, rushing off to explain the set-up the rest of the 'cast.' Junior would check the cameras, and the limo driver, who was a Harry-of-all-trades, was responsible for the lights, primitive though they were.

I heard activity as I dressed in my best clothes, hoping George would join in the fun. He did eventually get changed, grumbling all the while, before we went downstairs together. Junior explained the basic plot, telling everyone that there would be only one take for the initial scenes. It wasn't worth the expense or the time to do more; after all, it was merely to set up the ramshackle plot, itself an excuse for much fucking and sucking.

George and I climbed aboard the limo, with Junior and his camera on the seat facing us. All we had to do was pash on like newlyweds, fiddle with our rings courtesy of Junior's props bag, and generally act horny, George oblivious to my eye contact giving Harry the limo driver the come-on via his rear-view mirror. Harry drove along the road leading to our honeymoon cabin as Junior got the shots, depositing us at the front door then drove around once more so Junior could get shots of the limo on approach.

All well so far. Then, camera rolling, George picked me up like the proverbial newlywed bride, kicked open the door to the cabin upon which entrance our 'friends' jumped up and yelled 'surprise,' offering congratulations on our married status. As I smiled graciously, I had to turn unobtrusively and grin lustily at the limo driver who stood in the doorway behind us carrying our bags.

It took about fifteen minutes to set up for the first sex scene: me and Harry. While George celebrates with our friends downstairs, I go up to our room with Harry to stow the bags. Once inside it gets very steamy and in no time at all, Harry is plowing my ass.

Beginning with a fairly private scene enabled me to overcome my nervousness and my fear I wouldn't be able to get hard. I might be the bottom in the movie but I have my pride and nothing looks hotter than a guy with a raging hard-on being fucked in the ass.

It was also a relief not to have George hovering, especially as Harry had a magnificent body and a cock that just wouldn't quit. It was supposed to be a rushed liaison as our sex scene was to be inter-cut with scenes of George worrying about my disappearance, his climb up the stairs, his walk along the corridor and his bursting into the room. Of course, by that time Harry and I would be emptying the suitcases, after he'd dumped a substantial load all over my chest.

That was a definite downside to porn: the audience liked to see the money shot whereas I preferred to collect cum up my ass. It was also unfortunate Harry had to rush his time with me. He was a skillful lover who made me feel things that had lain dormant for a long time. I hoped it showed on screen.

While I took a quick shower, Junior set up the scene downstairs. It was George's drugging. I wondered if it might be too raw for him but in the end, he played it like a professional, staggering enough that I wondered whether Junior had really spiked the wine for greater authenticity. It may have been for the better if he had as I could feel George tense as he lay in the bed pretending to be unconscious stressing over the next scenes. The first would be the worst. I hoped once that was out of the way, he could relax.

Dean crept in, naked and magnificent, his cock bobbing provocatively close to my face. I slept with my lips slightly apart which was an open invitation for him to plunge in almost choking me.

"Too much enthusiasm," Junior scolded, getting him to do it again. "Gently. You still don't know if the drugs have had the desired effect on the boyfriend. That's it, slowly push your cock into his mouth."

Junior kept up a torrent of instructions which he edited off the soundtrack later.

I awoke, startled, a strange cock between my lips. I wanted to call out but Dean begged me to be quiet. I nodded my acquiescence and he ran his hands over my naked body, pulling the sheet off me to reveal I was hard as steel. Licking two of his fingers, he attempted to insert them in my butt but I shook my head nodding that George would hear us.

Dean whispered, "We drugged his wine. He won't wake up until morning."

Of course, my efforts to wake my comatose boyfriend were all in vain, giving Dean the green light to indulge his fantasy.

Every sex scene began with a little oral before getting down to the hard core anal sex.

"You've got no idea how much I wanted to fuck your cute little ass," Dean said as he slapped my cheeks before hoisting my legs in the air and lining up his cock. I'm not sure if his dialogue was character or real. Or perhaps both. There was no attempt at foreplay; he rammed his cock straight into me as instructed by the director.

"There's no time for love and affection here," Junior said. "This is pure animal lust. Give it to him hard and fast."

"You little fuckin' slut," Dean sneered, his spit dribbling from his evil, curled lips. "I've seen you staring at my cock. I know you want me inside you, fucking you like those whores in the village."

I had to hand it to him, he was totally in character, giving a performance that was turning me on. As he pumped his cock in and out of my ass, he leaned over the prone George and whispered, "I've always wanted to fuck your slut boyfriend in front of you, George, ram him so full of my cock he won't be able to sit down for a week. Fill him with my hot cum."

George sucked in his breath, obviously close to losing it. In desperation, I put my finger over Dean's lips to make him stop his taunting.

"Give me more, Buddy, let me hear you enjoying it," Junior demanded as he moved around the bed to get better shots.

"Fuck my ass, you bastard," I grunted as I grabbed Dean's face, kissing him savagely. "I want your cock more than life itself. Fuck me into the bed, screw the shit outa me."

"More. More," Junior encouraged.

Dean kept up a string of expletives as I attempted to match him. I watched his face as he grimaced in an attempt not to come, his eyes opening widely as I squeezed my ass muscles around his prick. As we gazed into each other's eyes we both realized we were no longer acting, our emotions were as raw as our language.

That did it. Dean pulled out, positioning his cock over my face. I opened my mouth as he shot a thick stream across my cheek, then aimed the rest of it into my mouth where his spunk puddled on my tongue.

"You filthy fuckin' cum suckin' slut," Dean cursed, squeezing my cheeks until the camera could get a close-up of his spooge in my mouth. "Swallow it, cunt," he commanded until I gulped him down, wiping the residue off my cheek and licking my finger.

"Great work. Who's next? Ah, Brent. Wait right there near the door, I'll call you when we're ready. I want you to do him doggy fashion, okay? Buddy, love, think you can go without a shower between fucks here, it adds greater authenticity."

"Not a problem," I admitted. "I love the feel of dried cum on my skin."

"You're a trouper," Junior said, patting my ass. "You too, George."

While I was waiting, I snuggled into George. "You okay?"

"I guess," he said sulkily.

I felt for his cock. He was doing more than okay.

Brent's performance was awkward, probably because of the proximity of his fully conscious former best friend. At one stage as he fucked me he whispered, "I'm really sorry, George."

He blew his load on my back.

The remainder of them were a lackluster lot, nowhere near the standard of the previous year's effort when George lay unconscious beside me. A conscious George was putting them off. I wished now they had drugged him again.

The exception was Rutger who doubled with his boyfriend Simon, the two of them kebabbing me in the mouth and ass before changing positions repeatedly for variety. Rutger was like a little boy full of unfocused enthusiasm. He obviously enjoyed my ass even though it had lost some of its traction. He and Simon seemed most comfortable with the playful aspect of what they were doing and shot their loads over my chest at the same time.

"Thanks guys," Junior said. "Time to set up downstairs. Take a break everyone. Coffee, sandwiches, but don't go overboard, we have a strenuous scene ahead of us. Get a shower and freshen up, Buddy."

I sat up, spunk dripping off my body, my ass sore, ready for a good soak, when George grabbed me, threw me down on my back, yanked my legs in the air, and sank his cock deep into my guts.

"Fuck, oh fuck, oh fuck," he repeated like a mantra as he pummeled my ass. "I couldn't wait any more."

He didn't last long, coming with a kind of dingo howl as he shot inside before collapsing on top of me.

It was a pity Junior didn't capture the fuck on camera.

I got to rest my weary legs, aching from over use. And my ass, which had never enjoyed this much activity before. I wasn't complaining, fuck no! I was having a ball, if only some of the fuckers would relax.

In the end, it was almost three hours before we were ready to go again. Some of the guys wandered off to have a nap while others watched porn on the wide-screen TV to keep them in the mood. George ensured none of them got too up close and friendly with me. He was containing his jealousy pretty well but there would be no fucking of his boyfriend other than that agreed to for the filming. It was going to be difficult to get away for a private session with Dean during our stay.

In the end, the gangbang was a bit of an anti-climax. With better planning, there would have been a day or two between shooting the scenes to give them time to recover. Not that anyone was less than valiant in their effort. The scene was supposed to be a continuation of the previous bedroom tag team after which they all manhandle me down the stairs, throwing me onto the floor before a group session.

Not being professionals they found the stop-start nature of filming as they set up for different angles, essential for gang bang shoots, more difficult than expected. It was an ambition too far; although their attempts to dominate or else selfishly get their rocks off to the biggest advantage worked well. Had it been a professional porn movie there would have been hell to pay but the pushing and shoving and bad camera angles gave it an authenticity that matched my excitement.

George stood on the sidelines watching, his excitement obvious in his shorts. I was still hopeful the relationship would survive. I heard Junior whisper to him, "You're a very lucky man, George, to have a boyfriend like that. He'd do anything for you."

"Except keep his ass exclusive," George said sadly.

"Monogamy is a very over-rated commodity."

"Not to me."

"Time for your entrance," Junior said, probably to get George out of his funk.

As George climbed back up the stairs, the guys jostled for access to my body and my holes Junior called "Go for it, Buddy. Give me everything you've got. And guys, swarm around him like a mob of degenerates. Action!"

"Fuck me like the slut I am, feed me your cocks until I drown in spunk," I cursed. Dean took up the cry as a cock stopped my mouth from spewing out its demands. The camera panned to George appearing at the top of the stairs, surprised by what he's witnessing.

"You fuckin' slut!" he screamed with enough conviction that I knew he wasn't acting. "Go on guys, you heard him. Fuck the faithless cunt. Spread him out and fuck his treacherous holes till he can't take any more."

Junior was jiggling with delight. He obviously sensed the change of mood as did Dean and one or two of the others.

"Let me see you bust his ass open," George snarled, his face twisted in pain and lust.

Dean was only too happy to oblige and mounted me while others battled for my mouth. George continued his barrage of abuse as he watched the men attack my body like hyenas over a carcass, until he strode over to pull Dean off to sink his own cock inside me with a roar of triumph. I felt every inch of it as he slammed his balls against my ass. I was on my back looking up at his face, the face of a man I no longer recognized, saddened that I was responsible for his change.

The chant went up to fuck me into oblivion as the guys kneeled around me aiming their cocks at my face and chest. They were taking their cue from George, some of them desperately holding back but unable to contain themselves for much longer. George pulled out of my ass which was the signal for them all. Globs of spunk hit my chin, my face, my chest, like warm porridge. I shot my bolt at the same time. Junior moved in for a close up.

I sat up as he instructed, a huge slimy grin on my face as the cum oozed down my body and through my hair. I winked at the camera. I was hooked.

"That's it guys. Great stuff. Get yourselves cleaned up and we'll have a drink to celebrate."

George moved off without a word.

The film turned out pretty good, for amateurs, although it had very low production values in comparison to the sorts of widescreen high definition studio films I ended up making subsequently. One of the many good things to come out of the experience though was that it served as the storyline to my first big hit, *Here Cums the Groom!* The film, about a newly married couple who honeymoon at a ski resort where the other guests all have designs on me, culminates in a gang fuck in front of a roaring fire while my boorish groom sleeps off a hangover upstairs.

And that, dear friends, is how I became a slut.

What's your story?

Seven Card Studs

It had been a shit of a night. Lousy tips, obnoxious customers, not enough private shows, and to top it all off, some drunken bastard almost ran me off the road on the way home.

No wonder I slammed the front door in a fit of anger, rattling some of the fixtures in the hallway.

"Hey, Hank. You back already?" a voice called from the den.

Oh, fuck, that was all I needed. Hank is my dad and I'd forgotten it was his poker night with his boozy, smelly mates, all fellow workers at his security company. Sighing loudly, I headed off down the hall to the den where I was Daniel to their lions. They made no secret of their dislike of me, usually when my dad was not around, because I'd made the mistake of 'choosing' (their word) to be gay. They were embarrassed on my dad's behalf because they believed he'd been humiliated by my 'preference,' even more so when I took a job as a barman and a stripper to pay my way through uni.

They saw it as their lot in life to belittle me as much as possible, often egging one another on to behavior just shy of physical assault. It was sport for them to verbally assault me but I was in no mood this night. If I'd had a machete, I would have cut them into tiny pieces and fed them to the dog.

As usual, the room was full of cigar smoke, the smell of beer, and the odor of frustration. Hannah, dad's secretary, who doubled as poker night whore, taking care of the men's needs, was absent tonight. Pity. I liked Hannah immensely, mainly because we had one big thing in common – a love of cock. She also endeared herself by standing up for me. It was her intervention with my dad that finally got him to see reason when I told him I was gay. His first reaction, after shouting the place down, was to make me retract my confession, that way he wouldn't have to deal with it. His second, to toss me out on my butt.

Hannah calmed him down, explaining it wasn't the end of the world, that I was still the same person as I was yesterday so why had being gay made such a big difference? My dad was all testosterone and macho bullshit, that was the difference. And his mates were even more so. Hannah eventually placated my dad who called an unhappy truce, and everything reverted to normal as long as I left my gay life at the front door before I came inside. He didn't want to know about it.

So I owed Hannah big time. Plus she loved to gossip. Most of the women in the town shunned her because of her extra curricula sex activity but, hell, her husband had been dead for ten years or more, and her two sons had grown up and left the town for greener pastures. She was still very attractive in her late forties and thought it was about time she had some fun. She'd been to the gay bar I worked at, she'd even disguised herself as a man to attend a gay strip club where I was performing. She copped a feel and an eyeful that night before boasting of my dimensions to the guys without revealing how she knew.

I knew enough about those same guys that I could have reduced them to sniveling shells if I'd wanted to, just by using the information Hannah had let slip during one of her loose lip periods. I could see why she'd be game to take the guys on, most of them were built, they had to keep their bodies in peak condition for the job, and if they weren't exactly male model material they were certainly rugged and masculine and, according to Hannah, knew how to use their dicks to advantage.

"Well, if it isn't Twinkle Toes," Matt, the most attractive, most youthful and the most obnoxious of my dad's mates, said when I stuck my head into the room.

The other men around the table hooted.

"Well, well," I replied. "If it isn't Matt, the man who likes to screw women in the butt and then make them suck his dick clean."

All eyes turned to him, his reddening face confirming what I'd just revealed.

He tried to get the upper hand. "I bet you'd like me to show you what it's like, wouldn't you?"

"Been there, done that." I was not prepared to put up with any more of their games. My anger and frustration made me a formidable opponent that night.

His mates laughed. I detected an undercurrent: perhaps Matt wasn't as popular as he thought he was.

"Where's dad?"

"Took off to visit Hannah," Smitty said. "Something special going on there."

"A bit too special if you ask me. No happy endings for us tonight," Soot complained.

I heard the sound of boot connecting with shin under the table and a cry of pain from Soot. He glared at his mates. "Why d'you go and do that?"

They pulled funny faces, miming that it wasn't a fit subject to discuss in front of Hank's son.

I laughed. "It's okay guys. I know all about what goes on here with Hannah."

They looked startled.

"And, yeah, I know dad joins in as well."

They all relaxed to various degrees.

"It doesn't worry you?" Lew asked.

"Why would it? He's a grown man, can make his own decisions. Hannah's a good-looking woman and, from what I've heard, she's pretty hot stuff in the sex department."

There was general agreement on that.

I'd never had a conversation this long with any of the guys before without them cursing me. Most of them, Matt being the notable exception, were treating me like one of the boys, including an invitation to join the game.

"I think I'm a bit under-dressed for the occasion," I said, realizing I was still wearing my bar drag: workers' boots, white socks rolled down, very tight and very brief black shorts, a set of tux cuffs around my wrists and a tux collar around my neck. "All the better to show off your body to the bar patrons," the manager of Pure Class, the bar where I worked, said when I applied for the job. His leery look made it obvious I would need to show him a lot more of my body than I really felt comfortable with. But, I needed the work and it was easy enough to grit my teeth and suck his not insubstantial prick before he gave me my hours. I thought that would be the last of it but I soon discovered if you needed extra shifts, or to change with another barman, or you needed any little thing, you also needed to use your ass or your lips to ensure he would look favorably upon the request. The bar staff had another name for the premises, one that a disgruntled employee created by smashing the neon letters on the sign outside reducing the name to Pure ass.

Management never bothered to fix it as the sign and those attributes on the bar staff brought in extra trade. We were expected to liven up proceedings as the night progressed by dancing on a makeshift stage or on the bar itself stripping to our birthday suits, although the cuffs and collar had to stay, and allow members of the audience to give us a hand, so to speak. It was also common knowledge that if the payment was sufficiently large then the barmen were available for a 'private show' in one of the upstairs rooms. We had no choice in the matter and received very little by way of recompense. Still, the hours were good and the money better than I would have received stocking shelves at a supermarket or turning burgers at a fast-food outlet. And there was always the outside chance of finding a husband.

"No need to change," Smitty said. "Join us." He pulled out the vacant chair next to him and patted the seat.

I complied. It would help me unwind and maybe buy me some credit with the straight guys.

"Are we playing, or chatting like girls?" Matt asked sarcastically.

Soot dealt the cards. The situation was such a cliché. It was the stuff of homo fantasy. Or, had I been a girl, hetero fantasy. Seven hot, well hot-ish, guys and one horny gay boy seated practically naked at a table playing cards. If it went according to fiction I would lose all my money and bet my scant amount of clothing, then when I was naked I'd suggest sexual favors until it became one huge gangbang.

Yeah, right, real life doesn't work like that.

I soon discovered the game was more of a chinwag to wind down from the week's work. No one lost large amounts of money so there was never any ill feeling among the participants. It all ended with a bit of group fun with Hannah, mainly oral and some hand relief; she reserved anal and vaginal for special occasions. The guys seemed happy enough with that. So Hannah had told me.

The game progressed at a leisurely place, the guys discussing work, generally coming to a consensus on solutions to problems that had arisen, interspersed with gossip and malicious character portraits of unreasonable clients or opposition security companies. It was all such a relief after serving drinks to boozy, aggressive, gay men who believed it was their god given right to tweak my nipples, grope my package, goose my ass, or just generally lunge in my direction whenever they felt like it. As a result, I probably had too much to drink.

As the night drew on though, and it sank in that there was not going to be any happy endings that night, the men's demeanor changed. Perhaps that's why the conversation turned to my job.

"Is that what you wear all night in the bar?" Soot asked.

"Yeah."

Smitty was curious too. "You comfortable with that?"

"I wasn't at first, but after a while you get used to it and don't even remember what you're wearing. Like now."

"You must get hit on a lot looking like that," Lew said.

"Yeah, but most of them can take 'no' for an answer. If they become obnoxious then security removes them. It doesn't happen all that often."

The atmosphere and the grog had loosened my tongue but, even so, a little voice in my head kept asking if I was being indiscreet.

"None of this will get back to my dad, right?"

They all agreed although I had a niggling doubt about their sincerity. Still, what did it matter, dad knew the basics of how I made a living. I wasn't stupid enough to gab about the seedier aspects of my job. Or was I?

"I'd hate to get excited in those shorts," Lew said. "Be fuckin' embarrassing."

I laughed. "It can be when we're stripping."

Don spluttered his beer, "You're a stripper?"

One or two of the others seemed concerned about whether they wanted to hear the answer to the question.

"Yeah. Late at night to get the guys in the mood just in case they're thinking of heading off somewhere more exciting, management encourages us to...uh...perform for the patrons."

I'm sure Matt could use that information against me in the future. "And you don't mind degrading yourself in that way?"

He was howled down by a couple of the other men at the table, one of whom pointed out the hypocrisy of his attitude. "That's rich coming from you, Matt, considering the amount of time you spend at strip clubs."

Then they all turned back to me to listen to my reply. I suddenly realized I was the center of attention for a mob of boozy straight guys who, up until this evening, normally didn't give me the time of day except to heap abuse on me, and who would probably go right back to that behavior the next day.

Maybe, just maybe, they'd have a better understanding of my position. God, I'm so naïve.

"I can't afford the luxury of feeling degraded. I need to work to pay for tuition and books. I make a pretty good bundle from the tips. Management lets us keep that. And it's tax free."

"How far do you go?" Red asked.

"As far as we like. Obviously, the better our performance the bigger the tips. But we start from a pretty low threshold, it's not like we're wearing a lot to take off. Basically, it's just our shorts, which is why we wear a jock underneath."

Matt slammed a handful of notes on the table. "Come on, show us."

Some of the other men, probably bored by now, joined in, adding more cash to the pile.

"I don't think so. It's not the sort of thing you guys would want to see. It's faggy."

If I hoped that would turn them off, it didn't work.

"Live dangerously," Matt suggested. "You guys want to see a strip show? See how the other half lives?"

They all began to chant in unison: "Take it off! Take it off! Take it off!"

"Come on, guys," I begged.

"We don't expect you to do it for nothing. Here's the money." Matt's use of the word 'money' brought home the fact he was calling me a whore.

What did I care? He'd called me worse. His opinion didn't matter. I had no need to impress him.

"Keep your money, I don't need it," I lied. "I suppose it won't hurt to give you a sample."

The guys whistled and stamped enthusiastically, there was no animosity here, except perhaps from Matt who seemed determined to goad me. "How do the bar patrons tip you?"

I almost blurted out the secret of the upstairs private shows. Instead, I mentioned, "They usually put it in my sock or, in the waistband of my shorts or my jock."

Matt smiled but it came across as patronizing rather than encouraging. "Right then, that's what we'll do. Okay, men? I for one don't mind helping pay toward your further education."

When he put it like that, the men were unlikely to refuse and I would merely appear churlish if I didn't accept. No one at the table seemed reluctant to be involved. Hannah's absence was obviously creating a pleasure vacuum.

I wasn't really happy stripping for my dad's employees, not that I intended doing anything remotely like I would at the bar, and I guessed a few bumps and grinds plus a flash of ass would probably satisfy them. None of them would want my dick dangling in front of his face like a crowd of gay men would. I wasn't sure why I was prevaricating. It would be easy money.

Or so I thought.

I chose a CD track that I knew I could dance to. It was fairly brief. At the bar, we usually went for the longest tracks in order to milk as much money from the crowd as possible, but these guys were getting the family friendly version, not the X-rated one.

The den was fairly spacious, I would have enough room to move about and dance around the table. Once I lowered the lighting, for a semblance of ambience, the room became hushed, and I thought I could hear the men breathing. I pressed play, the CD screamed to life and I began my gyrations. I kept the crotch thrusting and the ass flexing to a minimum, concentrating on running my hands suggestively across my chest, pinching my nipples, and then groping downwards and into the waist band of the shorts.

The men whooped and hollered at first, especially on the thrusts and grinds, but their reluctance to part with any cash meant they were rampantly homophobic or, more likely, I was doing a lousy job. In fact, I knew I was doing a lousy job. When the track finished, Lew was the first to express his disappointment. "That's it? Christ. I'm surprised you make any tips at all."

Matt was smarmy. "Oh, I think you can do much better than that. You're holding out on us, aren't you, Twinkle Toes?"

I thought attack was the easiest defense. "I don't think you guys could handle the real thing."

He called my bluff. "Oh, I think we could. Right, guys?"

They replied overwhelmingly in the positive.

"I'm not in the mood for getting my head kicked in, thanks Matt."

"I don't think any of us would assault the boss's son. We like working for your dad. It's the perks that make it worthwhile."

"I'm not a perk."

"I'm guessing that the more outrageous your act, the more the audience is actually involved, the more you make in tips," Matt surmised.

"That's right."

"Correct me if I'm wrong, but I'm also guessing some of you bar boys, I'm not saying you, probably get down and dirty with some of the patrons. Put on a little show, if you get my meaning?"

I could see all this information in a typed report on my dad's desk on Monday morning. "Some of the guys do get carried away."

"I guess they allow touching in intimate areas?" Matt was slowly working his way up to something but I couldn't guess what it was as yet, except that it probably involved my total humiliation.

"That's a minimum."

"What else. A bit of rubbing? A bit of hand relief?" There was a strategic pause. "Maybe a blow job?"

The men's interest was piqued.

"Maybe."

"I hear gay guys give the best blow jobs, better than chicks because they know what a man's needs are," Lew added helpfully.

"I can vouch for that," Soot volunteered.

"How do you know that?" Smitty asked.

"You remember that young guy, Blake somebody or the other who worked with us for a couple of months last year?"

"What of it?" Matt demanded.

"I thought you all knew. He was gay. Whenever I was rostered with him, he'd blow me in the car as we did the rounds."

By the look on his face, Soot suddenly realized he'd put his foot in it. "I thought you guys were all doing the same. His throat was like fuckin' velvet. And he swallowed."

"Sweet," Don smiled.

"So, maybe some of the guys give blow jobs," Matt said, bringing the attention back to me. "Does that maybe include you?"

"Why don't you come down to the bar one night and find out for yourself."

"But we can find out right here and now, right guys?"

They were definitely in agreement. There was no way out of it. If I were to give them a good show it would have to be with all the trimmings.

"You want the works?"

"We want value for money. The higher the denomination, the better the performance, get my drift?" So saying Matt scratched the side of his nose with a bundle fifty dollar notes.

I shrugged. "Okay, you asked for it. Don't come moaning to me if you get embarrassed. Just don't take it out on me. If you don't like it, then end it or leave the room."

I was sick of the games Matt was playing. He wanted nothing less than my total disgrace; the other guys obviously just wanted a little excitement to end the night now that Hannah was a no show. I might as well give it to them, open a few eyes. Maybe even give Soot one of those gay blow jobs he seemed to like. He was pleasant on the eye and had never made the demeaning remarks the others had.

"Let me just get some more appropriate music, make yourselves comfortable while I'm gone, maybe clear the table, and I'll get started."

I heard a rumble of excited conversation as I ran up the stairs to get my collection of CDs, the ones I liked to dance to, I also grabbed a large plastic squeeze bottle of baby oil and an average sized dildo. It wouldn't do to embarrass the guys by comparison.

Back in the den, I programmed the tracks in the order I wanted them. I didn't expect the act would last more than ten minutes but just in case I set up thirty minutes worth of music. I had the oil and the dildo wrapped in a hand towel which I placed on the edge of the table they were seated around. They all had that look of expectancy on their face, but I don't think most of them had a clue what they were getting into. That would make it easier for me and I could use the table as my stage, then they would all have an equal view as I gyrated my pelvis and my...other attributes.

"Before I start, you guys are sure you want the full-on gay strip experience?"

A couple of them looked hesitant, but most of them were keen to get started.

I'd begin at floor level then hoist myself atop the table. The old house had high ceilings so I was in no danger of connecting with the light fittings, besides which, I would be doing a lot of the dancing on my back after the initial strip.

I nodded to Soot who pressed play, music blared out through the speakers, suddenly enveloping everyone in the room. It had an intense throbbing beat that precluded any talk, plus enough rhythm that I could bump and grind my way through it effectively; the sort of music I could lose myself in.

I started slow and sinuous, more like a belly dancer than a stripper although I did the usual crotch thrusting as well as wiggling my bubble butt as I made my way around the group. I had to choose carefully, I didn't want anyone to bolt. Soot was the obvious person to start with so I danced over to him and sat astride his lap grinding my ass against his hard on. I lifted his arms and removed his T-shirt over his head, flinging it in the corner. He seemed reluctant to touch me so I didn't push it. He had the sort of beefy, hairy muscular body that turns me on, so I couldn't help but run my hand across his chest, pinching his nipples briefly just to see his reaction. His nipples hardened immediately. I took them one at a time in my mouth, flicking my tongue across them before nipping them just enough to make an impression. I felt his cock twitch beneath my ass. I slid one of my hands down and gave him a good squeeze.

I didn't want to spend too much time on my first circumference of the guys so I gave his crotch a little pat and he slipped cash into my shorts, using it as an opportunity to squeeze my ass. Definite possibilities.

I had to judge the men carefully. Some of them would be getting off on the performance while others would be scared shitless conflicted by their emotions versus their disgust; that made for a volatile combination.

Red, so named for his ginger hair, was a young pale-skinned guy in his late twenties who looked as if he'd never seen the sun in his life. He was originally from Ireland and sat uncomfortably at the table. A lap dance was not for him even though I could see the outline of a bulge in his trousers. From what Hannah had told me of the guys, Red was as skittish as a rabbit. I stood behind his chair and ran my hands down his chest, tweaking his nipples through his T-shirt, until I reached his crotch, giving it a squeeze while I whispered in his ear. "Nice cock." His face lit up like the color of his hair.

Smitty was all confident smiles as I lay across his knees and whispered he should spank my ass. His slaps were not those of a connoisseur but the position did, at least, give me the opportunity to get a good view under the table. There were expectant bulges on all the men, two of them having already unleashed their pricks, casually playing with them, awaiting their turn. I rubbed my chest and stomach against Smitty's throbber, but it proved too much for him because there was a quick intake of breath and I felt his cock pulse as he obviously blew his load into his underpants.

I was careful to check the identities of the two guys who had already unleashed their cocks. No surprises there.

Don was eager as a kitten when I leaned back against the table and asked him to lower the zip on my shorts. I was glad to be wearing a jockstrap because he was in such a hurry he fumbled and would have caught my dick in the metal teeth if it had been unprotected. I placed my butt on the edge of the table, using my foot to massage his crotch as I slid the shorts over my butt and down my legs. He looked too close to orgasm for comfort so I withdrew my foot and moved on.

Now that I was minus my shorts, my ass was just about naked apart from the jock straps that kept the pouch in place.

Lew was ready for me. He'd unzipped his trousers and hauled out his cock, a juicy looking uncut prick definitely on the large side. He'd also helpfully removed his plaid shirt, tossing it under the table. I rubbed my ass cheeks against his sweaty hairy chest and his cute beer gut belly. The other guys at the table couldn't see he'd undone his jeans so I slithered on his lap so his cock was wedged between my ass cheeks. His little gasp meant I was doing something right.

Next up was Parker who'd remained quiet for most of the evening. He wasn't exactly unfriendly but he wasn't welcoming either. I couldn't read him and Hannah had given me little I could use from her gossip. He was quiet, seemingly unmoved, although when I sat in his lap I could feel his prick throbbing under my butt. I took a chance. Cold fish sometimes react better...with a bit of affection. I held his face and moved in for the sloppiest kiss I could plant on his blank face. I was unprepared for the reaction. His hands flew to my head and he grasped me so tightly I couldn't move as he fucked my face with his mouth with such intensity I thought for a minute his cock was in his tongue.

When we came up for air there was shocked silence around the table. I winked at him before moving on to my nemesis, Matt.

I knew he had his cock out to prove to me he was up for anything but, in this case, it would merely be punishment not pleasure. He was a very good-looking man, darkly Mediterranean in coloring with a tough little body that turned me on. He looked like he knew it too. I slid into his lap facing him, his cock pinned by my butt. He moved it, nestling it close to my warm hole so there would be no misunderstanding his intentions. He smelled of honest toil and citrus. I raised his hands above his head and held them in my grip while I buried my nose in his armpit, licking and sucking the hairs, slurping up the testosterone that oozed from his body, showing that I was ready to serve him, worship him.

It didn't go unnoticed, a menacing grin spread across his lips.

He was getting off on my attention to his pits, eager for a repeat on his neglected underarm but I surprised him by sliding effortlessly off his lap and down between his legs disappearing under the table at the last moment to wrap my lips around his cock, taking him into my throat.

He was so surprised he didn't have time to censor his reaction and cried, "Holy fuck!"

Gotcha!

Normally I would not spend this much time on individuals in my bar audience, because they weren't going to be getting the personalized attention these guys were.

So far, my dancing had been perfunctory, but now that I'd picked up a few pointers on my audience, I climbed on the table, thrusting my ass in their faces, and began gyrating suggestively.

"Okay, guys, this is the time to leave if you don't think you're up for the whole shebang. From here on in you'll only find my performance in the X-rated section of the store. Two of them looked ready to bolt but their curiosity or their horniness kept them rooted to their chairs. I picked up the baby oil and squirted it liberally over my chest, rubbing into my skin to give it a shiny look that is an aphrodisiac for many guys, while I swayed my body. I pulled out the waistband of my jock and squirted oil over my prick, massaging it until my cock flowered to its full bloom refusing to be contained in the flimsy material. I turned my attention to my ass, rubbing my cheeks, knowing that was of more interest to them than my cock.

With a slow backward somersault on the table top, I whipped off the jock. I wasn't at the bar now so my cuffs and collar quickly followed. I was naked except for my boots and socks and they were staying on so I didn't slip in the oil. There was enough of the stuff on the table top now that I wallowed in it so that it covered my entire body. It also meant I could spin around on my knees or my back.

I grabbed the dildo I had brought down with me, licked the base, and slammed it on the table in front of Lew. I kneeled in front of it, facing Lew, smiling my need. I stretched my cheeks apart so the guys on the other side of the table, including Matt, could get a good look at my butthole.

I didn't think these were the sorts of men who would appreciate subtlety so I leaned in to lick the rubber prick from the base making sure my tongue lapping was clearly visible. I noticed a few hands were now permanently under the table so I had to be doing something right. I licked up the rubber shaft to the head which I flicked with my tongue before putting my mouth over the pink knob to begin my face's descent until the huge fake dick was lodged in my throat. If it's one thing you need in my profession, it's good throat control. I remained still for a short while before breaking to breathe and then showed off my sucking action.

That was enough for a free demonstration. I crawled across the table to Soot, opening my mouth wide, licking my lips as an open invitation and as I reached the edge he stood, his cock already on display, and pushed my head down on it. It was mighty fine tasting. From the corner of my eye I watched as more guys shed their inhibitions and their clothes, crowding around for a better look at the action.

"Shit, he's good!" Soot said admiringly, not caring who was watching him get a fag blow job. Even shy Red had his cock out, tugging it in expectation of a turn.

"Better than Hannah?" Matt asked sarcastically.

"Fuck yeah. No comparison. What this guy does with his tongue is little short of a miracle." Soot wasn't going to stand for any argument.

Matt just grunted his disbelief.

"Hey don't wear him out," Smitty cried.

"Yeah, even Hannah had to stop because she got too sore," Don added.

"You'll all get a turn," I said, relaxing my jaw from around Soot's cock for a moment.

Matt had to add his two cents' worth. "From what I hear it's impossible to wear out this fag slut. He's insatiable."

From what he's heard? From whom?

I didn't have time to question him because Smitty took advantage of my mouth's vacant possession and guided my head roughly onto his cock. It was a thick fucker which pushed the boundaries of my lips. He was not the type to give me a chance to adjust and kept pounding at my face, forcing those gagging sounds out of my throat.

"Fuckin' choke the bitch!" Matt shouted helpfully, as if it wasn't hard enough already getting my breath.

What the...

I felt oil squirted on my back and between my cheeks, fingers spreading me open and fingers lubricating my sphincter. I couldn't check to see if it was who I thought it was because my face was currently being held by Smitty who had his cock buried in my gullet spurting his cum down my throat, while simultaneously shuddering, "Oh my god! That was fuckin' amazing."

One down, six to go. Smitty high fived his mates as if he'd fulfilled some great sporting achievement instead of just dumping a load. That gave me an opportunity to check my anal violator's identity. Yep, it was Lew. I wiggled my ass to encourage him. He responded by shoving the dildo into my hot passage hitting my prostate first go. Shit, I didn't want to come just yet.

I grabbed for Red, forcing his dick into my mouth although he was shaking so nervously I had to hold him in position as I set about my task. His comparative stillness gave me the opportunity to work my considerable skills. I'm a born cocksucker!

Lew withdrew the dildo and I felt his cock press against my ass. I relaxed but there was still a little sting as he entered me. It wasn't painful, just enough to relay that a cock was being wedged in my ass. I moved back to meet him, twitching my anal muscles, as he rocked against me gently, savoring the fuck.

"Jesus fucking Christ," he bellowed. "If this is what it's like, I'm only fucking fags from this day forth."

It was a hollow boast but I appreciated the sentiment, thanking him by squeezing his cock tight while he was inside me.

Red was a silent sprayer and only I knew when he blew his load in my mouth, his sweet nectar dribbling down the back of my throat. He shuddered as I sucked every drop out of him, his cock head so sensitive he pulled it from my mouth immediately he had made his deposit.

Yum.

Don stepped up to the plate to take his turn. His cock was average length and thickness but he certainly knew how to use it. He screwed my face with just the right amount of force to make it easy for me while giving him maximum pleasure. I wish more guys would learn. His steady rhythm enabled me to concentrate my attention on the cock in my ass; Lew riding me like a pro, my body responding automatically as he pushed all my buttons. I was beginning to enjoy this.

A voice whispered in my ear, "Don't swallow it, keep it in your mouth."

Don dumped and pulled out. I saw Soot about to take his turn again but just before he did, Parker stepped in and went the tongue wrestle on me, suctioning the spunk into his mouth swapping it back again. Snowball. That was unexpected.

"Eww, gross Parker," Matt said. "You're kissing Don's spooge."

Parker was shaking. He confronted Matt, his mouth dripping sperm. "So fuckin' what, Matt? I like spunk. Big deal!"

Matt thought he was on a winner. "What would your wife say if she knew you were a fag?"

"For your information, Matt. My wife does know. In fact, she likes to watch me suck other guys' cocks. And she likes me to drink their spunk out of her pussy after they've fucked her. What does that make me? I love women. I love pussy. I just happen to love cock. If women had cock, I'd be in heaven. If I was gay, I'd be blessed. But I'm not so I get spunk any way I can."

I high fived Parker in admiration.

"And you know what, Matt? I'm gonna suck Danny's cock later...um...if he'll let me."

"Any time, mate."

I think he was a bit overwhelmed by his confession because he broke away to sit apart from the action for a while.

Soot stepped up for his turn.

"Hey, Lew," he said. "Mind if we turn the fag over for what I have in mind?"

"No, mate," he replied, pulling out.

As I scooted onto my back, I noticed the numbers had dwindled to a more manageable four, although Matt looked anything but involved in the proceedings.

I didn't have time to reflect on it as I was on my back and Soot was arranging my head over the edge of the table.

Uh oh. I had a fair idea of what I was in for. Lew slid back into my ass, now with the added attraction of squeezing my tits like he would a woman's. I was about to give him some pointers to refine his technique but Soot slammed his cock down my throat as my head hung upside down off the table. He was going for the choke hold power face fuck. All the recipient can do in a case like that is hold on and hope for the best. It wasn't like I had a choice really.

I don't mind a rough face fuck on the odd occasion and this was one of the oddest I'd ever encountered. Taking the deepest breath I could before he cut off my passageway, my head was knocked back against the table top as he gagged me with the first deep throat plunge. I don't care how good a cocksucker you are, there's no way of keeping control once a guy has it in his head that your mouth is just a hole to fuck into submission. Everyone in those circumstances gags, gets snot and tears all over their face, and sometimes pukes. I was no exception.

It was one of the roughest face rides of my life. Soot slammed his cock every which way, cutting off my breath until I thought I would pass out. He was a master of control, judging exactly how long I could take it without breathing, then withdrawing his cock sticky with my gag juices, filaments of snot and tear-like membranes adhering to my mouth and his prick. The sounds of my mouth rape echoed through the house and I caught a glimpse of Matt watching intensely from the sidelines.

Lew eased off to watch my face being used as a cum dump and I wondered if this is what Parker wanted. I doubted it.

I didn't pass out and I didn't puke, I took a load straight down my throat direct from Soot's spigot. "Wow," he said patting me on the head like a good dog as he withdrew his slimy cock, wiping it on my face. "That was the best. No comparison. Fags can obviously take more punishment than chicks. Hope we can do this again, I've got a few more things I'd like to try."

"Look forward to it," I lied.

In your dreams.

Then there were three. Well, two plus Matt who didn't give any indication he intended joining the fun. I hoped, if he did, he'd settle for fucking my ass as my throat was raw from Soot's attempt to fuck me to death.

"Roll on your side, Lew," I requested.

Once we got in position, I told Parker to hop on the table and give my cock the blow job of a lifetime. I asked if he wanted me to blow him but he declined. "I only let chicks suck my cock," he said almost apologetically.

"I understand," I said, and I meant it.

Parker was good, very good. If the other guys at the security firm knew how good, I'm sure they would have been putting him to better use. I didn't want to come too soon as he obviously didn't get a chance to play too often. It was a tough life.

Lew was picking up speed so I knew he was close.

I grunted, tapping Parker on the head to give him fair warning although I didn't for a minute expect he would pull away. My breath came in little bursts and I held off as long as I could, then with a "Fuuuck" that lasted about ten seconds, I blew my pent up load in his mouth. I hoped it tasted good as it felt.

Of course, I couldn't control my ass muscles as I orgasmed and the twitch in my ass sucked Lew to the edge and over. He held me tight as his cock pulsed, squirting five times into my bowels.

"Thanks mate," Lew said, pulling out. "Awesome."

Parker was almost dressed. "Yeah, thanks Danny."

"My pleasure guys."

And then there was one.

I sat on the edge of the table waiting. I wasn't going to help him out. When the silence stretched out to breaking point, I hopped down, gathered up the sex toy and the oil, and headed for the door with the parting shot, "I need a shower. In case you're interested it's the third door on the right upstairs, I'll leave it unlocked."

I was having a good old scrub down when Matt joined me, still silent so I took control. I kneeled in the refreshing spray, sucking his beautiful cock, ignoring the rawness in my throat. He was hard so half my work was already done. He got enough of my oral expertise to know the other guys weren't exaggerating, and then I stood, soaped my ass, and backed up against his dick. It slid in easily.

"Uh…you don't have to speak but I do expect you to do some of the work," I said when he just remained motionless.

That sparked movement and he began fucking with just enough power to excite me.

"Is that okay?" he questioned.

Mr Confidence was asking me if it was all right.

"Just the way I like it," I said truthfully.

"Me too." I had an idea he meant more than just the pace.

I decided to take a chance. "Where did you hear about my reputation?"

"Just around. One of the bars."

"Must have been a mighty queer bar to have heard of me."

"Maybe."

I stopped the interrogation to concentrate on the fucking. There was something comforting about the way we fit together, the pace we maintained, the way we were receptive to each other's pleasure.

"Sorry." That was all he said but I knew he was apologizing for all the abuse.

"That's okay."

It wasn't, but I'd let it go.

"I don't like to share," he added, as if it was a condition of his application.

Application for what?

"Whoa. Way too early."

He laughed. "I know. Just putting it out there so you know where I stand."

"Less talking, more fucking."

He pushed my head down and commenced an onslaught on my butt that could only end one way. That he managed to make me come at the same time was little short of a miracle.

We were just completing the tidy up of the den when my dad came in with Hannah in tow.

"Good, you're home Danny. I wanted you to be the first to know. Hannah and I have decided to tie the knot."

Hannah's expression was one of deep concern that I may reject the idea because of her slutty behavior.

I hugged her tightly and kissed her. "I think that's great news. I couldn't be happier."

"What's been going on here?" she whispered. "You and Matt are in the same room without screaming abuse at each other and I distinctly smell spunk."

"Well, you couldn't make the poker night so someone had to fill in."

"You didn't?"

"Oh, didn't I?"

"No more poker nights for me, young man. I'm being made a respectable woman."

"I think someone wants to make a respectable man of me."

Hannah nodded at Matt. "You're kidding?"

"No, I'm not."

"What about it then?

"You mean make it a double wedding?"

"Why not?"

I looked over at Matt talking with dad. Strange, but I was already developing feelings for him. He looked across at me as if he could hear my thoughts. His smile lit up the room. He would be quite a catch. Still, he had a lot of forgiveness to beg before we'd get to that point.

Just as well then that I'm a very forgiving soul.

Dude, Where's The Bar?

Dude, I was sooo wasted. I woke up, face down, drooling into the grass, something slimy crawling across my tongue. Sweeet! As long as I didn't swallow.

I felt like Dorothy – somewhere over the rainbow. There sure were enough Friends of Dorothy cavorting about in sweet fuck all, their manhoods covered by the smallest strip of fabric they could wrap around it. The cheek of it. Yeah, those too. Most of the guys had their butt cheeks hanging out inviting others to openly grope.

Eww, gross. That's exactly what other dudes were doing. Where the hell was I? I didn't remember passing out in a park but that's where I seemed to be. A grassy square displaying pretty rainbow banners on huge flag poles.

I leaned up on my elbow thinking I might see a Kansas cabin splatting a witch wearing striped socks. Nope. All I knew was these Munchkins were fuckin' giants, until I discovered it was because I was lying on the ground. When I sat up, very gingerly, I could see they were just ordinary sized humans. Fags, but humans.

That's when I suddenly realized fags equal...OMG! The slime in my mouth could be man spunk. I spat it out, relaxing when I watched the lump of mucous crawl off into the grass. Phew, that was close.

I guess I'm not in Kansas anymore.

I'm parched. Plus, I've got the munchies. Dude, what the fuck did I take? I cleared my throat and gozzied in the grass, still not so sure there wasn't some ball juice mixed in with the saliva. My head hurt in that good way when the drugs are superfine, but they were making me confused.

For instance, how come I knew about the fucking *Wizard of Oz* and Munchkins and Dorothy? That's like, Gay 101. That's so not my life. Dude, I'm a Dude. With a big D.

In the distance, I saw dudes selling water and munchies but their carts were as far away as Emerald City and I wasn't sure I could make it. WTF? Emerald City? I think one of those sweet little colored pills I took gayed my brain. That's okay then, it'll wear off. Sweet. But what if it doesn't? Panic, like, but just for a second or two. My girlfriend wouldn't let me. She'd soon cure me. Though, when she's in a mood, she always accuses me and Chester, he's my best mate, of really being closet fags. Anyway, she wouldn't let me stay this way. Would she? They say it can't be cured. You're born that way or...

Maybe I'm bisexual. Cool! I always wanted to bone a lesbian.

Too much thinking, not enough drinking. I pushed myself up off the grass but fell back on my ass. I felt like one of those turtles you see on National Geographic channel who flail about on their backs trying to turn themselves over. That struck me as funny so I put my arms and legs in the air and imitated a baby turtle. I made a sort of squeaking noise like I think a baby turtle would make but I don't remember whether they do or not, it just sounded good to me.

A couple of guys walked past and laughed, one or two of them whistling what sounded like appreciation. "Nice costume, dude."

I think I heard myself say 'sweet', but I'm not sure.

Costume?

I could feel the grass against my back. Okay. I felt for my chest, moving my hand down to my nipples. Yeah, the left one was still intact. I could feel...OMG...I've got a metal bar through it. Sweet. I wished I had a mirror to look at it. It throbs. It wasn't there this time yesterday. Now I know it's there it hurts like fuck.

To take my mind off the pain, my fingers searched for my other nipple, and, well, something didn't feel right. I had to look, terrified of what I might find. I tilted my head, fumbled while I stared open-mouthed at my chest, one half covered in a light mat of fur, the other looking for all the world like scarred bushland after a fire. That sobered me up real quick. Half the hair on my chest had been singed off. I smelled the rank odor of burnt hairs and piss.

Then the drugs took over again and I wished I remembered how I got that way.

I was still lying on my back trying to get up when a face loomed over me. A woman's face.

"Hey, love, you okay?"

"Sweet," I replied, managing to turn it into a fifteen syllable word.

"Yeah, that's what I thought. Come on, I'll help you up."

She held out her arm, telling me to clasp it near the elbow. There's no way a little thing like her could lift me up. Not the first time I was proven wrong that day.

I'm whisked up and on my very unsteady feet before I even had a chance to tell her I was ready. I stared at her with new interest. She is totally my type. A lesbian.

Dude, I told myself, that's sweet. Get yourself a sex change and become a lesbian then you could be eating pussy all day.

"Get that idea out of your mind right away," she smirked.

I must have said it out loud.

"Look at me," she commanded. "What drugs did you take?"

"I can't remember."

"What color were they?"

I seemed to recall a rainbow mix, like a packet of peanut M&Ms. Then she asked me about alcohol. Then whether I had any known medical conditions.

"Who are you?" I asked. "My mother?"

She tapped a Red Cross patch on her chest.

"Nurse?"

"Uh huh. And my diagnosis is that you're severely dehydrated." So saying she snapped the clip on her fanny pack and handed me a bottle of water. "What? No Perrier?" I asked. Shit, since when did I ask for boutique mineral water?

"Water is water," she said, all professional like.

I practically guzzled the whole lot in one go but she wrenched it from my hand telling me to take it easy or I'd throw up. I did feel a bit queasy so I agreed to go slow from then on. She handed it back and I took a mouthful at a time. It revived me although my stomach rumbled.

She laughed. "I'd recommend something healthy but our budget doesn't run to feeding the masses." She looked at the forlorn collection of fast food vendors lined up outside the party venue. "You'll have to take your chances with that lot."

I took a few steps toward gastronomic salvation before she gave me the final okay, lecturing me on drug and alcohol dependency and blah! blah! blah! "Sweet," I said as I dismissed her from my mind, concentrating on the wafting smell of hot dogs, compelled toward them by some force beyond my control. My lesbian nurse shouted final warnings before giving up, telling me to come see her at the medical tent if I need anything.

I was only half listening as my taste buds were salivating over the prospect of delicious cock-shaped frankfurts in a thick phallic bun covered in spunk creamy mayonnaise. What the hell was wrong with my mind? I'm a cunt man. Please notice the lack of a comma in that last sentence.

Before even paying for the food, I plunged it into my mouth slobbering over the taste, the texture, and its similarity to a big orange cock sliding between my lips and teeth. I bit down.

If my life were a film, this is the part where there would be a whoosh of sound, like a mammoth steam train bolting from a tunnel, while everything went backwards in a series of montages of what happened over the past six or seven hours. I didn't need a cinema because my mind did the flashbacks and the editing. Some of the images were hazy and disjointed, probably reflecting the drugged state I was in. Others stood out in such embarrassing clarity I thought everyone around me could see them.

One thing was clear. I was at the Gay & Lesbian Mardi Gras.

Why, I still couldn't ascertain although I remembered years before a good mate told us there were so many fag hags there, hanging out for cock, even Quasimodo would get lucky. Especially if the chick thought she was turning a gay guy.

The emotions during the flashback were so numerous it was hard to associate them to the visuals. There was pain, pleasure, spewing, dancing, chicks, dudes, more spewing, drugs, alcohol, loud music, cocks...hold on...but my memory wouldn't...assholes, women with a suspicion of facial stubble, a woman with a dick between her legs, a guy in leather with a riding crop...fuck off, that hurt...beer, spewing. I wanted to scream for it to stop but suddenly all was calm and I got the funniest feeling in my stomach, that squishy queasy feeling when you really like someone. I felt hearts. I desperately wanted to know who was making my cock throb. I never felt so hard and so fulfilled. I heard a voice whisper, "Meet me back here for the Recovery Party. I want to do that again and again."

I groaned. "So do I."

I heard a voice through the fog. "Hey, mate. Are you all right?"

But I was not finished yet. More hearts but without affection this time. Whump! I was where it all began.

This was the past. Very definitely the past. The heart I saw was carved in Chester's pubes. Chester is my best mate, and his pissed off girlfriend, Wanda, had just shaved his crotch hair into a heart shape not because their relationship is going strong, just the opposite, it's her attempt to humiliate him. And me.

Wilma, my equally angry girlfriend was on her knees in front of me. My dick jumped to attention, showing its appreciation. She swatted it away. "Get that thing out of my face."

I looked down, my favorite way to watch her at work, except when what she's doing is trimming a heart in my pubes as well. I racked my brain to remember why they were doing it. Bingo! Neglect. That's it. We'd neglected them. Plus we'd forgotten we were taking them to the Mardi Gras Parade and Party. Shit! Just as well we'd bought the tickets months ago, because the whole thing's always totally booked out.

"We go to all this trouble to dress up and you guys are so stoned you're lying on top of each other with hard-ons. Eww!" Wilma screeched at full throttle.

"If you guys love each other so much why don't you just get married and leave us out of it?" Wanda was riled.

"Aw, come on," Chester whined. "We can be ready in no time at all."

Wanda looked superior. "Where are your costumes?"

Wombat in headlights time.

Chester and I looked at each other, hoping for a brainwave but we were so wasted there was not a single brainwave between us.

Wilma snickered. "Just as well we anticipated such an eventuality." She looked hot in a costume that barely covered sweet fuck all of her tits and a pair of shorts that left nothing to the imagination. Wanda was dressed like her twin.

I couldn't help myself. "Hey, dude," I said to Chester. "Get a load of the dykes. Maybe they'll give us a show."

"Sweet," Chester squealed.

"We might as well be for all the attention you pay us," Wanda moaned. She's always been a complaining bitch. Don't know what Chester sees in her.

"This is your last fuckin' chance, Jesse," Wilma snapped at me. I know she means it because she never swears unless it's serious. "We're going to find a good spot to watch the parade before they're all taken. You come looking for us—"

"In costumes. Or else."

"Or else what?" I asked.

"It's fuckin' over between us," Wilma yelled as if it was as obvious as the nipples on her breasts.

"Aw, come on," I complained.

Wanda laid down the law. "We'll be at the Parade, then the Party. If you don't find us by dawn, then get yourself new girlfriends. Cause we will have got ourselves new guys."

"Don't even think about turning up wasted. Or it's over," Wilma added as they flounced out the door, leaving our tickets behind.

"Aw, dude, we are so busted," I said to Chester, but he just stood there open mouthed looking at my crotch, pointing.

"Sweet cock, dude," he said.

My annoyance boiled over. "That's what gets us called fags by our girlfriends, dude. You ever realize that?"

"Your knob's dribbling," he replied.

I looked down and saw a string of spunk drool hanging almost to the floor. I rubbed my finger in the spidery filament dangling so dangerously. With both of us naked from our humiliation shaving, I chased Chester around the apartment trying to wipe it on him. When I caught him, I wrestled him to the floor and sat on his stomach trying to force the string of spoof into his mouth but all I succeeded in doing was wiping it across his lips. He wriggled to escape my clutches, our giggling way out of control, until I felt his cock, hard as ice, press against my butt cheek.

Leaping to my feet, I pretended I hadn't noticed, turning away as if I'm busy with something else to give him time to deflate. He went to stand behind the sofa so I can't see he has a hard-on.

Close call.

"Hey, mate, you gonna stand there all night? How about the money for the hot dog?"

The hot dog vendor was looking daggers, waiting for his money.

My hand went to my pocket. Except I didn't have one. Pocket, that is.

What have I got on? Oh, shit! I'm in a pair of silver lamé shorts that Chester and I found as matching pairs in a sex shop in the city – the only costumes they had available. They were eating into my crotch they were so tight. My balls felt like they had a dozen rubber bands wrapped around them. They bulged in my shorts. I could see the outline of my cock and it was hard. Apart from a pair of boots and socks, oh and my nipple bar, that's all I was wearing. Where's my money?

The vendor must have seen my confusion. He sighed loudly. "You guys are all the same. Come on, hand over the money. It's been a really bad night, I don't need this shit."

"Dude, I've lost my money."

"Don't fuck with me, mate. What's that stuffed down the front of your shorts? Looks like a bag of coins to me."

"That's all me, Dude."

He wasn't going to be placated that easy. "Don't believe you."

No one was around at the moment so I slithered the shorts down until my cock and balls sprang up in the cool morning air. It was the early hours by the Pavilion clock, therefore dark enough that my activity was in shadow. I'd only be seen if someone came looking for an early morning snack.

He laughed. "You think you're gonna get your shorts back up over that prick? I don't think so. You'll need help. I know, let me chow down on that monster and we'll call it quits."

"Throw in a can of soft drink and you've got yourself a deal."

Fuck! Where did that come from? I'm no fag. I never ever let a guy suck my dick before. Maybe them scientist fellers are wrong and gay is transmissible. Or maybe it was just this guy had his warm greasy mayo-speckled hand around my cock and was milking me like an expert. He was good and I needed my balls drained or they were gonna explode.

"Nice?" he asked.

I swallowed, unable to speak. I nodded my head, hoping he'd keep it up. Instead, he dragged me by the cock against the brick wall where we had a little extra privacy courtesy of a tree planted at the edge of the footpath. Instead of tugging at my dick, he sank to his knees and took it in his mouth.

"Dude, sweet," I hummed, as he sucked like he was drawing my brains out through my dick. He did things with his tongue I'd never felt before, taking me down his throat that gripped like a velvet glove. If Wilma ever sucked like this, she'd never be off her knees. I had to hand it to fags, they knew how to suck cock.

While I was wondering how I came to have a mouth full of cock phlegm when I woke up earlier, I blew my load. In the vendor's mouth. Holy fuck, dude. He swallowed. I waited for him to throw up but instead he got up licking his lips, wiping his chin with the back of his hands. I was glad I wasn't getting the next hot dog he made: hot dog with extra spooge dressing.

"Thanks, man," he said. "That's a great cock you got and your spunk is so sweet."

That reminded me: I had no idea where I'd lost Chester.

"Thanks mate. You could make a fortune with that mouth of yours." It was a compliment I was happy to pay. My cock and balls fitted snugly in my shorts now, still prominent, albeit not so painful. The only problem was the lamé chafed my legs. I'd ditch the duds if I could find something better to wear.

The vendor tossed me a can of soft drink which I chugged in one go just like those mountaineer types in the telly commercials. My burp was like an earthquake alert.

"Any time you want that manfurter of yours taken care of, just come looking for Julio. I'll never let you down," the vendor smiled.

"Deal, dude," I said, meaning it.

What was wrong with me? I didn't go round seeking out blow jobs from dudes. Where was my Eww factor? What the hell, I enjoyed it. Live dangerously, that's my new credo.

My best bet was to walk back toward the city which unbeknowns to me would put that credo to the test. Oxford Street and the gay Golden Mile lay ahead where I hoped I'd find Chester, or our girlfriends, but preferably that mysterious person who got my heart as well as my dick pumping. If only I could remember what she looked like.

I was half-way across the park to the main thoroughfare into town when I ran into a group of guys huddled on the grass doing some serious shit. They looked like they were about to bolt, they must have thought I was a cop, until one of them looked up and recognized me.

"Hey, aren't you the dude who caught fire?"

If I was, I remembered nothing about it.

"Sure you are." He stood up to examine me more closely, running his hand across my chest. "Look your chest hair is all singed. You were lucky."

"What happened?"

One of the others in the party answered. "Dude, you were so wasted. You were sniffing poppers, trying to light a cigarette at the same time. You spilled the shit all over your chest and stomach and then set yourself alight with your lighter."

"How come I'm not barbecued?"

"The amyl burnt on the surface and Henry here had the presence of mind to put you out."

"How?"

The guys all laughed.

"He doused the flames by pissing on you. You smelt terrible, piss and burnt chest hair. Henry didn't collect his reward you were so rank. You went to wash up. Then we lost you in the crowd."

"Thanks, Henry," I said looking around the group until this cute fucker – since when have I noticed men are cute? – put his hand up before using it to wipe excess powder from under his nose. "I appreciate it, dude. Hope to see you around."

As I went to leave I felt a strong grip on my arm. "Just a second. That's it? You promised Henry a trip to paradise and back, and I think he wants to collect before you disappear again."

"Okay," I said, holding my hands up in what I thought was a placatory gesture. "Not sure what I meant by a trip to paradise, but I don't welch on promises."

"Come on, guys, let's help Henry claim his reward."

Manhandled onto all fours, my shorts peeled from my body, I was naked apart from my footwear. There was a lot of activity around my crack and I was worried that Henry's reward might have something to do with my asshole. Yeah, I was right. I felt something cold and wet probing the entrance to my bowels and I knew it wasn't one of those new, lightly moistened ass wipes.

It was okay, I had obviously turned gay for the night so I'd know how to handle this latest assault on my gay virginity. What a fool I was. I felt Henry prod his thumb and one or two of his fingers into my lubricated hole. I was feeling no pain because one of the dudes in the gang had held some of the powder to my nose instructing me to snort. I'm not one to turn down any mind altering substance, particularly if it will help me through something that could radically warp my mind. Like Henry using his battering ramrod on my guts.

The guy dispensing the powder assured me I'd have more fun with it careening around my system and it would make me practically insatiable. Insatiable was good, right? What dude wouldn't give his right testicle to keep it up all night? Of course, being only a temporary gay, I had no concept of what 'insatiable' meant in gay dude-speak.

I found out. What it meant was Henry rammed his thick frankfurter between my hot buns. If they can hear dingoes for miles out in the desert then my howl of pain must have been heard on the moon.

"Shut up," someone whispered. "You want the cops to hear you?"

"Holy fuck, dude. You guys get fucked in the butt for pleasure?" I asked. Now I knew why Wilma flatly refused every time I asked. I would never ask again. Unless I was wasted.

"Is this your first time?" Henry panted over my shoulder.

"Yeah," I said impatiently. "Do I look like a dude who takes cock up the ass on a daily basis?"

A couple of guys snickered but no one answered the question.

Then something odd happened. The pain went away and having a dick in my butt seemed like a really good idea. And after Henry blew his spunk inside me, it seemed like an even better idea if each of the other guys had a turn as well. My largesse knew no bounds. I was also happy it seemed to have any number of guys porking my mouth including, I was told later, any strangers who happened to pass by.

I don't remember much of the experience apart from begging Henry and his gang to 'fuck me like a whore' which, it seems, they were happy to do. That explained the sore asshole and the stream of cum that oozed down my leg when I stood up. It also explained the unusually large amount of mucous that coated my mouth so that I was clearing my throat every few minutes, swallowing gobs of sperm.

Gay dudes sure have a lot of hot sex, I thought as I pulled up my sparkling shorts and headed off on my journey, just like Dorothy following the Yellow Brick Road. Yep, I was still feeling the effects of the gay drug someone must have slipped me because I was channeling Judy Garland.

The sun was coming up now and in a few hours the pubs would open for those who were too peaked to go home or those who still hadn't got their rocks off as many times as they wanted. Like me. I was buzzing on all four cylinders, my cock looking for action. I wasn't sure what I'd done when I was wasted at the party, apart from getting a nipple bar, but while fully conscious I'd been sucked, been fucked, and had sucked cock. My own prick felt left out from the anal stakes. I would have to rectify that before the night was finally over.

Mark me down as a failure in that respect. I stumbled as I headed to gay Mecca, realizing I needed sleep. It wasn't hard to find a good possie, even though there were sleeping and unconscious bodies strewn through the park and in shopfronts everywhere. I found my own darkened shop entrance and curled up to sleep only waking when the water truck sprayed the gutter to wash away the night's colorful debris, splashing me with the excess.

Staggering to my feet, my asshole throbbing, my mouth tasting like, well like what I imagined my asshole would taste like if I was stupid enough to stick my tongue in there but I couldn't because I wasn't ambidextrous enough and even if I were I wouldn't. Dude, was I ever hyper.

I heard some passers-by mention the Recovery party and I asked them where it was. They looked at me like I was some sort of alien. Was I speaking in a foreign tongue? They seemed to be expecting me to say something else so, "Dudes, I'm from out of town," I lied. That broke the ice and they were happy for me to tag along. Seems every pub on the strip was opening early and had its own recovery-style booze up. Hair of the dog and all that shit. From what I saw, it was more like hair of the whole fucking pound.

Nothing looked familiar. No one looked familiar, either.

I realized gay dudes were getting more sex, more booze, and better drugs, than straight dudes. And they were far more adventurous than Wilma or any of the chicks I'd fucked. Guys didn't want to sit around discussing feelings, they compared dick sizes. Mine, it seems, was considered premium sausage. I was wondering where I could sign up.

Wandering the streets, I had so many propositions for various sex acts, some I'd never heard of and some that made my eyes water just thinking about them, I could have filled my dance card for the next few months.

There were so many people around, I knew it would be impossible to find the chick that got my heart pounding and my balls churning. Now all I wanted to do was find Chester and debrief on our adventures, see if he'd been gayed for the night like me because we'd both taken the same drugs.

I left the biggest recovery party till last. It was held in a laneway between two main streets into the city, a pub on the corner at each end catering to the crowds drinking and chatting in the gutters and on the asphalt roadway, currently closed to traffic.

It was difficult to see anyone but I pushed my way through the wall-to-wall bodies, getting groped and goosed as I went. Gay guys are so damn horny all the time. No different to straight guys, I suppose. We all think with our dicks.

I saw Chester. He was sitting on some dude's lap in the gutter swapping spit. He was really snogging the guy, bouncing his butt on the guy's crotch. Sweet. He was so gayed.

Then something snapped. I didn't want that stranger snogging my best mate. I tried telling myself sucking dick, taking it up the ass was okay, but kissing. Eww! But really, I felt a hole open up in the pit of my belly. I was pissed off. Chester was my mate. Hands off!

I towered over them and coughed loudly. Chester looked up. "Dude, where have you been?" The stranger looked daggers at me, but some of his mates moved so I could sit next to Chester, their hands lingering on my ass as they helped me down.

Chester introduced me around but all I was interested in was his tales of the night's events. He hadn't seen our girlfriends either and had spent most of the night with Marty, the one he was snogging, and his mates, the ones who were pawing my family jewels.

Just then, one of the DJs from the party fired up his turntables and the laneway really got into party mode, Marty seemed to find dancing a good substitute to Chester, at least until I pissed off. I remained seated and Chester transferred on to my lap, space being at a premium, so Marty could get up to boogie.

When we had a modicum of privacy I blurted out, "Dude, I think I'm in love."

Chester looked at me sort of disappointed. "Who?"

"That's it, I don't know. I was so wasted, all I remember is we met around here somewhere and she made me feel special. We must have made out because I can still feel the fluttery shit in my stomach from when she kissed me. She made me feel special. I want to see her again. To feel that hearts and flowers shit, dude, that everyone talks about but I never felt. I'm fucking twenty-three and I never felt it before."

Chester's eyes opened wide. "And you don't know who she is?"

"No, dude. That's what sucks. Hey, do you remember who I was making out with last night? You must have seen us."

"Yeah, I know," he admitted.

"Sweet."

Chester made no effort to tell me.

"Come on, dude. Spill the beans. I'm panting here."

He leaned in to whisper the secret, but instead held my face and planted his lips against mine, at the same time grinding his butt against my cock. I was so shocked, I started to push him away then the hammering in my chest began and the hammering in my gut and the hammering in my dick. I let him kiss me a while longer before responding, trying to work out what was happening. When we broke our lip lock, I held him away from my body to look in his eyes for the truth.

"It was you, dude? There was no chick?"

"Uh huh," he said. "It was me all the time. You were so wasted, well, I thought I'd take a chance. I've been hot for you since high school, dude. And I couldn't hold it in any longer. I didn't think you'd remember and it would give me enough ammunition to jerk off over for months."

"You jerk off thinking about me?"

"Yeah."

He looked as if his whole world was starting to crumble.

I chanced it. "You take it up the butt?"

He must have thought I was criticizing because he rose to his full height while still sitting on my lap and spat, "Yeah, what of it?" Then he must have felt my dick hardening in my shorts, because he smiled.

It was so crowded in the laneway no one would even notice. I pulled his shorts down so his ass was bare then pulled down the front of my own until my cock sprang free. He pulled a sachet of lube from the band of his shorts and ripped it open with his teeth, lathering my cock with the cold grease and prodding a little on his hole.

He positioned my prick and slid his ass down on it until I was gasping for air the feeling was so intense. I had never felt anything like it in my life.

"Du-ude."

When he was seated with my cock totally inside him he leaned over to whisper, "I've been in love with you half my life. This is even better than I dreamed it would be."

I couldn't speak. I was paralyzed with new feelings for my best mate whose ass muscles were gripping my prick as I pushed in and out slowly. Chester kissed me again and my stomach did that flip flop thing that I had to believe was love.

"Sorry to disappoint you," Chester said sadly.

I was puzzled. "What do you mean?"

"You're obviously wasted if you're fucking me, dude. You won't remember a thing tomorrow."

"Dude, I'm so not disappointed. Fuck, we've lived together for years. I'm used to you. I don't have to change anything and I've got sex on tap seven days a week. All we gotta do is move your stuff into my room."

"Or move your stuff into my room."

"Maybe we use my room when I root you and we use your room when you root me," I suggested.

Chester's mouth dropped open. "You serious?"

"Shit, yeah. You're my best mate. And just between you and me, the best fuckin' kisser ever. And I do believe you'll turn out to be the best fuck ever, too."

"You're not embarrassed?"

"Only that we didn't do this years ago."

"We got a lot of time to make up for, dude."

We both sighed together. "Sweet."

New Year's Steve

"So what's it to be this year?"

I sidled up to Billy who was writing out his New Year's Resolutions. He always took the task so seriously. After Christmas, he would get out the previous year's list. Those resolutions that he'd not managed to achieve had not been crossed off and he would transfer them to his new sheet, provided they were still relevant. It was an annual ritual more important to him than sex. And just as secretive.

He would never divulge what was on his lists, his failures or his successes. As if to reinforce the secret nature of his resolve, he wrote them out on paper, never trusting them to the computer even with a password. That was due, in part, to his taunting my inquisitiveness.

"A boy has to keep some things private, keep a little mystery in the relationship," he said as if to confirm my very thoughts.

I couldn't control my eyebrow which arched automatically at his comment. Billy attempted to keep everything secret from me, usually failing abjectly, and usually causing me the utmost public humiliation. Okay, he had help from our countless friends and enemies who all wanted a piece of his succulent ass. I wondered whether his resolutions for the coming year had to do with strangers and friends coming inside it.

"What?" he said as he watched my eyebrow rise to the heavens. "You just have to know everything, don't you? It would kill you to let me have just a few secrets of my own. You manage to stumble across everything I ever get involved in. Just once, I would love to have a secret you don't find out about."

This Billy was familiar. This was the one who had a guilty secret and was attempting to deflect attention. Billy was the world's worst poker player.

"What's up?" I asked as nicely as I could muster.

"Why would anything be up?"

"Okay, if you don't want to talk about it." I turned to walk away.

I could almost hear the synapses in his brain sizzling, attempting to work out just how much to tell me. In the end, he just blurted it all out. "I can't come to the New Year's Eve party with you, I have a job. Really good money. And we need it if we're ever going to take up Uncle Ram's tickets to Italy." His confession was followed by a relieved sigh.

"Is that all?" I smiled, anticipating there had to be more.

"I know how much New Year's Eve means to you," he put his arms around me and nuzzled my nose. If he believed that he really didn't know me at all well. The welcoming of the New Year meant nothing; I would have been equally as happy staying at home to watch television coverage of the event from around the world. "I didn't want to disappoint you. I wanted to tell you but I was afraid you'd make me turn it down."

"Did I make you turn down the pizza delivery job, even after I found out what it involved?"

Billy turned a shade of red that looked good with his complexion.

"Does this job entail that sort of...um... activity?" I asked warily.

I watched him closely. I'd be able to read the lies on his face. "Hell, no! That sort of behavior is behind me. You know why I did it. For you."

Billy was adept at justifying his activities on the grounds that it helped me. It was wearing thin. I couldn't see any evasion in his face. It had to be legit. I could relax.

"What's the job?" Being the supportive lover was the way to go.

"Nothing special. Just being a waiter for an all-night New Year's Eve party in some rich guy's apartment on the harbor."

"Do you know him?"

"Nah. I got the job through a company that supplies casual waiting staff. Seems I was recommended from one of my previous jobs and they were desperate." I was about to object but Billy went on. "That worked to my advantage. Nobody wants to work on the biggest party night of the year so they were having trouble finding someone. When I hesitated, the woman from the agency quoted a price that literally took my breath away. She must have mistaken that for reluctance because then she doubled it. I was still speechless and she added another two grand to the total. She told me that was her final offer. When I found my voice, I accepted it."

I was suspicious. "How much?"

"Twelve thousand dollars." Billy could scarcely contain his glee.

"Who do you have to kill for that sort of money?" I was only half joking.

"It's legit. I checked. She gave me the phone number of one of the other waiters. I sort of know him to nod to so I gave him a call. He ummed and ahed a bit, wanted to know how much I was getting. I lied and told him eight grand. He told me that he was getting the same but I could tell he was lying too, he was getting more. In the end he confirmed that it was all legit. The guy is wealthy beyond our wildest dreams and what he's paying the wait staff is petty change to him."

Points to Billy for checking. Now it was my turn. I rang the agency, *Hors d'Oeuvres*, during business hours the next day to ask for prices and availability. Their charges were reasonable if on the expensive side, they obviously catered to the top end of the market, but they became astronomical during major holiday periods. 'No one likes to work those days,' the manager, Brian Noirish, revealed. He admitted that for New Year's Eve, their permanent staff were totally booked and he'd had to bring in outside help at considerably inflated premiums. Sometimes, he told me in rather shocked tones, he had to work himself if absolutely no one else was available. He had gay and lesbian friendly staff for those special occasions although, when I pressed him for how special the staff would play I got his back up and when I pushed a little further about their 'availability' he said rather tersely down the line, 'If you require that sort of service, sir, I suggest you consult the back pages of your local gay newspaper under escorts', and hung up. Points to *Hors d'Oeuvres*.

Billy was even more appreciative as I became positively keen on the job and began making tentative plans for our European excursion in the northern summer. It did leave me at a rather loose end for New Year's Eve, however. It was one thing staying at home with Billy; it was quite another staying home alone. We'd received a large number of invitations to parties but I realized a lot of those were contingent on Billy's attendance in the hope he would indulge in modest amounts of alcohol or party drugs, even small doses were apt to release his pent up libido, resulting in less than modest amounts of infidelity. It wouldn't hurt to ring around to see if I was welcome solo.

My ears were almost bleeding from the rejected suggestion that I attend alone. Some of them said straight out the invitation had been for Billy, others prevaricated by saying the party was for couples only, a few asked if Billy could, perhaps, turn up after work, a minority asked expectantly whether we'd split up, while an all-too-small minority welcomed the suggestion I come alone. Yes, I made a list of the bastards.

In the end the choice was taken out of my hands. I got a phone call from a former boyfriend to say he and his would be in town on New Year's Eve and for me and mine to pop in for a drink. They were being put up in a luxury hotel owned by the company he worked for so he had the penthouse suite with an uninterrupted view of the fireworks.

Billy was far from impressed with my choice of New Year's companion as he detested Bith, short for Bithell, the sort of pretentious name you give to the scion of an old money family. I had split up with him because I couldn't stand his family, they hated me with an equal vengeance, and I grew to detest the patronizing way Bith treated people of a lower social standing than himself – that included me. He oozed privilege and expected to be treated with the utmost deference, even by his lovers. He could not believe that I would give up untold wealth and a life in the lap of luxury. I'd only stayed with him because he was good sex but even that became perfunctory toward the end, as if he were doing me a favor by consenting to fuck me or, even more so, when he 'allowed' me to fuck him.

When Billy and I hooked up a few months later, Bith was still smarting over the rejection doing everything to split us up, right down to attempting to steal Billy right out from under me. They'd both detested each other since. But it was a brighter, happier Bith that rang to say all had been forgiven, how like him, and that he was insanely happy and wanted us both to meet the new love of his life, Ethan. Billy was not unhappy to miss the momentous event but told me he wanted a full report on how bloated and fat Bith had become and how ugly his new boyfriend was. Nothing bitter about Billy.

They were going on to a party after the fireworks to which they invited me but I begged off although, depending on how the evening went, I might change my mind.

On New Year's Eve itself, Billy was a flurry of activity getting his immaculately cleaned and pressed shirt and trousers to hug his svelte frame. He was mouthwatering, the material stretched tight across his butt, and revealingly across his crotch. The shirt hugged his pecs like it was making love to his chest. The little black bow tie was a nice touch to one hot looking dude. His spiky blond hair gelled in place like plaster. He shucked on his black coat, pecked me on the lips, we'd had our big new year's smooch before he'd got dressed, and rushed out to the cab he had waiting.

"See you in the morning for our belated party," he shouted as he headed for the lift.

Later, I made my way over to Bith's hotel, feeling totally intimidated in the foyer, so tongue-tied by the affluence I could scarcely bring myself to speak above a whisper to the receptionist when asking to be announced to Bith. He had to ask twice for me to speak up.

"He's expecting you, sir. The private penthouse elevator is the one on the right just around the corner here. Just enter and press his apartment number, he will key you up."

The lift was more opulent than my entire apartment, more chrome, more velvet, more everything. Put in a bathroom and I'd happily live in it. I was still admiring the decor, since when do elevators have decor, when I reached the spacious foyer of the thirty-third floor penthouse. It was the sort of place where you expected an impeccably groomed butler once you'd rung the bell. Instead I got a shouted 'Come' from inside.

I pushed open the door to be greeted by a disheveled and scarcely dressed Bith, buttoning his shirt over a somewhat corpulent frame. Billy always maintained the wealthy got fat because they never had to look their best for anyone; their money did that for them.

"Oh, I'm early," I said, startled as much by Bith's weight gain as I was by his lack of preparedness.

He swept over to me, engulfed me in his arms giving me an up close and personal feel of his body, something I could have done without. "You haven't changed a bit, Steve," he said kindly. "In fact, I think you're better looking than ever. And that body."

"And you're still the same old Bith," I smiled. I was lying, of course. I couldn't bring myself to say he hadn't changed when obviously he had.

"Ever the flatterer," he said. "I've put on a little weight since we last met. It's the contentment, I think. Puts weight on a man." He patted his 'little weight' gain like it was a favorite pet.

I hadn't seen him in almost five years and he'd really stacked it on in that time. He was no longer the hot stud whose name I'd screamed out as he plowed me.

"Should I go and wait in the bar until you're ready?"

"Good lord, man. Of course not. We're old friends. We're just running a little late because, well, Eth and I got a little carried away and, well, one thing led to another and we lost track of the time. You know how it is when you're in love."

Ah. It was all a set-up, to show me how happy he was in his new relationship. Call me cynical, I knew I was right when the door to the bedroom opened and a hot young stallion with only a towel wrapped around his waist to cover his modesty wandered into the living room ostensibly to ask Bith a question.

"Come and meet Steve. Steve, this is the love of my life, Ethan. Steven was the love of my life before you."

Ethan shook my hand. He had a strong grip and an even stronger effect on my cock. He was gorgeous! Hollywood leading man gorgeous, *Men's Health* magazine muscle ripped, Colgate dazzling, and, if the bulge in the front of the towel was anything to go by, he was porn star hung.

The fake question that had supposedly brought Ethan into the room was quickly forgotten as Bith ran his hand across his boyfriend's chest and abs and made him pose so his impressive biceps strained in all their glory. Bith knew I was a sucker for men muscles. He swatted him on the butt, ordering him to go get dressed, the show for my benefit over, although as he walked toward the bedroom door the towel managed to slip off his waist to reveal a succulent ass.

"Very impressive," I said once we were alone.

Bith pretended ennui. "He makes me happy. Exquisitely happy. What more can we ask of life?"

Less pretentious bullshit, I thought, but actually said, "Indeed, what more would you want with someone like Ethan by your side."

"How right you are," Bith said from the bar. "Your usual?"

I would hate him to think I hadn't changed so, on the spur of the moment, I said, "A vodka and bitter lemon please."

"My, you've changed in some respects. I like it." He handed me my drink. "And how's," he hesitated as if he had to think of the name, "Billy, isn't it?"

It was going to be a night of games and one-upmanship.

"He's fine. Sends his love, but he has to work tonight," I said cheerily.

"I would never allow Eth to work on such an important occasion as New Year."

"New Year means nothing to us. Besides, Billy is getting penalty rates for the night, almost enough for us to book that trip to Europe we've been talking about."

"Is that the same trip you were talking about five or six years ago? No, it couldn't be. Eth, honey," he called. "How many times is it now we've been to Paris since we met?"

"Five," Eth called from the bedroom. "We go every year."

I wasn't going to play the game so I just said, "We haven't had the money, what with the global recession, and me being out of work for a while, so it will be our first."

Bith clasped my arm. "Oh, how sad at your age never to have travelled. How do you manage? Life must be awfully dull."

"You could never call life with Billy dull."

That was the opening he was waiting for. "Yes, we've heard rumors. You poor, poor man. What he must put you through. Frankly, I'm surprised you're still with him after what I've heard about his behavior."

"I wouldn't believe everything you hear."

"You don't have to pretend with me, Steven. We're old friends. You can tell me anything."

"I don't know what you want me to tell you, Bith." I kept my temper under control.

Bith shook his head. "The truth, Steven. Just the truth. It will go no further."

"The truth is we're extremely happy, but our friends and enemies aren't. They like to spread sordid stories about us. There's nothing much we can do about it."

"You know the old saying, 'Where there's smoke there's fire.' You may think everything is rosy, but who knows what's going on behind your back? He probably has secrets so bad he's never told you about them because you would throw him into the streets."

"I trust Billy. He tells me everything."

"Like where is he tonight?"

"He's doing an all-night party," I said.

"Are you sure?"

"It would be pretty hard to fake the amount of money he's being paid," I said with a superior smirk.

"If it's as good as you say it is, what does he have to do to earn it? Hmm?"

I was getting tired of this and thought about throwing the drink in his face and storming out, but Ethan interrupted our little tense moment. He had changed into expensive casual wear which hugged his body as closely as Billy's hugged his. Bith was a lucky guy.

"I saw shots of Billy when he modeled for that T-shirt promotion. He's hot," Ethan said, sipping a cocktail.

"What was the promotion again, something like Slut wear, wasn't it?" Bith's sarcasm uglied his face.

"One hundred per cent Pure Slut it was called," I said proudly. "Made the company a fortune."

"Gave Billy a rotten reputation, I know that," Bith said. "You deserve better."

"Why don't you go and finish getting ready, darling," Ethan said. "I'll keep our guest company."

Bith grunted and headed off to fix his shirt and tie and put on his shoes.

"Sorry about that," Ethan said. "He loves needling people."

"His least endearing feature," I said.

"One of," Ethan laughed.

We wandered out on to the huge balcony that came with a view down the harbor to the bridge above and around which the famed fireworks would light up the night sky culminating in a waterfall of color and light cascading from the bridge roadway into the murky waters below. This was the perfect vantage point. We could hear the sounds of people enjoying themselves in the foreshore park adjacent to the hotel but none of them would be allowed entrance to the prime views in front of me. It took wealth for that, but I suspected the people crammed into the park were having more fun than us, thirty-three stories above them.

There were two telescopes positioned on the balcony. They had clear sightlines to the bridge but I suspected they were mainly used to track the peccadilloes of the occupants of the neighboring high-rise apartment buildings. One was positioned toward a nearby penthouse apartment, a floor or two lower, so close you felt you could reach out and touch its railing. The partygoers there seemed occupied with a late-night swim in the outdoor pool on the large sun deck on the pleasant balmy night, or guzzling drinks shouting to show what a good time they were having.

No one would be getting any sleep tonight.

I'd deliberately arranged to meet Bith as late as possible so that if things did not work out, and they weren't, I could quickly slip away once we'd rung in the New Year. When he came out of the bedroom, he was dressed almost identically to Ethan who pursed his lips in irritation. "Just this once could we not go out dressed like Tweedledum and Tweedledee?" he said with an edge to his voice.

Bith shot him a warning look which I caught but pretended not to see. "I thought you liked us to go out as a couple." He sounded whiny.

"A couple yes, not as book ends."

"Fine, I'll go change." He started to flounce off when Ethan sighed.

"It's all right. Don't worry about it. I guess it's the humidity. I need another drink." Ethan went to the bar and I saw him pour a rather large portion of liquor to a very small portion of ice and mixer.

"Some view, eh?" Bith said, more relaxed now although somewhat florid in the face from his alcohol consumption. He obviously intended getting plastered.

"A view like this would set you back a pretty penny," I said leaning against the balustrade, looking toward the city.

"The view from this side," Bith said guiding my view to the raucous party in the building opposite. "is even better. The things they get up to at night beggars belief."

He seemed pleased that it did.

"The middle-aged gay couple who live there certainly have a fine eye for hot young men. And lots of them. We were told their New Year's Eve parties are something else. As many fireworks over there as there are on the harbor." Bith was watching the activity through the telescope.

"Come and take a look," he encouraged. "I remember you used to like watching."

I didn't remember I was that obvious with Bith. My fetish was obviously showing. No point in being shy about it. Ethan and I wandered over and I bent slightly to peer through the device. "Can't they see us?"

"No, there's a shadow falls over the balcony and if the lights in the living area are off, we're in darkness. Besides, I doubt they care, you can see almost as well with the naked eye."

What I hadn't seen with the naked eye before was that shock of spiky blond hair carrying trays of drinks amongst the revelers.

"The waiter's mighty cute," Bith said. "Need to see a bit more of his body though."

"Let me see." Ethan pushed him aside. "Very cute from the back. Nice ass."

I nodded because my voice caught in my throat.

"What? What am I missing here?" Bith feigned surprise. He took a look through the telescope again. "Oh my god! Isn't that your Billy?" He had a look of triumph on his face.

"Yes. I didn't know his waiting job was right next door."

"Job? You really are naive, Steven. But then you always were. That's no waiting job." Bith laughed in my face.

"What is it then?"

"You really don't know. Your little Billy who keeps no secrets from you didn't tell you?"

"Bith," Ethan warned.

"I saw the caterer's van this afternoon. Billy is doing the job for *Hors d'Oeuvres*, am I right?"

"Yes," I answered, fearing the revelation to come.

"Everyone in the trade knows them as *Whores d'Oeuvres*. W.H.O.R.E.S. That's what their waiters are."

"Billy doesn't know. I've got to warn him." I got my mobile phone out and punched in Billy's number only to be diverted to his voicemail. I left a message for him to ring me and hung up.

"You really didn't know? Oh, poor love. Billy is their party entertainment."

I looked over to the apartment again. Sure, a few drunken guys were attempting to grope him but he pushed their hands aside easily. There was no sign of any group sexual activity although some of the guests were quietly consummating friendships in the darker corners.

"It all looks pretty tame at the moment." I was trying to put the best face on it.

"He's quite a stunner," Ethan said. "I can see why he would be popular."

Just then there was a shout of Ten! And the countdown was on. I joined in feebly all the while casting my eyes back to the adjacent penthouse patio. Billy was quaffing a glass of champagne while joining in the fun of the occasion, obviously oblivious to what was to come. Provided what Bith said was true. He seemed to know a lot about it.

As the countdown reached its conclusion, there were horns and whistles and shouts of 'Happy New Year' as well as tinny radio versions of 'Auld Lang Syne.' Bith kissed Ethan with a passion that seemed to surprise him. I watched a number of the partygoers kiss Billy with the sort of drunken familiarity that goes with these parties but that was as far as it went. Then everything was drowned out by the first loud explosion heralding the fireworks display. Just about everyone stopped to watch them although I noticed Billy scurrying about getting drink orders. The second waiter was nowhere to be seen. He'd chickened out or was a ring in to calm Billy's fears.

It was the longest twenty minutes of my life as I was eager to leave and try my luck at gaining entrance to the party opposite, to drag Billy home. I'd give him the benefit of the doubt because he hadn't given me the slightest inkling of impropriety. Maybe I was over-reacting. Perhaps Bith was attempting to destabilize my relationship again.

I glimpsed Billy arguing with an older partygoer, obviously one of the two middle-aged men who had hired him, shouting and gesticulating wildly, encompassing all the men at the party. He shook his head a number of times. Each time the older gent seemed to be pleading. I wished I could lip read. After shaking his head vehemently again Billy turned to walk away but the gent grabbed his arm and held him. He reached into his pocket to retrieve his wallet then opened it for Billy to see. Billy paused. He looked at the older gent and then pointed to the other older man at the party who was currently watching the fireworks. He took some bills from the wallet and pocketed them. The older man pointed to the others at the party and Billy shook his head.

The older man grabbed Billy's arm and dragged him into one of the other rooms so I could not see what was happening any longer. I had been so preoccupied I hadn't noticed the fireworks were over. Ethan turned to me, "Nice meeting you. I can put a personality to the name now." He went out to the lift with a bottle of alcohol wrapped in a paper bag for the party to which they were headed.

Bith was close on his heels. "See yourself out, mate. Pity about Billy. I guess all good things must come to an end. Pity it had to end so publicly like this." I heard him chuckle as he turned his back. "I'll leave you to stew over it. Just let yourself out when you're finished. Nice catching up. I'll look you up next time we're in town. Maybe by then you will have found a boyfriend who doesn't keep secrets from you. Who isn't a liar when it comes to relationships?" He closed the door and was gone.

I'd forgotten to ask him if he knew the number of the penthouse opposite. I didn't intend to wake the entire building in an effort to track down Billy. There was no concierge so it would be impossible to penetrate without the correct apartment number. I went to see if Bith was still at the lift but the door would not open. I tried again. I banged my fist but there was silence from the foyer. They'd obviously gone.

Something in the apartment building opposite caught my attention. The first older man emerged and sought out his partner who walked back into what I could only assume was the bedroom where Billy must have been waiting for him.

It must have been no more than ten minutes later when two new guests were ushered into the apartment, one of them glancing toward my telescope and waving. I felt sick. Bith and Ethan had gone over to the party where Billy was. We'd both been set up.

My mobile phone rang. It was Bith.

"Hi Steve. By now you will no doubt have discovered that you are locked in the apartment. Even if you did manage to escape into the foyer it will do you no good as the lift is on security in the basement, and the fire stairs are wired through to security. I've warned the front desk to be extra vigilant because we'd had strangers attempting to access our floor during our stay. You will be arrested if you are caught and I'm sure I can find a few items missing from the room, obviously stolen by your good self in revenge. If you sit tight and behave yourself we will return in good time and let you out. We might even bring Billy back with us if everyone here has finished with him. Oh, he might be a bit sore but, hell, he's a slut and probably used to it by now. Oh, and don't bother with the police, unless you want Billy to end up in jail for prostitution."

"You mongrel, Bith. What have I ever done to you?"

"You split up with me, Steven. No one ever splits up with me."

"What about Billy? He's never done you any harm."

"Oh, that's for the fun of it. You think he despises me, so that will make it so much more exciting. My friends Griff and Tony organized the whole thing. Aren't they divine?"

"I'll get you for this, Bith."

"Don't go making threats because I'm recording this conversation."

"Bastard!"

"Why don't you sit back and enjoy the show? There's nothing much else to do. Grab yourself a drink and some nibbles. Drag a chair out to the balcony, focus the telescope and watch us all plow Billy's hot ass. Oh, I'm not one for silent movies; I always find sound so much more exciting so I'm going to leave my phone on, that way you can hear every grunt, groan and cry of pain from your slut boyfriend while we fuck the shit out of him. Enjoy."

I was shaking so badly I went to make myself a stiff drink to calm down, also raiding the fridge for a little food so as not to get too intoxicated. I did pull up a comfortable chair, making sure to keep it in the darkness. I didn't want Bith to see me perving on the action. I put the mobile on speaker phone so I didn't have to hold it to my ear.

Bith waved and walked out on to the balcony. A few minutes later Billy emerged from the bedroom after, I had to assume, sex with Griff and Tony, back in his waiter costume once again although it looked less pristine than when he first arrived. He was in the kitchen, where I had a perfect view, pouring drinks. He looked disgruntled. He was about to look even more so because Bith was creeping up behind him. I could not see Ethan anywhere.

Billy tensed as the hands went around his waist and I could see he was about to hurl some pretty graphic abuse. I was in for a shock, a very unpleasant shock. I could hear the conversation as Bith had the phone in his breast pocket.

"Bith!" Billy greeted him with delight, flinging his arms around him, kissing him full on the lips. Bith looked toward the balcony where I was fuming. Some of what he'd said cryptically earlier in the evening was now beginning to make sense.

"How long have you been in town?" Billy asked excitedly. "Why didn't you call?"

"Only got in yesterday and I knew you'd be here."

"How long are you in town?"

"A couple of days."

"Great. Listen, I have to mingle and serve drinks. I'm working, fuck the luck."

"As of now, Griff and Tony have given their permission that you're all mine for the next half hour. The guests can get their own drinks." Bith was unbuttoning Billy's shirt in full view of the window. "I really missed this beautiful body of yours, Billy. I keep forgetting what a stunner you are."

"Mmmmm, I like that, Bith. Pinch them. Make them hurt."

Bith pinched the nipples much harder than I ever had, screwing them around violently. Billy sucked his breath in pain but did nothing to stop the agony. Bith tongued the reddened tips, licking before sucking each one into his mouth, biting hard. Billy groaned. Bith repeated the action. Billy unbuckled his belt and unzipped, his trousers fell to the floor, his underwear following shortly. He kicked them away.

While he tortured Billy's tits, Bith pushed him back against the kitchen table, shoving his hand between his legs. He must have pushed his fingers into Billy's asshole. "Did Griff and Tony fuck you good, Billy? Did they fuck your cute little ass and make you yell like I do?"

"No one makes me yell like you do, Bith," Billy said opening his legs to give him better access.

"Did you like their cocks inside you?"

"You know I always like cock in my hole."

Bith began to remove his own pants. "Your butt is the best, Billy. I told you that night I fucked you while Steve was out. Remember that? I made you scream so loud I thought someone would call the cops. You were begging for my cock in your slimy hole. Steve had just gone to work and you left the door open for me, remember? I let myself in and you were lying on the coffee table, your ass spread open waiting, dripping lube you wanted me inside you so bad. I fucked you for three solid hours, Billy. You said no one had ever done that before and given you so many orgasms without even touching yourself. You were covered in spunk. I filled your fuckhole three times, like I did all those other times you left the door open, like I'm gonna do tonight, Billy."

I couldn't believe what I was hearing. Billy had been fucking Bith, my evil ex-boyfriend who he professed to loathe, on a regular basis. Not for cash, not for revenge, but for the pleasure of it. And even while I listened to Billy's confession, I knew it was going to continue whether I liked it or not.

Billy spread his butt cheeks apart to give Bith access and he slid right in lubricated by Griff and Tony's spunk. "Mmmm, so sloppy, Billy. They opened you up nice." Bith took his time, fucking in a circular motion, slowly. It must have been plumbing the depths because I knew that look on Billy's face; he only got it when cock was embedded deep inside him, pleasuring his guts.

"Fuck, Billy, your butthole is hotter than it ever was. What's say we skip the party and you and me go back to my hotel room for a real fuck session?"

Billy moaned like a bitch in heat. "I really want to, Bith, but I can't. If I don't stay here and finish the job I don't get paid."

"Fuck the job. I'll pay you."

"It's too much money. Besides, I'd hate for you to pay me for something I want to do with you for free."

"Good boy."

Even though I was sickened by what I was hearing, my cock was leaking in excitement. I stripped off my clothes and sat naked, I'd already ensured all the lights were off. I stroked my cock slowly, it was going to be a long night and I wanted to pace myself.

"Need some help with that?"

The voice came from behind me.

"Help yourself," I said, taking my hand off my shaft.

I heard the rustle of clothes falling to the floor. He came and kneeled in front of me.

"Why'd you come back?"

"I thought it was a lousy thing to do. I didn't like the idea you were trapped and couldn't get away."

"You'll miss out on fucking Billy."

"Nah, it will take hours for them all to go through him. I'll be back in plenty of time to join the queue. He doesn't know yet, does he?"

"I don't think so," I replied.

"Do you mind?"

"What?" I asked. "That the whole party will fuck my lover? Or that you'll join in?"

"Both, I suppose."

"Billy can take care of himself," I said.

He laughed softly. "You didn't answer the question."

"Does it look like I mind?"

"It looks like you enjoy watching Billy get fucked."

"Mmmm, I do. Though not particularly by fat ex-boyfriends whom, I discover, have been fucking him for years behind my back."

"I suspected as much." Ethan stood to watch the action through the telescope. "So that's what Bith looks like when he's fucking me. Not a pretty picture."

"On the table on your back, fuck slut," Bith ordered.

"Yes, sir!" Billy snapped into action and was on the table with his hole exposed in record time.

"Very fuckable," Ethan murmured.

I reached forward and stroked his bubble butt. "He's not the only one."

Ethan turned and smiled. "I hoped you'd notice. Let me get a drink and prepare myself. I'll be right back.'

He disappeared into the darkness while I watched Bith penetrate Billy again.

"I love the look on your face, Billy, when you take my cock. No one else but you has that look of sheer fucking pleasure."

"That's because nobody else loves cock as much as I do."

"Who writes their dialogue?" Ethan called from the bar. "It's atrocious."

"Especially your cock," Billy added.

"You could have this cock all the time and not just when I get away from Ethan," Bith added.

"This I've got to hear," Ethan said, coming out on the balcony and sitting in the deck chair beside me.

Billy's curiosity surprised me. "How?"

"Move in with me."

"You've got a boyfriend. I've got a boyfriend."

"I'm over Ethan," Bith said.

"Not as much as I'm over you, honey," Ethan smiled.

"I'll pay him off. You could move in tomorrow if you want."

"You'd get sick of me..."

"No--"

"Yes, you would," Billy insisted. "Everyone does. Except Steve. He takes me as I am, doesn't try to turn me into something I'm not. I love your secret visits, Bith. Lying on the coffee table with my asscunt exposed waiting for you to push open the apartment door, strip in the hallway and then discover me panting and naked. I can't get that thrill from Steve. He knows that, he lets me play around, though he doesn't know about us."

"He does now, mate," Ethan said to the night.

"It would gut him if he knew about you and me."

Bith chortled.

"Bastard!" I muttered as I took another mouthful of Scotch.

"I think the word you're looking for is *cunt*," Ethan said. "No offence to feminists among us."

"What if I tell him?" Bith was playing for high stakes here.

"Then it will be over between us."

"He'll throw you out, and then you can move in with me."

"Nah," Billy said. "He'll be really super pissed off at me. He'll fuck me into the ground in order to hurt me for what I've done and I'll get the best sex with Steve ever. Then it will all calm down and I'll find someone else to replace you."

Ethan looked at me and I nodded my head that he was correct.

He whistled his appreciation. "You are some piece of work, Steve."

"I have a piece you can go to work on here any time you're ready," I said, waving my prick about.

He slid to his knees and had my cock in his mouth. He took it as slowly as Bith was fucking Billy, not wanting to miss a word.

"I don't take too kindly to rejection, Billy," Bith said, his temper getting the better of him. "Why do you think I fucked you in the first place? It was to get back at Steve for dumping me. I was gonna tell him I fucked his sweetheart. Fuck it up good for both of you."

"Yeah, I know," Billy said. "I'm a slut, I'm not a fuckwit."

Ethan laughed even while he had his mouth around my cock.

I smiled. "Good one, Billy."

"But your ass is something else. It's addictive," Bith continued.

"So I've been told." Billy sounded bored which meant this could only take a turn for the worse.

"Move in with me. I won't take no for an answer."

"Look, Bith. I've tried it with others. It doesn't work. Only Steve has the secret. Sure, he gets bored, gets boring sometimes, but he knows how to play me. It's always interesting with Steve. Neither of us knows what will happen next but we're both up for it. Pain or pleasure."

Bith turned nasty. "If you turn down this offer, Billy, I can guarantee you the pain. You'll never get another offer like it. This apartment could be yours, Billy. I own it. All you have to do is move in here and have your asshole ready every time I want it. I'll sign it over to you lock, stock and barrel. You'll have everything you need. Just leave that loser boyfriend of yours. I'll look after you. Money problems over. You'll see Paris every year. Latest fashions, all yours for the asking. I might even let one of those dirty French boys stick his cock in you, Billy. You like that idea? Yeah, I see you do. Turn me down, Billy, and the whole party will fuck you. Your mouth and your asshole. No one can save you except me."

Their fucking had slowed to a crawl by this time. Bith pulled out and sat at the table. Billy lowered his legs and sat up.

"So, Bith, you're giving me a choice? Move in with you and live in the lap of luxury even though you would get bored with me in a matter of weeks and I'd be bored shitless with you in a matter of days. Or, correct me if I'm wrong, have all the men at the party use me as a cum dump over the next six or seven hours. Hmmm." Billy was in full sarcastic mode. "Decisions, decisions."

Ethan had stopped sucking my cock awaiting the outcome.

Billy hopped off the table and bent down to retrieve his clothes. "You know, I think I'll go for Box B. It sounds like a lot less whiny and self-indulgent and much more my style. How many would you say there are? Fifteen? Sixteen? They won't all want to fuck me, them I'll blow. Some won't want me at all. More's the pity. Oh, and forget dropping by for a freebie when Steve's at work. It's over. Now, if you'll excuse me, I have to get back to work."

Grabbing Billy by the hair, Bith roared like a bull, dragging him back into the kitchen, banging him against the table so that his man hole was vulnerable. He slammed his cock in roughly, fucking like a madman, trying to squirt some sense into Billy.

"You cunt," Bith swore. "No one, but no one, rejects me. He pulled Billy's hair just enough that he could spit in his face.

"By the time we've finished with you your ass will be mincemeat. Even Steve won't want to go slops."

Bith was fucking him so hard it was pushing the table against the wall, making enough noise that Griff, or was it Tony, came to investigate.

"He turned me down, Griff. Can you fuckin' believe it?" Bith was on the verge of tears by the sound of it though I suspected they were tears of frustration. "I offered him the world and he fuckin' turned me down. Well, I'll show him what we do to guys who don't respect their betters."

There was no way Bith could hold off for long at the pace he was going and, while Griff watched Billy's humiliation, he banged hard enough to screw Billy into the wall, making a loud deep growl like a wild animal as he pumped his cum into his prey. "Take it you fuckin' lousy slut-cunt. Take my spunk in your slut hole. Fuck yeah."

"That was so fuckin' hot," Ethan said, kneeling in front of me. "I think it only fair that you get to do with his boyfriend what he just did to yours. With just as much force if you don't mind. But please don't leave bruises."

Being an obliging soul, I sank my prick inside him, fucking him smoothly and expertly. I was hard, but I was hard for Billy. Ethan was a stunning looking man, built like the proverbial brick shithouse but the whole time I was buried inside him I was remembering Bith buried inside Billy's guts. That feeling when the bottom falls out of your stomach, when your boyfriend is cuckolding you with someone you detest, an image that gets your cock so hard it threatens to explode.

"Take my cock, you mongrel cunt," I swore at Ethan, banging sharply into his guts, impaling him on my dripping prick. Sure, I recognized there was scarcely a spunk's breath of difference between me and Bith. Maybe that's why we detested each other.

"Feel it, you slimy piece of slut shit. Feel it ramming your ass, probing deep inside your slut-hole. Beg for it, baby. Beg daddy to fuck your slime-hole."

"Fuck yeah, daddy. Split me in two. Let me see your face as you fuck me. Please."

I pulled out so he could scramble on to his back. I hoisted his legs roughly on to my shoulders and my cock found its way home. I knocked the breath out of him as his eyes glazed over from the deep and brutal penetration. He groaned, just like Billy, so I plowed him like I wanted to torture-fuck my boyfriend for his infidelity. I grabbed his throat and choked him as I spat in his face. He opened his mouth to take my abuse and swallow any saliva that I hoiked there.

I squeezed his balls until he gasped in pain, and then slapped his hard drooling cock with the back of my hand. It was liberating to treat him like a piece of shit just like Bith was treating Billy at the party. Pinching his nipples, smacking his pecs until I left a print on his skin, I wanted to defile his beauty. He was begging for it.

"Make me your slut-cunt, daddy. Use me. Abuse my hole."

Suddenly I could hear the words as if they were coming from Billy.

"Rape my fuckin' asshole if you dare, you motherfuckers," he was yelling at the partygoers. "Who wants to be first? Think you're man enough for this prime pice of boycunt?" I heard him slap his butt. I imagined the meaty red hand print and slapped Ethan.

"Take it fucker! Feel my daddy prick in your boy ass," I joined in.

I heard Billy gagging through the phone, someone riding his mouth, as I pumped into Ethan's wet, tight shithole, feeling my cock squeeze into his chute. I grabbed the telescope and watched as some big fucker lined up at the gate to Billy's guts and with no preliminary warning gave one almighty push and disappeared into his butt.

Placing my hand around Ethan's cock I began to milk it slowly but he stopped me, smiling, he said, "Don't. I want to save it to pump inside Billy."

During my adventures with Billy I'd met a few guys I took to. Ethan was one of them. If he hadn't been in a relationship with that fucker Bith, he could become a friend. He 'understood.' And that was rare.

I concentrated on dropping my load. The visuals of my boyfriend surrounded by a group of hot guys eager to gangbang his hole that was already oozing man-snot, the sound of dirty talk through the phone and Ethan begging for his daddy to fuck him senseless – it doesn't get much better than that.

"Fuck him, you cunts," I yelled, knowing they couldn't hear me. "Make him bleed. Drown him in hot spunk! Fuck the bastard! Rape his ass while his daddy watches."

It was a beautiful fuckin' sight. A hot sub who wanted nothing better than to be defiled had my cock wedged in his tight muscular ass, while I watched the same sort of cock and cum degradation being visited on my lover. One by one they lined up to pound into him until he puked up a stomach load of their spunk, his hole leaking slime, some of the guys feeding it to him, watching him swallow the funky cream.

With an enormous bellow of satisfaction I dumped in Ethan. I remained still after the last squirt of my load settled inside his bowels. It had been intense. He felt it as well and as I slowly lowered his legs, he let out an exhausted breath. "Wow. I couldn't do that every day. Billy's right. Better the occasional fuck that's so intense you think you'll die of pleasure."

I slapped his butt. "Second only to Billy," I said.

"That's high praise coming from you." He was unsteady on his feet as he went to get his clothes. "Sorry to fuck and run but I want to sample the only ass, I have it on impeccable authority, that is better than mine."

I laughed. This guy was fun.

I pulled him into my arms, planting a wet sloppy tongue in his mouth. He hummed his appreciation.

"Now that Billy's looking for a new man to open the door, you may like to apply. I might even drop in unexpectedly and catch you at it and be forced to teach you both a lesson," I suggested.

"I do like the sound of that, but let's see if I'm man enough for Billy."

"You're a good guy, Ethan."

"Ditto," he said as he headed for the lift. "You gonna stick around to watch my performance?"

"As long as it's soon. I've gotta get back home. This lot are strictly by the book gangbangers."

In the end I did stay around to watch him. He was as great a top as he was bottom and I could see he perked Billy's interest. Whether it was enough to offer him the vacant slot, so to speak, I didn't wait around to find out. I would stumble across it soon enough.

Back at our apartment, before I showered and climbed into bed, I dug out Billy's New Year's Resolutions from its secret hiding place, took my pen and crossed off number one on the list: *Break up with B.*

He'd got the year off to a great beginning.

Of course I read his resolutions. It's the only way to stay one jump ahead of Billy.

Lydian

ABOUT THE AUTHOR

Barry Lowe writes about love and sex so he won't forget how to do it. When he's not scribbling his adventures for the Sydney gay weekly SX, or out doing field research, he's writing about love's wonderful variations for a series of smut eBooks, novels and anthologies for Lydian Press.

He lives in Sydney with his partner, Wally.

Check out his website at www.barrylowe.info

Also available from Lydian Press

YOUR BOYFRIEND IS HOT

Is it cheating if it excites your boyfriend?

In this collection of gay cuckold erotica you'll meet men who are complicit in their own 'betrayal' and those to whom it is a wake-up call. Whatever your taste you'll find a story here, from a man at a college reunion who watches as his boyfriend cuckolds him with the bully from his former frat house; a young toy boy whose sexual favors are part of a takeover bid for his lover's company, a callous actor who will hawk his virginal ass to his boyfriend's employer for a chance at the big time, a young man who resorts to tarot in order to experience a threesome, a world famous television chef who enjoys watching his lover put out for fans, and a boyfriend who loves to secretly watch the humiliation of his lover at the hands of his friends and enemies alike.

Your Boyfriend is Hot: Gay Cuckold Erotica includes: *From Here to Fraternity, Stripping His Assets, Indecent Exposure, Middle Man for Madame Blavatsky, A Cook's Tour,* and *Topping the Pizza Delivery Boy* (originally titled *Christmas on the Rocks*) - all previously published as individual eBooks by loveyoudivine Alterotica.

THE BOY IS A BOTTOM

Some guys will go all the way to get to the top.

In some cultures it's still seen as 'unmanly' to take a cock up your ass, although it's hard to associate the image of someone supposedly 'less than a man' with some of the muscle studs who grunt like a pig to get dicked. Let's face it, oft times it's the bottom who's the power behind the fuck, using his sphincter in such a way that a whole universe of pleasure resides in one tight black hole.

In these eleven stories you'll meet power bottoms from Victorian England and the Renaissance, vampires, marines, men at the top of the world, an elf who discovers humans make the best tops, a group who take out their frustration on a mate's boyfriend's ass, a straight boy who'll do anything to get ahead, a net date who's horny for Satan's dick, and a student aching for hard Arab cock.

The Boy Is A Bottom includes, *Marine Biology, Marine Animals, Attack of the Ass Bandits, The Arab Downstairs, The Extraordinary Victorian Clockwork Derriere, Creaming the Party Dip, Top of the World, Route 666: Signal Driver, The Butler Did Him, Fifty Shades of Fey,* and *Spinning the Bottom* - all previously published as individual eBooks by loveyoudivine Alterotica.

ANTHOLOGIES By Barry Lowe

BUSTING BILLY'S BUTT - eBook & Print

Four On The Floor
Jolly Rogering
The Devil His Due
Never Take Candy from Strangers
Done Like A Dinner
In The Family Way
Right Up His Alley
Group Therapy

THE MAJOR AND THE MINERS - eBook & Print

A Serpent in Paradise
Desperate Remedies
Joshua's Story
Emerald City
Danny's Revenge
Future Tense

ROMANCING THE BONE - eBook and Print

Carbon Dating
Let the Games Begin
Taking the Bait
Party Whip
Team Player
Davy Jones' Locker
Here's to You, Mr Robinson
Gay Dungeon for the Straight Boy
OMG! Santa's Got a Six-Pack
AVlad the Impaler
Meta-Analysis of the Effects of Love on Tofu

LIKE FATHER LIKE SON - eBook and Print

Man of the Hour
Like Father Like Son
Sonny & Shared
Sonny Side Up
Eclipse Of The Son
Son & Games
Where The Sun Don't Shine
The Sun Shines Out Of His Ass
Have Son Will Travel

YOUR BOYFRIEND IS HOT - eBook and Print

From Here to Fraternity
Stripping His Assets
Indecent Exposure
Middle Man for Madame Blavatsky
A Cook's Tour
Topping the Pizza Delivery Boy

THE BOY IS A BOTTOM - eBook and Print

Marine Biology
Marine Animals
Attack of the Ass Bandits
The Arab Downstairs
Clockwork Derriere
Creaming the Party Dip
Top of the World
Route 666: Signal Driver
The Butler Did Him
Fifty Shades of Fey
Spinning the Bottom

BEAR SKIN - eBook & Print

Carbon Dating the Bear
Bumming a Fag
Four on the Bear Floor
Beauty, Mate
There's a Bear in There
Busting a Gut
Steam Punk
Piss Elegant
The Bear's Guide to Depilatory Wax

ROUGH & READY - eBook and Print

Stocks & Shared
Scarface
Ceps: Mad about Muscle
The Plumbers' Mate*
Climbing Up the Wall
Little Red Rides da Hood
The Dex Factor
Jailhouse Cock
The Skinhead Upstairs

COCK-EYED OPTIMISTS - eBook & Print

A Red Rose Before Crying
Too Frocked to Care
The Three Spooges
Love and the Odor of Red Leatherette
It's All Greek to Me
Hard On His Heels
Salted Mixed Sluts
The New Dad's Club

OMG! NOT ANOTHER GAY EROTICA ANTHOLOGY?

OMG! My Dad's a Stripper!
OMG! The College Jock's a Nudist!
OMG! Put Some Clothes On!
OMG! My Uncle's a Fairy!
OMG! Satan Wants a Blow Job!
OMG! My Dad's Got Tits!
OMG! Santa's Got a Six-pack!

BABY, I'M NOT A MONSTER - eBook and Print

The Vampire's Guide to Dental Hygiene
Stupid Cupid
Gadigal
Pride & Joy
Seeing Things
My Dad's a Vampire
Guys & Trolls

THE GRAVY TRAIN - eBook & Print

In the Soup
Salad Days
Whores d'Oeuvres
Beefed Up and Porked
Torte A Lesson
Café or Lay

For all Barry's titles please visit his page at:

lydianpress.com

Lydian Press is dedicated to bringing you the
finest GLBTQ erotic literature on the web.

Visit us on the web at:
http://lydianpress.com